HOUSEBOAT HERMIT

of the Everglades

No Refuge in Wilderness

Marvin Cook

The author thanks, first and foremost, Lee Cook for proofing, editing and encouragement. Test readers of the draft provided valuable comments and suggestions that are most appreciated. Thank you to Sue Doker, Pat and Frank Hankins, Pat and Judy Ball, Doug Bailey, Bill Kent, Anna and David Grossman, Maxine Glenn, and Pete and Pam Scalco. Dr. Felicia Coleman is due special acknowledgment for her contributions and suggestions. Thank you to Kendra Greis for her assistance with the cover.

Marvin Cook has traveled throughout the United States and Caribbean working to connect people to natural and cultural history at parks, museums, and wildlife refuges. Fiction has liberated his imagination, allowing him to invent characters maneuvering through dramatic circumstances in interesting places. When not writing or painting Florida and Maine landscapes, Cook sails the coast of Florida and spends summers aboard a boat in Downeast Maine with his wife, Lee.

Other books by Marvin Cook include

Across Florida Straits
From Cuba to Key West

Blue Goose Passport

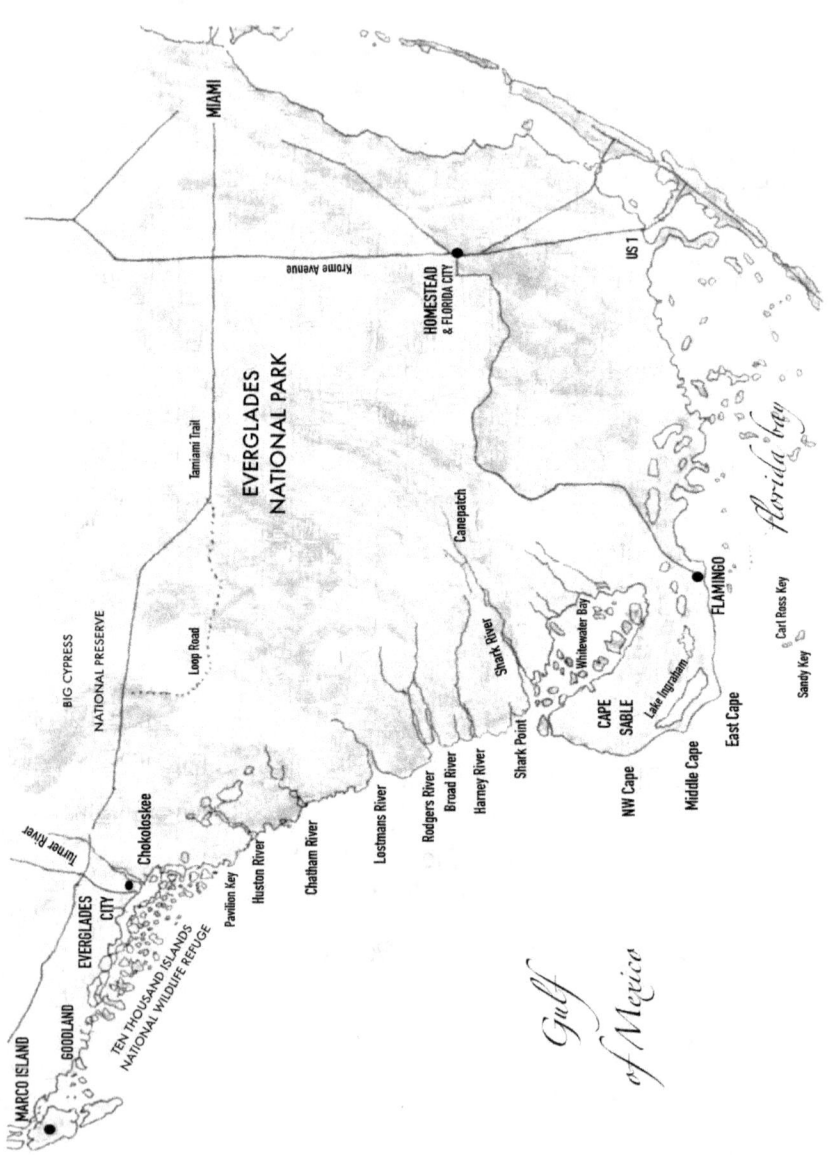

ONE

Gliding over flat still waters perfectly reflecting the bright morning sky, Ranger Bob felt as if he were flying. Only the drone of the outboard motor and hissing of the water spray intruded on the surreal ride through the wilderness. The skiff skidded sideways through each turn in the labyrinth of mangroves. Wading birds launched from their perches, expressing their annoyance at his intrusion with raucous protestation, squawking a hoarse "caw-caw-caw-caw".

Bob's spirits were soaring in the excitement of the sprint through the placid back-country. This was the work he relished, out in nature, having a wilderness to himself. The purpose of his excursion tempered his euphoria. Still, until he reached his destination, he could enjoy the ride.

On the thirty-mile run out to Ponce de Leon Bay on the Gulf Coast, Nelson had time to reflect. He thought about his time at the University of Georgia studying natural resources management and wildlife biology and how he was overjoyed to be hired by the National Park Service. He recalled his decade of working at different parks until he had settled into his ideal position at Dry Tortugas National Park in South Florida. Ideal, until the daily routine became overwhelming.

During his tenure at Dry Tortugas National Park, Bob had advanced to Chief Ranger. He had served in the Tortugas for years, through seasons and storms, through isolation and visitor inundation. Over the years, the occasional arrival of Cuban refugees landing in the Dry Tortugas had become a regular occurrence. Emergencies became a 24/7/365 burden. Often, a hail would come in from the Coast Guard or Homeland Security, calling the Park to assist with search and rescue or accommodation of detained Cubans. Each call was urgent and panicked. All manner of watercraft were towed to the beach at Garden Key. None of this is what Nelson had signed up for.

His interest in being a park ranger was founded in protecting the park and facilitating visitor enjoyment of public lands. He was weary of the circumstances that were distracting him from his duties as a ranger. He knew it was time for him to leave.

Bob Nelson transferred to Everglades National Park from the Dry Tortugas. Everglades National Park was an escape from the changes at Dry Tortugas that were eroding his passion for the job. Duty at Everglades National Park restored his passion and was a respite from the extraneous distractions and crisis demands at Dry Tortugas. While he missed the history of Fort Jefferson and the amazing coral reefs of the Tortugas banks, there was new beauty to be immersed in in America's unique biological national park.

Nelson piloted his sports skiff patrol boat across the open waters of Coot Bay to Whitewater Bay and on through the winding passages toward Shark River on the northwestern tip of Cape Sable. He loved traversing this section of the park, one of America's last true wilderness areas. The mangrove-fringed shore, stretching a hundred miles from Flamingo, bordering Florida Bay, to the coast of the Gulf of Mexico, up to Marco Island, was devoid of development. The millions of acres under the stewardship of the national park and adjacent national wildlife refuge preserved the natural environment, avoiding the transformation from swamp to coastal condos as had occurred in Miami Beach and Naples.

Slowing as he approached the Little Shark River, Nelson traveled at idle speed, appreciating the stands of the tallest red mangroves found in the continental U.S. Each time he came to the Shark River he was amazed at the mangrove's arching prop roots and impenetrable intertwined bases that knitted the forest together. He noted a raccoon at the shore, washing his meal of blue crab. Little blue herons and snowy egrets perched on the roots, watching Nelson's boat move slowly down river. Hidden in the darkness of the forest understory, night-herons searched the exposed mud for food.

Nelson wondered what this place might have looked like before being knocked back by hurricanes. Even more than 60 years after the direct hit of Hurricane Donna in 1960, the forest had not recovered to the magnificence touted in the historic natural history narratives. Now, the swamp was healthy and growing. Perhaps the forest would reach the towering heights of 120 feet again, but it would take time and luck that another hurricane would not cause widespread devastation.

Rounding the last bend in the river, the water opened into a protected cove at the mouth of the river where it meets the Gulf of Mexico. Three sailboats and two cruising trawlers were anchored in this natural basin. Nelson motored past them, waving at the few boaters who were out on deck. They returned the gesture. Nelson would check in with each boat's captain after he finished his primary task, finding the "houseboat hermit."

Nelson exited the river, passing the navigation aid at the river's entrance from the Gulf. Throttling up the motor to get on a plane, he decided to head north around Shark River Island, to search some of the likely haunts of the hermit.

The first place he checked was a bust, but off in the distance he spotted the eccentric craft, the homemade houseboat. Nelson set a course.

The hermit's houseboat was a creative assemblage of a small, plywood-patched travel trailer, sans axle, and a portable, blue-tarped aluminum storage shed mounted on a pontoon boat frame. A bent tuna tower, salvaged from a large sportfisherman boat, was mounted between the trailer and shed. A wood frame connected the two structures and was covered with sections of pool screen, decorated with a string of lobster pot floats. A little back porch had a chair and table, neatly stacked driftwood for cooking, and a barbecue grill and a gas stove. A new outboard motor on the stern had a Rube Goldberg-inspired steering system connected to a wheel on the tower. The whole conglomeration was painted with various shades of tan and green in a camouflage pattern. A small plywood pirogue hung on the side of the shed. The houseboat's name, *Épave*, was crudely painted on the pontoons, behind the up-to-date FL boat registration numbers.

Nelson approached, giving a wave. "Hey there, Mr. Thompson! Good to see you again."

The old man reached down to catch the boat, while Ranger Nelson handed him a line.

Thompson's white hair was neatly trimmed. Baggy tan work pants were drawn tight to his waist and a "wife-beater" undershirt hung loosely on his wiry frame. His dark leathery skin revealed a life lived in the sun. Nelson guessed he might be 70 or even 80.

Thompson replied with his usual brusqueness, "What is it this time?"

Nelson replied cheerfully, "Oh, I was just missing visiting with you. I see you have a new engine."

"Yep, what of it?"

"It looks good! Congratulations!"

The old man's demeanor eased up a little as he answered, "Yes, I needed to get something that works for me, more than I work for it. But, I don't know nothin' 'bout all the extra stuff on this engine. It's not as simple as my old Johnson."

Nelson interjected, "I know what you mean. But the 4-cycle motors are supposed to be a lot better and won't smoke you out with oil fumes."

Thompson said, "Reckon you didn't come out here to talk to me about boat engines. So, what do you want?"

Nelson asked, "May I come on board? Do I smell coffee?"

Immediately, Thompson barked, "No, not without a warrant."

"OK, OK. I didn't really think anything had changed from the last half dozen times we've been together, but I thought I'd ask."

Thompson sneered, "We can talk with you on your fancy boat and me on mine. I'll get you a cup of coffee."

With the park patrol boat tendered to the makeshift houseboat, Nelson leaned back in his seat, while Thompson sat in his rocker on the back deck of his castle on the water. Ranger Nelson sipped the strong coffee and gently got into the purpose of his visit. "You recall I visited you last month?"

Thompson nodded.

"Well, there are some new regulations for boaters that the Park started last year. The limit on anchoring in the park is 30 days. We've not been active in enforcing the rules, but a new superintendent is more a by-the-book kind of guy and he's directing rangers to be more diligent."

Thompson snarled, "What are you talkin' about? I've been travelin' this coast ten years and ain't hurt nothin' and I ain't bothered nobody!"

Nelson said, "I know, I know. You've got quite a long history here, but I need to let you know what the rules are. I might not agree, but it's not my call. Here's what we need to do – and I'll help you with this. OK?"

Thompson frowned.

"There's a test you have to take to get a permit for boating in the Everglades. I can go over it with you and when I get back to my office, I'll fill out the form on the Internet for you and print your paper certificate. Then, since you're over 65, you're eligible for a senior pass that gets you into all the national parks in the country, so you won't have to worry about the fees for anchoring. And, same goes for a free Florida fishing license to avoid problems with the Game Commission."

After some more sniping at the restrictions and intrusion of government on his lifestyle and freedom, the old man calmed down a little and accepted that Nelson was trying to help him. Just when it all seemed to be settled, Nelson added, "You will have to limit your stay in the Park to thirty continuous days."

That rekindled the fuming complaints. "Why? I'm not taking up space here. This is as desolate as the desert. A few boats pass through and I see the campers in their kayaks and canoes, but there aren't many. It's not like this place is in high demand. So, what's the problem if I stay more than 30 days?"

Nelson assured him that he was correct, that it's a big, wild space with very few people passing through and his houseboat wasn't taking a space from anyone. "If it was my decision, I wouldn't ask you to move, but you've got to understand it isn't only me on the park patrols. There are other rangers, especially junior rangers, who are less understanding and more focused on being "park cops" and writing citations. Can you work with me on this?"

Thompson leaned back in his rocker, wiping his hand over his forehead. He sat for a minute and was quiet. He then asked, "Where do I have to go?"

Nelson had a suggestion ready. "I've thought about this. Easiest thing is for you to move on up to the Ten Thousand Islands. I think the national wildlife refuge might have the same restriction for staying in one place, but if you spend a day or two outside of the Park boundary, you could return for another 30 days, before leaving again for a few days. Or, less preferable, is to go south to the back-country of the Keys, like the Contents, or off Little Pine Key. But you know it's a long haul across Florida Bay and you need good weather to make that run in your houseboat."

Now with something concrete to ponder, Thompson reacted. "You know, I can go up to Chokoloskee and Everglades City. That's where I get my mail and buy provisions. They don't have a problem with my houseboat."

Nelson nodded in approval. "Yes, that would work. Just plan your timing to avoid staying in the Park over 30 days at a time. I'd suggest you keep a record of your stays on a calendar so you can show it to a park ranger if you get hassled."

Thompson exclaimed, "Damn-it! Calendar? I don't have one. It's in my head! I live by the sunrise and sunset; every day is a Saturday for me. That's the life I want, the life I have."

Nelson opened a watertight ammunition case to retrieve some park literature on the new permit program and went over the test with Thompson. With a little reluctance, Thompson complied and answered the simple and common-sense questions about how to operate a boat in the park and Florida Bay and seagrass areas.

"Thanks for the coffee and your patience with all of this." Nelson continued, "I think you are fine here for the next couple weeks, but when the weather is right, move on up to the refuge for at least a couple days before returning. I'll have your certificate next time I see you, and if you've got 50 bucks, I'll get you a Golden Eagle Senior Pass and a free calendar."

Thompson started to get up. "I'll get your 50 dollars – just a minute."

Nelson said, "Pay me when I see you and give you the pass."

Thompson barked, "Hell no! I don't want to be beholdin' to anyone. I'll get you your money."

Nelson respected the independence of this old guy, even if he was an eccentric, grouchy curmudgeon. Somehow, he just fit in, in the wild west coast of the Everglades, the kind of character that was part of the ecosystem.

Untying the patrol boat, Nelson tipped his cap to Thompson, "Good luck. See you next time."

Then slowly motoring off, Nelson sighed in relief for accomplishing a task he had been dreading. In his imagination, he envisioned a scenario that could have played out badly.

Hitting the throttle, the boat jumped to a plane and he headed back to the Little Shark River anchorage. Nelson would make courtesy visits to the cruising yachts he passed earlier to explain the new rules for boating and overnighting in the Park's waters. He knew this would not be popular with the boaters, but their transits were temporary. They were likely to object but not be as entrenched as Thompson.

When he entered the basin, only two boats, both sailboats, were still at anchor. Nelson knew that the cove was a popular stopover for people traveling to or from Key West because it was a safe place to wait out the weather for a comfortable passage of Florida Bay or a convenient overnight stopover. He was keenly aware that, during lobster season, Florida Bay is full of traps that entangle the props and rudders of boats. Because traveling at night risks ensnaring the trap lines, most cruisers wait at anchor for daylight to transit the Bay.

He also knew the anchorage has a well-deserved reputation for insects, having personally experienced the ferocious mosquitoes. With the wind blowing, and during daylight, the mosquitoes are tolerable. But, at dusk, an invasion ramps up to an overwhelmingly unbearable onslaught of biting arthropods, both mosquitoes and black flies. There are so many bugs that boats are enveloped with relentless assailants. By dawn, their carcasses litter the boat decks. Unsuspecting cruisers might spend a miserable night or two while they wait to travel east to the Keys or west to the Ten Thousand Islands. Cruisers who have experienced one overnight's stay know a mosquito net tent over the boat is a necessity.

Nelson checked with the boat captains at anchor and handed out the leaflets explaining the new boating restrictions. They were polite, if not overjoyed to learn of a complication to their use of the reliable stopover.

A family on one of the sailboats was suffering from their overnight stay. They had not secured their hatches before dark and had been overwhelmed by the bugs. The lady was weary as she explained, "We were up until midnight before we were able to kill enough of the bugs to be able to sleep. I wish we had taken the warnings of biting insects more seriously, but we wanted to have the hatches open to catch the breezes. That was a mistake! The overheated cabin isn't as bad as being eaten alive!"

Nelson smiled in agreement, "Yes ma'am. I can't imagine surviving a night out here without screens. The mosquitoes are brutal. Have a safe sail on to Key West." He departed for the ride back to Flamingo, retracing the track on his GPS plotter.

Back at the Park's service area dock, fellow rangers met him to help tie up and off-load the patrol boat. Expecting a story of an argument, Buddy Smith, a seasoned ranger asked, "So how'd it go with the old hermit?"

Nelson said "It wasn't bad. He didn't like it, but it turned out OK. We just need to lighten up on the old man. He's made his life in the back-country for a long time and this is a big change for him."

Buddy was disappointed that there wasn't more to it. Huffing, he remarked, "I thought it would have been a real fiasco. You must have hit him on a good day. He's never been hospitable to me."

Nelson shrugged, "Just lucky, I guess. He will move on up to Ten Thousand Islands in a few days and probably be back again. I'm getting him his permit and a Golden Eagle Pass."

Buddy shook his head, "You're just enabling him. This can't be good. A derelict junk like that is just a wreck waiting to happen."

Nelson didn't want to argue. Old man Thompson was a fixture in the Park and deserved a place as much as any sport angler or wilderness paddler and Thompson was right. He hadn't hurt anything or bothered anybody, only offended the aesthetic sensibilities of park purists.

TWO

Faint pastels of dawn brightened to a warm glow and then radiant sunshine. The blue sky was dappled with white clouds, tinted with the amber wash of the south Florida sun. Thompson sat in his screened patio under the tuna tower sipping coffee and watching another day begin while waiting for the torrent of insects to subside.

He started his new motor. A twist of the key and it turned over immediately and murmured to a hum. It was quiet. Water pumped with the pisser steadily streaming cooling water. This was easier than pulling on the starter cord on his old motor and there was no strain and fussing with the choke.

Heading to the bow, he surveyed the horizon. No other boats were visible, only clear sky and calm water. It would be an easy run up to Everglades City. He knew this coast, probably as well as any, after more than a decade of plying the shallows and edges of the mangrove creeks. Mentally he knew these waters, but he still kept an old paper chart to check himself or plan his route.

In mid-morning he began the trek north. After starting the outboard motor, Thompson left it in neutral while he went to the bow and bent over to pull the anchor. It was tight, so he climbed to his helm to put the motor in gear, bumping the houseboat ahead until he could see the anchor line slacken. Then he slipped the motor back into neutral, allowing the momentum to glide the boat forward. Retrieving the anchor, he stowed it on deck. Although it came up covered with thick clay-like, gray mud, he decided he'd clean it later.

A lot of his navigation knowledge was from trial and error. He checked the depth with a long pole, notched for feet. He needed just over 2 feet to skim by. If the water was clear he could eyeball the depth, but turbidity in the water often disguised it so the pole was useful. Going slow was essential to avoid getting stuck and stranded.

Setting a course north, he leaned back in the chair on his perch and steamed ahead slowly. It was good to move on, even if he resented that it wasn't by his own choosing. Maybe he'd make it about half-way up toward Everglades City. If not, it didn't matter. It could take another day, or even more.

He made 20 miles by early afternoon and was east of Pavilion Key, between the unnamed islands and Duck Rock. He said aloud, to himself, "Might as well anchor for the night and maybe fish a bit."

Once the anchor was set, Thompson launched his pirogue to paddle over to Pavilion Key to fish the cut between the islands. He netted a couple of pinfish to use for bait and hoped for a redfish for dinner. If he was skunked, he'd just pop open a can of tuna and boil some rice. But a nice redfish on the wood-fired grill would be better.

The tide was running through the cut, the pirogue drifting with it. He hooked a pinfish through the backbone to serve as live enticement to the reds. With no success on the first pass, he paddled forward against the current to make another drift. This time a fish bit and he had a decent redfish on the line. He boated it quickly. Talking to the fish, he said aloud, "Fine, you will do nicely." Before returning to the houseboat, he beached his pirogue on one of the unnamed islands and walked the shore to collect a little driftwood to replenish what he would use for cooking dinner.

The shore was sandy. He noticed that the wrack line of seaweed had trapped too much litter - plastic bottles, plastic bags, fishing lures (which he kept), and some lobster trap floats. Stepping over the weeds, he walked up the dune to collect a few dry sticks.

As he returned to the houseboat anchored near Duck Rock, he noticed in the distance a small tent and two kayaks pulled up high on the beach of Pavilion Key where the Park had a designated campsite with a porta-potty at the north end. Knowing that Pavilion Key is a popular stop in the 100-mile canoe route from Flamingo to Everglades City, he confirmed in his mind, "Yep, paddlers on the Wilderness Waterway Trail. I guess I won't be alone tonight." With campers a couple miles away, he considered his world crowded.

The redfish filet on the grill was ready in no time. Thompson laid it on his plate, over a bed of rice, accompanied with hot, steaming coffee. Before eating, he closed his eyes and said a prayer, "O Lord, Bless this food to our use, and us to thy service, and keep us ever mindful of the needs of others. In Jesus' name, Amen."

As he ate, the houseboat swung on its anchor. Thompson could see the campers' fire glimmering on the island. The bugs were not too bad, but inside his screened room, he didn't have to fight them. Perhaps the campers were in the lee of the smoke, if they were not in their tent. Otherwise, he knew they would be swatting.

19

As night fell, the moon rose. The sky was clear and winds were gentle. Thompson read his Bible for a while before retiring early. As he moved into the trailer, he checked to see if the kayakers' campfire was still burning.

Morning delivered a damp dew, coating his boat. The air was still and the water was like glass. On this very calm day, it would be hot. Thompson decided to delay departing until a little sea breeze came up. While waiting, he dropped a line through his floor hatch, baited with an artificial shrimp lure. He could fish in the shade inside his screened room. As he waited for a fish to bite, he was in a day-dream.

He was startled from his trance by the sound of kayakers. A young couple was close by, sneaking a look at his unusual houseboat. Thompson shouted out, "Hey! What do you kids want?"

They were spooked by the gruff voice coming from the dilapidated houseboat until he emerged on the back deck. Seeing an old man, the kayakers were a little less apprehensive, and replied, "We are paddling to Flamingo. Just wanted to check out your houseboat. Do you live here?"

Thompson growled, "Yep and I don't much care for company."

The kayakers looked at each other and moved on, waving, "Goodbye. Sorry to have disturbed you."

Thompson watched them paddle away. He was always cautious about strangers. The coast had a notorious reputation for harboring illicit activities. Some were minor offenses like illegal fishing, but some were more serious and dangerous crimes like smuggling drugs or piracy. The remoteness of the area offered a vast expanse for clandestine operations with little law enforcement. Because of this, Thompson always laid low and minded his own business, steering clear of people and suspicious boats. Being alone and on such an unusual houseboat, he wasn't a likely target. He might only get in trouble as an accidental observer of some crime or other.

Thompson started his outboard and pulled anchor to move farther up the coast. Since he had gotten a late start, he aimed to reach Russell Pass near the channel into Everglades City before sunset. He rationalized that it would be fine to go into Everglades City fresh in the morning. The channel was not tricky, but it was narrow and his houseboat was unwieldy.

Everglades City has its own history. It had been the locus of marijuana smuggling in the past and many of the residents had been in on the enterprise. Feds broke up the ring and set the small community back with the incarceration of a lot of smugglers and RICO Act confiscations of property. Now it was back to its hard-scrabble fishing heritage and being a remote outpost for anglers.

The next day Thompson carefully navigated the channel up to town, looking for dock space to temporarily moor his houseboat. His boat was so unconventional that most people along the seawall stopped what they were doing to gawk as if it were a parade float.

The easiest place in which to moor the houseboat was the Everglades Rod and Gun Club dock. As usual, there was plenty of space for the awkward *Épave*. Thompson maneuvered the houseboat slowly, approaching the dock at an oblique angle, carefully adjusting to the strong current in the Barron River. A worker saw him coming in and ran over to grab a line. *Épave* bumped the dock. Thompson hurried down the steering tower to

21

throw a line to the dockhand before the boat drifted away in the current. This barge was not easy to single-hand in tight spaces.

Once *Épave* was secured to the dock, Thompson retreated to his trailer to put on a collared shirt and run a comb through his hair so he would be more presentable when he asked for permission to dock for a while.

As he walked through the doors of the Rod and Gun Club, he heard Maggie, the desk clerk, exclaim, "Mr. Thompson! So nice to see you again. How long has it been? Months, I know, at the least."

Thompson tipped his cap, "Yes, back a few months. I didn't plan to come back so soon, but I have some business to attend to. I don't plan to stay long, but would be obliged if I could tie up to your dock. Maybe for a few hours?"

Maggie said, "Let me check," and laughed. "It's summer. There are only a few boaters tough enough to visit here with the heat and mosquitoes. Our dock is empty until next weekend, so stay. I won't even charge you."

"Much obliged, Maggie. I'll be off soon so I don't overstay my welcome." Thompson returned to his boat, pulled out an extension cord long enough to reach the dockside electricity pedestal, and plugged in a box fan to circulate the air in his trailer. Out on the water, at anchor, it was cooler and he didn't need a fan, but in the still heat of the town it was a necessity.

The post office was closed so he decided to walk over to the bar on the east side of the city, if you could even call Everglades City a city. Walking along the streets was like walking through a ghost town. Nice little houses with neat and well-kept yards lined the vacant streets. But there were no people around. The few who lived in Everglades City year-round were probably inside air-conditioned homes, watching TV, rather than outside, living. At the bar there were a couple of visiting fishermen and a bored waitress talking with a local. Thompson pulled up a bar stool.

"Whatcha want Pops?" the middle-aged server asked. Thompson answered that he wanted a cold soda.

"Only a Coke? This is a bar!"

Thompson laid down $2.00 on the bar. "Just a Coke, please."

He enjoyed being in the air conditioning even if he didn't like the stale tobacco smell and cigar smoke wafting from the fishermen. Finishing his soda, he said thanks and left to walk back to his houseboat. As he walked, he made a mental list of what he would need to do while in this remote outpost that was his link to civilization.

Thompson was waiting to collect his mail at the post office when the postmaster arrived and unlocked the door. She told him, "Let me open up and I'll be right with you."

Years ago, when Thompson first came to Ten Thousand Islands, he rented a large post office box in Everglades City. Since then he visited Everglades City every few months to pick up mail and reprovision his boat with staples. Since there was no bank, he had to do his banking by mail, so he bought a package of pre-stamped envelopes. Typically, he would find his post office box filled with lots of junk mail and a few important papers and checks. But, nothing in his life was urgent.

Thompson returned to the boat to carefully go through his mail. There were advertisements and catalogs cluttering what was important. There were checks from the government, a few statements from his bank in Marco, and some letters from the Veterans Administration. He filled out mail-in deposit slips and addressed an envelope to the bank. He would cash one check at the City Grocery to pay for his purchases. Sometimes he would have to wait for days for the store to be able to cash his check. It wasn't a matter of whether the check was good or not; they just didn't have the cash on hand.

Over the years he had accumulated a significant stash of cash that he kept hidden on the boat as an emergency or reserve fund. His bank account was flush as a result of his austere lifestyle. Thompson knew eventually that he would have to make other arrangements for banking, like getting an account that would let him use an ATM. But he did not want to go all the way to Marco Island to do his banking or move his postal box address from Everglades City.

When, earlier in the year, he bought the new 50 HP motor for the houseboat because the constant battle with his undependable outboard had worn out his patience and perseverance, the boatyard in nearby Goodland was skeptical about his ability to pay for it. But when he put down a $1,000 deposit in cash, they took a chance. However, just to be sure, when the motor came in, they wouldn't let him leave until his check cleared. He spent an enormous sum to repower his houseboat, but clearly he could afford it.

The next day he returned to the post office and mailed his letters. He purchased his supplies at the grocery store and borrowed a shopping cart to transport them back to the Rod and Gun Club dock. He filled water jugs from the dockside spigot and all of his gas tanks by making multiple trips to the gas station. Tired from the exertion, he treated himself to supper at the Club. A restaurant cooked meal and shower in the marina restrooms recharged his soul. He told Maggie he would be leaving in the morning and gave her a ten. She said thanks and told him "Come back again when you get lonely." She knew that was a joke. If she knew anything of Thompson, it was that he was a loner.

Thompson was off early in the morning, casting off without help to swing the boat around and return to the channel. He motored past the western office for Everglades National Park and sneered because he felt that he had been chased out of the park.

He moved slowly out the channel into the Gulf of Mexico. Turning north towards Gullivan Bay and the Big Marco River, he picked an anchorage near Dismal Key. It was a place he had spent some time when he first arrived in Southwest Florida. Most of this area was a national wildlife refuge. Thompson didn't want to run afoul of another federal, or even Florida, wildlife officer. All he could do was try to stay out of their way. It was hard not to attract attention with his unique houseboat but, if he stayed out of the main boat traffic areas, he hoped they wouldn't notice.

Setting the anchor in a dead-end cove near Dismal Key, he was surrounded by mangroves that made him invisible to the fishermen racing in the marked channel out to the bay or back home again after a day's fishing. There was no reason for anybody to poke into his anchorage. After a few days in this location, he'd head back down to Everglades Park to his favored haunts.

Thompson mused that, despite its foreboding name, Dismal Key had a storied legacy as an important place to the pre-European-contact native Calusa tribe. The key towers a dizzying 20-feet above the surrounding mangrove islands occurring at sea level. It must have taken untold thousands of baskets of sand and mud and shell to build up the elevation of this village site.

Thompson untied his pirogue and paddled it to the island where he could walk the paths through the tropical hardwood forest that grew on the elevated island. There was not much to scavenge there, at least nothing really useful. A few coconuts and key limes added to his larder none the less. Fishing in the cove was fair; a few mangrove snappers were keepers.

After a day or two as he was about to depart, a skiff came into the cove and motored close to his houseboat. Two men in some kind of uniform were seated at the helm. They passed slowly, giving the houseboat an intense look-over. They beached their boat at Dismal Key and he could see that the boat was labeled "Calusa Research Project." At least they were not police, but archaeologists instead. Thompson quickly pulled anchor and got underway.

Not wanting to go far, but wanting to get back out nearer the Gulf, Thompson went to anchor near Rabbit Key. He set the anchor and resumed his routine of fishing, collecting firewood, and reading either his Bible or new books he picked up while in Everglades City. Once settled at anchor, his slight anxiety about feds eased. In his screened shelter, he watched the sun set over the Gulf and enjoyed a sunset rum.

Up before dawn again, he could see kayakers were at Rabbit Key, starting their wilderness adventure. Rabbit Key was the first stop for them, after launching at Everglades City. The wide beach was a great spot for pitching a tent and acclimating to the Ten Thousand Islands environment.

He grumbled to himself, "More kayakers! I can't get away from these pests."

Having recently had interaction with people in Everglades City, Thompson was a little more relaxed with people being around, accepting that the kayakers were not a threat. They were simply outdoor people seeking adventure. But he still resented people intruding upon his wilderness domain.

The paddlers broke camp and came toward the houseboat. His boat was an eccentric attraction that always drew the attention of the curious. Thompson really didn't appreciate this. It was his home and he was accustomed to its appearance, considering it to be normal. The kayakers came close and Thompson came on deck to watch them.

Friendly voices called "Good morning, sir! It's a beautiful day. Wonder if you could tell us if we are headed the right way."

Contrary to his usual gruff demeanor, Thompson nodded, as he answered. "Well, that depends. If you are going to Flamingo, head over to that marker. That's the start of the Everglades Wilderness Waterway trail. If you are finishing the trail, you need to turn around to reach Everglades City."

The kayakers paddled closer. "Thanks, we are just starting out. I'm Ashley and this is my new husband, Cameron. We're from Atlanta and we just got married. We did a canoe trip through the Okefenokee last year and wanted to do this trip. It looks awesome."

Thompson nodded, not really caring to engage more with them, but the enthusiasm of the kids kept them talking and asking questions. The young man looked fit and his girlfriend was pretty, with red hair, and slender, but not outdoorsy looking. She was looking all made up like she was ready for going out on the town.

"We've heard there are snakes, alligators and even crocodiles in the swamps and you can get lost and never be found," the young man said.

The young lady chimed in before Thompson could answer. "Is this true? Like, really, how dangerous is it?"

Thompson replied, "As far as the critters go, if you don't bother them, they ain't gonna bother you. I don't know much about the canoe trail, but I see markers all up and down the mangroves,

27

and the Park has a bunch of campsites and outhouses set up along the coast. If you're careful, I don't know that it's a problem for y'all. It's just a long way to Flamingo."

With a little more trivial conversation, the young couple was off on their way. They were on their honeymoon. Thompson watched them reach the marker and disappear into the mangroves. He was glad they were gone and hoped not to be bothered by any other people. Solitude was his refuge.

Later in the day, four young men, two each in larger canoes, were powering by, off in the distance, on their way to the marker at the mangroves. They didn't bother with coming close to the houseboat, barely giving *Épave* a glance. They were strong paddlers, moving in steady synchronized strokes. It seemed like they knew what they were doing and where they were going. Thompson took out his binoculars and noticed each canoe seemed heavily loaded with gear. He thought, "These guys seem prepared for the trip."

Barron River

EVERGLADES CITY

ENP West Entrance

CHOKOLOSKEE

INDIAN KEY PASS

Lopez River

Camping Site

Gulf of Mexico

Huston River

Camping Site

DUCK ROCK

PAVILION KEYS

Chatham Bend

THREE

Ashley and Cameron, truly Atlanta urbanites, paddled their kayaks through the mangrove creeks. She followed behind, letting her new spouse lead the way. The winding waterways snaked through the wet-footed forest. It was beautiful. The water was flat calm; neither the slight current or wind slowed their progress. A few birds flew from the woods only to disappear again. Fish, probably mullet, launched from the green water and landed with a splash. So far it was a good start, kind of like their recent experience in the Okefenokee. Their Okefenokee trip was just overnight and she found it tolerable; sometimes, even enjoyable.

The trip on the Everglades Wilderness Waterway trail, from Everglades City to Flamingo, would be ten days, according to the plan Cameron plotted – over a hundred miles compared to the 15 miles from Folkston to Suwannee State Park. Unlike the Okee trip which was fully supplied by an outfitter, who oriented them to the canoe trail, made the camping platform reservations, and provided all the gear and food for their adventure, the Everglades trip was planned all on their own.

If Ashley had her way, they would be in a resort in Hawaii or maybe an island in the Caribbean for their honeymoon. They would be getting room service and enjoying a sandy beach, under a cabana, sipping umbrella-garnished fruity cocktails. But she knew how much Cameron wanted to do something different, out of the ordinary and build memories they could tell their kids and grandkids, creating a tale that would endure for generations. A resort beach would be nice, but a kayaking adventure would be special. He promised they would go to a cushy resort on their first anniversary.

The paddlers were comforted to see markers for the trail, especially at a fork in the channel. They rafted up to drift together while checking the map. Cameron said, "Looks like we've made three miles and have about three to go to the camp. Are you OK?"

"Sugar, anywhere is wonderful, so long as I'm here with my big, strong, handsome husband," she teased, in her saccharine-sweet southern-belle voice. "Seriously though, it hasn't been hard so far, and a lot more fun than I expected."

"Cut it out, I know you are doing this for me." He drawled sarcastically, "Honey, you are such a fragile flower, so beautiful to behold. I'm the luckiest man in the world."

They both chuckled at the sappy dialogue. They knew each other well and were equally devoted to one another as lovers and partners.

"Let's get going again, on to the camp, so we get set up and eat before dark. If the sky clears, we can lay outside to watch the stars. It should be really dark." Cameron pushed off and dipped his paddle into the water. Ashley followed close behind.

As they moved on, the scenery became monotonous. It all looked the same, making the thought of getting lost a little intimidating. There were no landmarks, only the trail route markers. Occasionally, they paddled through tunnel-like passages in the mangroves. The narrow waterways were bounded on both sides by thick tangles of arching roots with tree trunks reaching up to a canopy of leaves and branches nearly obscuring the sky. Shafts of light streamed down through sparkling gaps in the leaves.

Ashley and Cameron paddled slowly through the vegetated tunnels. In one of the canopied waterways Cameron stopped abruptly and Ashley's kayak bumped into his stern. "Jeez! Sorry!" Ashley apologized.

"Look. It's an alligator. No...it's a crocodile!"

Laying atop the tangled roots, a 5-foot American crocodile lounged like a couch potato. A mere ten feet away and resting at eye level, this olive-green reptile might as well have been twenty feet long. It was all teeth with cold, beady, slit eyes. This was a scary encounter for these novice wild-wilderness explorers.

Cameron slowly tried to back up his kayak, getting a little off course and bumping one side of the narrow passageway. Ashley did the same, pushing her paddle against the mangrove roots. Cameron turned to look back at Ashley, when, splash! In a flash, the reptile exploded from its perch to hit the water and disappear.

Startled Ashley exclaimed, "Where did he go? Oh my God, this is so small and shallow. Is he under us?"

Cameron had no idea. "I can't see anything in this murky green water. There's just a cloud of mud stirred up from the bottom. I don't know where he is!"

They stayed still for a couple of minutes, without conversation, just surveying the water ahead, behind, and under.

"No sense just waiting here. He's either gone or under us." Cameron suggested, "Let's hurry up and get out of here!" Ashley nodded vigorously in agreement.

Exiting the tunnel, their course opened up to a wider river. Another marker reassured them they were still on the right route. Still a little rattled by the crocodilian encounter in a tight space, each of them watched the shoreline carefully and surveyed the water, which was rippling from a light breeze.

Turning a bend, they could see the camping platform ahead, perched on the edge of the mangroves, on pilings about 3 feet over the water. The portable toilet was a visual buzz-kill to the otherwise idyllic scene. As they approached, they could see a ladder hanging down into the water. The site was empty and they hoped nobody else would arrive to share the deck with them. It was their honeymoon and they should have time alone!

A clear bright orange sunset illuminated the sky. The gentle breeze stalled and the bugs began their siege. The couple retreated to the tent, talking about how wonderful their wedding had been. So many people, family and friends, celebrated with them. Even Ashley's father seemed to enjoy the celebration, accepting that he was losing his baby girl to someone he thought was clearly not worthy of her. The band played on well past their contract and guests were slow to depart the reception revelry. The bridesmaids and groomsmen paired off; perhaps a few romances were kindled.

During the ceremony and celebration afterwards, Cameron had expected some jokes from Chad, his best man. Voicing his thoughts to Ashley, he said, "Chad was sure sedate - so out of character. He was on his best behavior and didn't pull off anything crazy. I expected he would make some kind of scene."

Ashley agreed, "He's such a prankster! I really expected him to give us a roast rather than a toast! I'm so glad he didn't make a spectacle."

As darkness settled in, the wind picked up, keeping the bugs at bay so they could go outside and watch the stars. They emerged in their underwear and pulled out a sleeping bag to lay on the deck for a while, watching the stellar display. A few constellations were clearly evident, identified by an app Ashley had downloaded on her iPhone. Cameron was delighted to see the Milky Way in all its splendor, clear and shining bright in the dark sky. He hadn't seen this since he had thru-hiked the Appalachian Trail in the summer before graduating. It had been too long since he'd had a true outdoor adventure, and now he was sharing it with the love of his life.

The moon began to rise, dimming the astronomical display, while tempering the darkness, allowing them to see the shadows of the wild landscape surrounding them. After a few glasses of wine, Ashley rose and positioned herself over Cameron. She was dancing suggestively in a cute silk teddy nightgown, beckoning him with her finger. "How 'bout it, Mr. Clark-Greene? Mrs. Clark-Greene will be waiting for you in the bedroom." With that, she tugged on the sleeping bag and dragged it into the tent. Cameron stood and bent back for a final farewell to the night sky.

Off in the distance, the display didn't go unnoticed. Four men, in two canoes, had been watching them. With binoculars they took turns ogling Ashley's feminine curves. The silky fabric shimmered highlights of her figure.

One whispered, "Hey man, don't hog the binoculars. She's hot!"

The alpha male lectured, "Don't grab! And be quiet." He hissed, "We need to hang loose, until the opportunity is right. We can't ambush them until they are at a real campsite."

The men were under a suspended mosquito net, using their paddles as tent posts. The canoes were tied together and tethered to the mangroves, just around a bend from the platform. They bantered about the plan. Each guy had his own idea of what they should do and patience was running thin.

One said, "Damn, this is uncomfortable, but probably we can catch them tomorrow. I think they will be out on Pavilion Key if they follow the canoe trail, and don't stay here."

Mitchell said, "They better be moving on or we should just do it now. I don't think I can wait another night this way. They are so much into each other, we can catch them off guard, even on this platform."

The leader of the group said in a loud whisper, "Shut the fuck up! We will overwhelm them when they least expect it and we have cover. If we are going to capture their camp, we have to wait for the right time! A time they will be most vulnerable." He snickered.

"OK, OK, I'm just not into peanut butter and jelly and sleeping in a wet canoe, stalking them."

The ringleader reminded them, "When we made this plan, we all agreed on it. Nobody needs to get hurt and we want to pull this punk off." The other three grumbled agreement. They would all give it one more day. Maybe they could catch a fish and have something hot to eat after they did the deed.

The honeymooners woke early with the sunrise. Sticking his head out of the pop-up tent, Cameron was immediately attacked by a swarm of ravenous pests. He zipped the opening quickly and swatted at the few that had invaded the tent.

"Ashley, honey, we're going to have to stay in the tent until the wind picks up and blows the bugs away." Ashley was happy to sleep longer, warm in their sleeping bag. They both napped a couple more hours. When they woke again, the bugs were tolerable. As they were breaking camp, eager to get underway, they were a moving target for the bugs.

The men in the canoes were still in the mangroves, waiting. Miserable from a damp night in a cramped canoe, they were eager for the couple to leave. After they left, the men went up to the platform where they could stretch their legs, use the porta potty, and even make some coffee. Secure in the knowledge that they could easily catch up with the honeymoon couple, they needed to take this little break. Drinking beer late into the night, they were all moving a little slowly.

Their sleeping bags were laid out to dry in the sun. Each took a turn at casting a top lure from the platform. Jonathan caught a fish, a little one. But he caught more flak from his buds. "Hey man, that's a really big catch. How'd you ever haul it in?" All hoped they might land something that would be suitable for a feast after they ambushed the couple. "Hey, if we don't get anything, I'm sure we can score some of their food. Even build a fire on the beach! We have some brats and still have a little beer."

The coffee was good and stretching their legs prepared them for the chase. Tonight would be their chance. They waited until noon to depart. With only 7 or 8 miles to get to the island camp, there was no need to hurry. They needed to arrive at dusk or later to avoid being seen.

Ashley and Cameron were delighted with the beach campsite. Walking the pristine beach, they collected shells and waded in the breaking waves. Pavilion Key was a wilderness paradise. The water was clear and warm, a welcome change from the green murky waters in the mangroves. They stripped down and frolicked naked in the shallow water until several large dark forms appeared just offshore, about 50 yards away from them. Fearing a group of sharks, they scrambled from the water only to see a coconut-sized head lift up and exhale a breath with a spurt. "Manatees!" Ashley joyfully shrieked.

They glanced at each other, laughing at their brief trepidation, and watched the manatee parade move south until they disappeared. With the sun getting low, they put their clothes on and collected driftwood for a fire. They made a ring with the shells and dragged a larger log for a bench seat. The onshore breeze was tamping down the hordes of insects. Lighting the fire, they watched the sun descend into the Gulf of Mexico, hoping for a green flash. They were two young lovers, basking in nature. Ashley confessed, "This might be a more genuine experience than a Caribbean resort."

From his anchorage near Rabbit Key, Thompson saw the four men paddle by. The old man was on his back deck cooking his dinner, pausing to give them the "skunk eye." He watched as they paddled south toward Pavilion Key.

The four men could see the newlyweds' tent at the north end of Pavilion Key and the campsite portable toilet, standing like a lighthouse. They paddled east of the unnamed islands and entered the cove on the south end of Pavilion Key. Seeing the glow and smoke of the fire, they carefully chose a landing that was out of view. Pulling the canoes up onto the beach and tying painters to some shrubs, they prepared for the invasion. It would be dark soon and the couple would then be retreating inside the tent, or so they thought.

It was hours before Ashley and Cameron stood up from their fireside bench, kissed and retired inside the tent. Now the crew could put their plan into action. They stealthily positioned themselves about 100 yards south of the camp. The wind had shifted and the waning campfire smoke wafted between them and the tent.

The couple had just stripped to get into their sleeping bag. The guys could see the silhouettes of the couple on the tent illuminated by an LED lamp. When the light went out, they started their slow walk towards the camp.

Ashley asked "Do you hear that?"

"No, what?"

"Listen."

"Maybe it's something flapping."

"No, there's music or drumming or something."

"Yes. I hear it now. It's getting a little louder."

Cameron reached for a hiking pole and unsheathed his dive knife.

"Quiet! Get me some zip ties from the pack."

Ashley found the zip ties. Cam secured the knife to the end of the hiking pole.

"Quiet."

The sound was getting louder. "Bump, bump, thump, thump. They could make out "Demons, Demons." It was a remix of scary, spooky songs. They were both frightened. "Shhh, we're not alone. We can't be trapped in the tent." Half dressed, they crawled outside.

They were dimly illuminated in the fading glow of the fire, easily in view of the approaching men. The assailants had made a soundtrack for their march, playing it on a portable speaker, adjusting the volume to be louder as they got closer.

"Bump, bump, thump thump…. spine chillers. You can't outrun us demons."

Cameron and Ashley sneaked around the edge of the tent, seeing four shadowy figures in ski masks and dark shirts, stumbling towards them, moving like zombies. They kept coming, through the smoke.

Cameron was not going to succumb without a fight. He yelled, "Hey! Get out of here!"

They kept coming. As they got closer, the music got louder. He could see the four figures' erratic, jerking movements.

When they were within thirty feet, they emerged through the smoke. He yelled again. "STOP!"

The men kept coming forward. The glow of the campfire and smoke was eerie.

Cameron stood and heaved his cobbled together spear at the closest figure. The man saw the projectile and raised his hand to deflect it from hitting his chest.

Stopping immediately, he dropped his portable speaker and grabbed his hand. His thumb was nearly severed and spurting blood. He screamed out in agony, frightening everyone.

"Damn it, you cut off my thumb!"

Cameron paused, "Yes, and I'll cut off your dick next!"

"Cameron, it's us!" yelled one of the men. "You hit Chad!"

Confused about how the hell Chad could be there, he recognized the voice. "Bill?"

The men pulled off their ski masks and rushed to Chad. One pulled Chad's mask off and asked, "What happened?" Another man turned the loud thumping music off.

Chad said, "My hand is cut. It's really bad," while squeezing his hand together as tight as he could.

"Come over here. Ashley, get the light." She was panicked, perplexed and perturbed. Getting into the tent, she retrieved the light and grabbed Cameron's long-sleeved shirt to cover herself up.

The wind seemed to pick up. Jonathan took out a small flashlight to shine on Chad's hand. They sat him by the fire on the log where, just a few hours ago, everything was so ideal. Chad's hand was covered in blood.

"Let me see it."

Chad shook his head no and drew his arms closer to his chest.

Cameron said it again, more forcefully, "Let me see it!"

Chad extended his hand. In the light cast by the flashlight they could all see his thumb was askew, the blade cut to the bone between his thumb and first finger. Blood oozed and dripped. They could see little white tendons squiggling.

Chad looked down and got dizzy. Grabbing back his hand, he gathered his thumb back into position and gripped his injured hand with his other hand. He fell back to sit on a log.

Standing over Chad, the five of them were dumbfounded. Ashley asked, "So now what do we do? He needs medical attention and we are way out here." Chad's three conspirators shuffled their feet and looked at the ground. "We know we don't have cell service. Maybe we can go to the houseboat and ask the old man if he has a radio to call the Park."

"That's a good idea. Mitchell, you and Jon paddle over there. It's maybe a mile or so. Tell him what's going on." Cameron was taking charge. Ashley interrupted, "No, Cam, you and I should go. We talked to him before. Two strange guys in the night will just scare him. He'd probably shoot them."

Mitchell said, "I'll go get the canoes. They're around on the other side of the island." Jonathan and Bill were quick to agree to go too, so they could be doing something and exit the awkwardness of the situation of their failed stunt. Ashley decided she and Cameron should stay with Chad. While they waited for the others to return, they got dressed and prepared their kayaks to go to the houseboat.

All three pranksters raced to where they had left the canoes. Pushing one of the canoes into the water, Bill yowled and fell back. Mitch and Jon couldn't tell what was happening but there was thrashing and splashing water and thumping on the side of the canoe Bill had been pushing. Jon shined his light in the direction of the commotion, only to be horrified to see that a crocodile had a death grip on Bill's thigh. Bill was hammering the head of the crocodile hard with his fist. Frightened, the other two guys jumped into the fray.

The crocodile was writhing violently, instinctively trying to secure its prey. When the two men began beating on it too, the large reptile transitioned from offense to defense, releasing its death grip on Bill and snapping at Mitch and Jonathan. Then, it burst back into the dark water.

Jon and Mitch dragged Bill up to higher ground from the water's edge. They could see his pants leg was torn, with puncture-ripped flesh on his thigh where he'd been bitten. He wasn't bleeding as much as Chad's injury, but he was bloodied from the attack.

"We need to get back to the camp so we can get help!"

The prank they had orchestrated had turned into a full-blown nightmare. Now the joke was on them and it wasn't funny.

Jon raced up to the campsite from the lee shore, breathlessly exclaiming, "Bill's hurt!" Huffing, he continued, "A big alligator attacked him when we got the canoes."

Thinking Jonathan was joking, Cameron yelled, "God damn it, no more bullshit!"

"I'm not kidding. He's hurt and in one of the canoes. Mitch is with him but he's hurt bad. We need to get help."

While Jonathan was running to the campsite, Mitch paddled Bill around the island's edge to Ashley and Cameron's campsite. Gathering at the fire that Ashley refreshed with more driftwood, the situation was a surreal horror. Bill was laying back in the canoe with a t-shirt wrapped around his thigh, held in place by a belt. Chad was on the log, his head hung down, holding his hand. Cameron held Ashley tight trying to comfort her. Mitchell and Jonathan were standing by, dumbstruck, waiting for instructions.

Cameron broke the silence. "OK, we need to do something to get ourselves out of this mess. Ashley and I will take the kayaks and paddle to the houseboat and see if the old guy can help or call for somebody to help. You two stay here with Chad and Bill. Keep the fire going."

Ashley and Cameron launched their kayaks, each taking a flashlight. "Stay close, Ashley." She replied, "Don't worry! I'm scared and won't let you out of my sight!"

Fortunately, the moon was rising. Although not a full moon, at least it would not be pitch black for their emergency run. They paddled off into the night, into a shimmering ripple path of light reflecting the moon. Their purposeful paddling was boosted by adrenaline. Aided by a fresh backwind, they arrived at the houseboat quicker than they had imagined.

Approaching the houseboat, Ashley yelled, "Hello! Hello! Can you help us?" Coming alongside she repeated, "Hello! Hello! Can you help us? We have an emergency!"

Cameron chimed in, "Mister, please help us! Are you there?" He rapped his knuckles on the hull.

A bright light hit them from the bow of the houseboat. They heard a distinctive sound of a pump shotgun, chunk-clunk. The light was blinding. A gruff voice called out "What do you want?"

They both answered, talking over one another. "We need help. We're camping on Pavilion and have an emergency."

Pondering this and seeing it was the same two kids he'd met a couple days ago, he lowered the shotgun, and million-candle-power Q-beam spotlight.

"What's the problem?" Relieved that they weren't shot, Cameron explained that four guys came up on them, one was cut by a knife and one had been attacked by a crocodile. "Do you have a radio? Can you call for help? We don't have any cell phone signal out here."

Thompson said, "No, no radio. Your phones ain't gonna work this far out. The park patrol may be out in the morning to check on things but probably not tomorrow. Probably not until after the front passes. We've got some weather coming."

This was not the answer, not the quick solution, the couple sought.

Ashley asked in desperation, "So what should we do?" She started crying. "I don't think we can kayak to Flamingo from here tonight." Sniffling, she continued, "or even tomorrow."

Thompson growled "Tie up your little boats and come aboard. We can figure something out."

Once they were standing on the boat, they took a seat in the screened part of the houseboat. Thompson asked, "Where are they now? At your camp?"

Cameron nodded. Thompson was quiet for a moment and looked with disdain on these two pathetic kids intruding upon his hermitage. Slowly, he drawled, "Well, I reckon I'll just have to take y'all to Flamingo. But we need to go quick, before the front hits."

With that he sprang into action and barked orders. "Kid, pull up the anchor when I tell you." Thompson started his new motor and bumped it into gear. "Now, kid, pull on it!"

Cameron tugged on the line, hand over hand, retrieving the anchor.

Thompson throttled up and motored to the north end of the island. The wind was increasing, so he stayed off the beach to avoid getting blown onshore and stuck in the shallows.

"Go get your friends. Can you get back into your boats out here? I don't want to pull up to the beach in this wind. I won't be able to get back off."

Cameron told Ashley to stay on the houseboat. He paddled fast to the shore and to inform his former buddies of the plan.

As he approached the beach, Cameron yelled instructions to Mitch and Jonathan. "Take Bill out to the houseboat. Then come back for Chad."

They paddled Bill in the canoe to the houseboat where Ashley waited. Nearly capsizing the canoe, they got Bill rolled onto the deck and then returned for Chad.

Cameron instructed, "Jonathan, you stay here. I'll go with Mitch and Chad and get Chad on the houseboat. Then Mitch, you go back. You and Jon stay at the camp while we take the guys to Flamingo. We'll send help. Are you OK with this?"

Neither of them liked the idea. They wanted to go too, but neither was in the position to argue. They were OK and they could survive a night alone. The most important thing was getting Bill and Chad to a hospital.

Once Chad was on the boat, Thompson revved-up the motor and started down the outside of Pavilion Key. In the moonlight, Cameron could see Mitch make it back to shore and the two men standing by the fire. Their tent and the porta-potty reflected the fire glow like neon monuments.

Thompson was up on his steering perch piloting his craft past the south end of Pavilion Keys, noting a compass course. Cameron and Ashley were attending to their patients below in the screened enclosure, trying to stay out of the wind which was now a little chilly.

"Hey, Kid," Thompson shouted. "Come up here."

Cameron climbed up the tuna tower and looked to Thompson for orders.

"I want you to steer this boat so I can check out your friends' injuries. Think you can do that?"

"Yes sir!"

Thompson showed him how to steer the boat and pointed out a couple flashing lights on the horizon to use for reference. Barely visible was a line of land ahead and to the left. "Don't over steer to adjust your course. Just make small turns of the wheel and be patient. This boat doesn't turn on a dime. It takes a while to respond. Got it?"

Pointing to the dimly lit compass, Thompson added, "This is the course you want to keep."

"Yes sir."

Thompson backed down the ladder and started triage on the two injured men. His bedside manner was characteristically rough. "Let me look at you."

Thompson surveyed the trauma each had suffered. He cleaned their wounds and poured some of his precious bourbon on the cuts. Wrapped up with gauze from his old first aid kit, they were stabilized. The bleeding had stopped. Bill's bite was more worrisome; his thigh was bloated from internal bleeding. An infection could explode into sepsis. Fever was starting to set in.

Thompson returned to the helm and told Cameron to go take care of his friends and be nice to that little woman he was with, chiding, "This is no honeymoon for you to take your beautiful bride on."

The line of the weather front was approaching fast. The low cloud line was ominously advancing and catching up. It was a race down the Gulf side of the state to turn into Florida Bay where there would be safer sea conditions. It was only a few more miles to the turn. Thompson pushed forward at a higher speed. He'd never had a reason to open up the throttle on the houseboat. Ambling along had always been fast enough. Now he wanted to beat the weather and get these victims off his boat and into medical care.

The wind increased and seas kicked up. The front hit with a fierce strike, rocking the houseboat, making it pitch and roll for a few minutes. The passengers on deck huddled together and tried to get out of the wind, spray, and rain. Chad was seasick and holding back retching.

Finally turning east, they rounded West Cape Sable. At the turn, the water was turbulent where the waves were big from the long fetch before the front. In the lee of the Cape, blocking the northwest wind and with no distance for the waves to build, it was tolerable. Now the rain was the only impediment.

Ashley had been checking her cell phone to see if she had a signal. One bar flickered on and then off. She showed Cameron, saying, "Check your phone. Do you have anything?"

Cameron checked. It was the same with him, no solid bar. Ashley kept checking. In a few minutes she had one bar and dialed again.

"This is 911. What is the nature of your emergency?"

Ashley started rambling, stuttering, "I am on a boat in the Everglades. My friends are hurt. We need help. There was an accident."

"Ma'am, may I have your name. What is your location?" The 911 operator was calm and clear.

"I am Ashley Clark-Greene. I'm on a boat in the Everglades. I don't know where..."

The 911 operator said, "This is Marathon in the Florida Keys."

The call dropped. Ashley said "Hello, can you hear me?" Then she screamed into the phone, in desperation, "Hello! Hello?"

Looking at the phone, she could see the low battery symbol was flashing.

She dialed 911 again, asking Cameron, "Where should I say we are?"

"South of Cape Sable on the way to Flamingo, close to the beach."

"Hello, this is 911. What is the nature of your emergency?"

"I was just talking to you. I am on a boat in rough weather. My husband says we are south of ... Hello! Hello! Can you help us? Cape Sable headed to Flamingo."

"This is Marathon Emergency Center. Would you like the number for the Everglades National Park?"

Ashley screamed, "No! I am almost out of battery and we need help. Please call the Park or Coast Guard or anybody to help us. We have…" The phone was dead again. Barking at Cameron in her frustration, she asked for Cameron's phone and tapped 911 in again.

"Hello, this is the emergency response center in Marathon. What is the nature of your emergency?"

"I am on a derelict houseboat south of Cape Sable, near the beach, and really need help." Ashley was almost in tears.

"OK, honey, calm down. Can you provide more details about…" Cameron's cell phone went dead too. She hoped the EMS operator had enough information to send help.

The Marathon EMS operator wasn't convinced these calls weren't some kind of hoax. Why was the call coming from so far away, in the Everglades. Pausing for a minute, she decided she should call the emergency number at Everglades National Park. After a minute on hold, she was connected to Ranger Nelson.

She relayed all the information she had. Deciding he had to investigate, even if it was hoax, Nelson mobilized a search and rescue team. Heading out in a Park patrol boat and a larger boat with a cabin, they proceeded out the channel from Flamingo and headed into the weather approaching from the north. Steering by only the GPS plotter, the search team met the hermit's houseboat only a couple miles from Flamingo.

Nelson pulled alongside, shouting into the wind, "Thompson, do you have a problem?"

"Hell yes, Nelson! I've got a couple hurt kids on the boat and this weather is making it tough to keep this boat on track."

Nelson asked, "Do you want to off load them here, or keep going on in?"

Thompson yelled back, "Say again, I couldn't hear you!" while making a motion to hold his hand to his ear.

Nelson grabbed the bullhorn speaker and repeated his question.

Thompson gestured ahead, moving his arm forward.

Escorted by the two park boats, they docked in the marina boat basin. Rangers hurried to move the injured to shelter. Nelson ushered Ashley, Cameron and Thompson to the office.

They took turns briefing him on the events of the day leading to the tragic ending. A ranger came in and said the med-evac helicopter was on its way from Homestead. Rangers were doing what they could to keep Chad and Bill calm and warm, trying to avoid their going into shock. Bill was not looking good. The EMS personnel on the copter would be better able to render medical attention.

Nelson had a lot of questions, but those could wait until later. Having an overview of the situation, he made arrangements for a room in the Park's staff village for the young couple and suggested that Thompson stay at the Park dock. He told the assembled group that the canoers stranded on Pavilion would be rescued as soon as the front passed and rangers would retrieve everything possible from the campsite.

Nelson walked with Thompson down to the dock. "Thank you for your help. Those people would not have had a chance without it. It certainly would have been a different outcome."

Thompson scowled, "Yep, guess so." He continued, "You can replace the bottle of bourbon I used on their wounds, but I just want to get back to my peaceful life."

Ashley and Cameron retired to the small studio apartment, usually made available to VIP guests. They showered, rinsed their clothes and laid in bed. They were so worked up, they couldn't sleep. Staring at the ceiling, they told each other how lucky they were to be together. Cameron summed it up, "I think if we get through this, we can get through anything. While this might seem like a really rocky start, it's a solid foundation for our lives together." Ashley hugged him and whispered, "I hope you got your wish for a memorable honeymoon we could tell our grandkids about."

Spent and exhausted, they slumbered together.

FOUR

The storm hit Pavilion Key an hour after the houseboat departed. Mitch and Jonathan took shelter in the tent. It was a small shelter; fine for a honeymooning couple but not quite enough personal space for two mid-twenty-year-old men. They settled in to wait for rescue, using whatever Cameron and Ashley had left behind. Their own gear, sleeping bags and packs with food and water, had been emptied on the beach where they had originally landed so they could make space for Bill in the canoe.

Mitch said, "I sure hope they make it. Bill was really bit bad. Can you believe it – an alligator bit him. How many people get attacked by an alligator?"

Jonathan said, "It wasn't an alligator. It was a crocodile."

"A crocodile! We're not on the Nile or someplace in Africa. We're in Florida!"

Mitch replied, "No, it's an American crocodile. They only live in this small area in South Florida and people don't usually step on them at night."

Jonathan was incredulous that it was a crocodile. "How do you know it wasn't an alligator? It was large, had a big mouth with lots of teeth, and took a chunk out of Bill's leg. It tried to kill him!"

Mitch explained, "Alligators are mostly in fresh water, while crocs are mostly in salt water. Bill probably intruded on her nest on the sandy beach. I read somewhere that gators make a pile of rotting vegetation in the marsh for their nests, not out here on the shore like crocs do."

Jonathan accepted that it must have been a crocodile then. He tried to reassure himself and said out loud, "The guys will make it. That old man is helping them. If we had to rescue ourselves, it would have been a couple of days. Bill might not have made it and Chad would have had no chance at keeping his thumb. Now maybe there's a chance that both will be OK."

The tent shuddered with each wind gust, and waves of rain struck the thin fabric like bullets. "The storm is pretty nasty. I hope they're not caught in it, that they got to Flamingo before the weather got this bad."

They found a bottle of rum that Ashley and Cameron had already opened among their belongings left in the tent. "Since the rum's already open, I'm sure they wouldn't mind us sharing." Mitch said. Finding the couple's Yeti cups, Mitch poured each of them a generous drink.

Jonathan toasted their bungled venture. "Mitch, here's to an epic failure of bad intentions gone wrong! Skoal!"

Mitchell echoed, "Skoal!" Taking a sip, he continued. "We had such a good plan. It wasn't an outcome I could have ever imagined. This was supposed to be a big joke and tribute to Cameron's deep devotion to his family history."

Jonathan said, "You know when he first told us about his family story, I wasn't so convinced it ever happened or that people did such insensitive things."

Mitchell replied, "Yeah, it seemed a little creepy to me, but Cam took such pride in his great-grandparents honeymoon story. I checked it out, researching the practice on the Internet."

Mitch refreshed the rum and began recalling the story Cameron told him years ago. "Cameron said his great-grandparents were married in Atlanta at the turn of the last century. They barely had cars back then. On their wedding day, they had a ceremony in a church and then each went home to their separate houses to stay with their families on their wedding night. They each packed a bag for the next day.

"The next morning, Arthur called upon his new bride, Susie, at her home and together they boarded a trolley to take them down to the Chattahoochee River. He had a surprise for his bride, a boat trip and camping down the Chattahoochee River to start their new life together, alone. Arthur had built a skiff and stocked it for their adventure. He had everything they would need. Perhaps they would land in Columbus, Eufaula, or even Chattahoochee down in Florida.

"Arthur had his savings. Susie had put away some money too from her job at a chocolate candy factory. Maybe they would find a new place to live, maybe they would return to Atlanta. Either way they planned to live in a boarding house until they found a place of their own.

"They launched the new rowboat Arthur built and proceeded down the river. When they were ready to stop, they selected a site and set up camp. They were about to be intimate when yelling and banging pots and pans interrupted their postponed wedding night. It was Arthur's friends practicing something called 'shivaree.'"

"Shivaree?" Jonathan looked puzzled.

Mitch continued, "I found a lot of information on the shivaree practice. It was an old ritual that evolved over time from a genuine objection to a couple's marriage to the kind of thing Cameron's great-grandparents experienced. Shivaree became a harassment of newlyweds as a joke to disrupt them from consummating their nuptials."

"Sure was different times," Jonathan remarked. He then smiled as he realized that shivaree is exactly what all of them had planned to do.

"Arthur and Susie's 'friends'", Mitch continued, using air quotes, "followed them down the river, letting them escape during the day and catching up at night to repeat the annoyance."

Jonathan recalled, "Cam said this went on for a week. Can you believe it? But he said the family lore tells about how, while on the river, his great-grandfather and great-grandmother learned a lot about each other and started a long life together. Though he never met them, Cam was fascinated by their honeymoon shivaree story."

Mitch continued his story by commenting, "I think the outdoor adventure Cameron planned for Ashley was founded in his romanticism about his kinfolk. I can't imagine any other reason a couple would go out here instead of some cushy resort or even visit a city in Europe."

Jonathan kidded, "Oh, yeah. Why not go to some interesting vacation spot like Haiti or Afghanistan?"

Mitchell asked, "You recall how Cameron said it ended up? Cam told me they spent a week rowing down the Chattahoochee, camping, fishing, and enjoying the solitude of just being together. They stopped before they came up on rapids and falls near Eufaula,

Alabama. Arthur sold his boat to some locals for enough money for the two of them to buy passage on the train back to Atlanta."

Jonathan cut in on Mitchell's story. "But the guys chasing them didn't know his great-grandparents left the river and headed home! The guys continued down river and wound up on the rocks. Their boat busted and sank. His shivaree tormentors didn't have enough money for the train so they had to walk back to Atlanta. When they first set out, they figured they would row upstream to get home."

Mitch said, "Kind of like us. Chad instigated our shivaree scheme. Best laid plans; it seemed like a good idea at the time. We were all in. If everything worked, it would have been funny. His groomsmen coming out of no-where acting like zombies. What could go wrong?"

Jonathan lamented, "Now that I think about it, I don't know if it would have been funny. Even if it had worked out, I'm not so sure Ashley would be laughing. I bet she's not laughing now. I bet she's pissed!"

Mitch said, "I know Cameron will be pissed, especially about how bad things turned out. He didn't mean to cut off Chad's thumb. Cam, hell, both of them, must have been scared to death. Our plan wasn't just an annoyance – it was too much!"

"Do you really think he thought we were zombies?"

Mitch was vehement, "Hell no! I bet he thought we were attackers, maybe redneck rapists, murderers, or worse."

Jonathan chuckled, "What's worse than murderers and rapists? Ready for another shot? We're going to have to buy them another bottle when we get back, if they will still be talking to us ever again."

Mitchell said, "Yep, hit me! We'll get them a case! I wonder where they are now and how the guys are doing? Sure hope they made it, not to mention hope they will be sending someone back for us."

Jonathan offered, "For sure, it won't be tonight. It's pretty frisky outside. It's blowin' like crazy. I'm glad we have their little tent and are not sleeping in a canoe tonight! Let's go to sleep and wait this out. I'm ready, it's been quite a day! How 'bout you?"

Mitchell said, sarcastically, "No, think I'll go outside and see if I can shine up some gator eyes." He followed his remark with, "Yes, I think we should rest up. Who knows what will happen tomorrow."

Dawn broke to the east. The weather changed and was much cooler, with a strong wind out of the north. Jonathan found some matches so they could restart the fire. Looking through the camp supplies they also found some food. Once the fire was started, they made coffee and a little breakfast of energy bars and cookies. Now, all they could do was wait and keep the fire burning until help arrived.

It wasn't long before help did arrive. Two rangers in the large park patrol boat edged up to the beach at the campsite. The guys were happy to see them, rushing to ask how Chad and Bill were doing. The ranger who was obviously in charge responded that they had been airlifted to the hospital in Homestead, but he didn't have any news of their condition.

The other ranger said, "We're here to get you and your stuff. Can we help you gather things up?"

Jonathan said, "Yes, thanks. We are grateful y'all came for us. I'll get the canoe and our gear from the other side of the key."

One of the rangers said he would come along to help. Arriving at their landing spot, Jonathan saw the place where the crocodile attack happened. There were tracks in the sand from the reptile's feet and Bill's boot. It gave him pause.

After putting the supplies he and Mitchell had off-loaded back into the canoe, Jonathan grabbed the painter on the canoe and started dragging it along the shore. The ranger suggested it would be more efficient for them to paddle it around, back to the campsite.

The trip to Flamingo passed through the Shark River into Whitewater Bay, Coot Bay and down the canal to the NPS Service Area boat basin. Ashley and Cameron were waiting when they docked. Jonathan and Mitchell had no idea what to say.

Mitchell started, "We are so sorry. So, so sorry. What's happening with Chad and Bill? Any news?"

Ashley said nothing but her angry eyes pierced their souls. They couldn't look at her. Cameron, on the other hand, was reserved as he answered. "They are both OK. Chad's hand needs surgery and Bill is going to recover. He would have died from internal bleeding or an infection if he hadn't got to the hospital for antibiotics.

"I have no idea what you were thinking - that you could pull something like this on us. It is one giant mess. I guess I made very bad choices for groomsmen and a best man. I don't know how we will ever get over it."

Ashley finally spoke in an angry tone, "You four ruined our honeymoon and Cam has been hurt by his best friends. I'm glad you are OK, but don't expect us to help you get to Homestead. For all I care, you can walk back to Atlanta."

After Ashley and Cameron sorted and packed their things from the pile of camping supplies offloaded from the Park boat, they drove off in the car they had shuttled to Flamingo. Sitting in his office, Nelson then interviewed the two survivors. He told the two remaining prank perpetrators, "Seems no laws have been broken. If Chad doesn't press charges on assault with a deadly weapon, there won't be any."

Nelson thought to himself, "The only thing the four fools were guilty of was a stupid, foolhardy attempt to prank their friend to resurrect a memory."

Nelson smiled and resumed his conversation with the two men in front of him. "You're free to go. You can collect your stuff. I think it will be a long walk back to your car in Everglades City or you could take your canoes and go by water." Nelson and the other rangers were not anxious to provide any assistance beyond what was minimally required.

FIVE

Ranger Nelson drove around Flamingo to check out the campgrounds. Being early winter, there was a good bit of activity. Because winter provided decent temperatures and stiff breezes, keeping the legendary horde of insects away, campers usually had a pleasant stay.

As he drove through the new camping areas developed after a recent hurricane had devastated Flamingo, he noted the infusion of disaster recovery funds was having a positive impact by updating the tired and well-worn facilities. Though the Everglades Park hosts a million visitors a year, spread over the three main entrances, Flamingo is at the end of the road. For most visitors, it is more of a day trip than a vacation destination. For locals, Flamingo is the launching place for fishing in Florida Bay or the freshwater back-country. Few locals would choose camping at Flamingo over, say, the Florida Keys. More often the campers come from far away, the Midwest or Northeast, drawn by the image created by tourism promotions or PBS nature programs. Some are dedicated birdwatchers making seasonal pilgrimages to observe the remarkable variety of birds.

Nelson made note of the license plates on the parked vehicles, subconsciously playing a game of license plate geography, noting the furthest distance or the state having the most visitors. Driving through the parking area at the visitor center, Nelson saw a nice Mercedes backed into a space at a far corner of the lot. It had no license tag on the front bumper, which was not unusual as Florida does not require front tags. What seemed a little off was the car being covered with leaves and bird droppings. It must have been parked there awhile. Nelson stopped and walked around to the back. There was no license plate, front or rear.

Nelson was a little curious. It wasn't unknown for stolen vehicles to be abandoned in the park at remote locations. But, he never heard of a stolen vehicle being dumped at Flamingo. It was too far for an easy get-away or thieves who would be stripping parts. This Mercedes Benz was intact, only very dirty.

Looking inside the windows, he saw an empty hiking boot box, a Patagonia puffy winter coat, and a bag printed with an REI logo. Some fast-food rubbish could be seen on the passenger side. He copied the VIN number so he could check a database for stolen vehicles.

His database search revealed that the Mercedes was registered in New York to Ronald Donald Bradford, III, New York, New York. The vehicle was not stolen and there were no warrants for Bradford. An Internet search showed that he was a financial advisor in New York City. His website looked professional, claiming that he owned a small firm giving personal attention to "high net worth" clients. His portrait photos revealed a handsome, smiling mid-30s man, looking casual, sitting on a desk with the New York skyline visible in the background.

Nelson tried the phone numbers listed on the website. The phone went to an automatic recording, "The number you have reached is no longer in service. Please check the number and try again." Next, Nelson sent an email to the email contact listed, asking for Mr. Bradford to please contact him regarding a vehicle registered in his name. He attached a .jpg image of the car. It was a mystery, but not an urgent problem; follow-up could wait. In the meantime, Nelson would keep an eye on the car.

After a couple days with no response to the email, on a hunch, Nelson decided to call the New York Police Department to request a wellness check. It would be good to know if Bradford was in New York or if he might be lost in the Everglades. He found the precinct close to the address on the registration. The duty officer answered "NYPD 13th. Can I help you?"

Ranger Nelson introduced himself and explained about finding the car in Everglades National Park with missing tags. He asked if they could do a wellness check and perhaps tell Mr. Bradford that his Mercedes has been located.

The Officer was incredulous. "What? We've got more to do here than 'wellness checks.' Do we take his temperature when we find him?" The demeanor was not quite what Nelson expected from a fellow law enforcement officer.

"Yes sir. Please let me know if he's running a fever." Nelson returned the sarcasm. "Seriously, would you please see if there is anyone at that address who might clear up why his car is seemingly abandoned in our parking lot."

The NYPD duty officer called back a few hours later. He was more serious and professional. "Ranger Nelson, this is Sgt. Patronis. I had an officer visit the address you gave me. The place is in kind of an up-scale neighborhood. He found door tags on the brownstone indicating that the electricity and water had been shut off for non-payment. The mailbox was overstuffed. The house looks abandoned. My officer checked with a neighbor and she reported that she hadn't seen Mr. Bradford for a month. The neighbor also said his wife and daughter left a couple months ago in a cab, but she didn't know where they might be."

Nelson thanked him for the help. "Please call me if anything else comes up."

It wasn't long before Nelson had another call from New York. This time, it was a detective on the phone about Bradford. "Hello Ranger Nelson. I'm Detective Ramos with the financial crimes investigative unit. We've been looking into Ronald Donald Bradford regarding some suspicious business activity. There's no arrest warrant yet, but it looks like he got fooled by a Ponzi scheme and then created his own Ponzi scheme to cover up his mistake. If you have his car, it's helpful to know where we might start looking for him. We would like to talk to him."

This surprised Nelson.

"We found his former secretary. She knew something was up with what he was doing, but apparently not in on it. She quit after missing two paychecks and seeing the business account overdrafts, and a mountain of late payment and final notice letters in their mail. He was a one-man show, making the pretense of a wheeler-dealer. We think he got in way over his head."

Ranger Nelson's curiosity increased. "Why would someone from New York run to the Everglades?" He asked the detective, "Do you know if his wife and daughter might be with him?"

"No, they're in Rhode Island with her parents. Appears she didn't have any involvement with her husband's business affairs. From what we found she is a total socialite, involved in a different world. She and her daughter are safe, so if you find him, please let us know. There's no warrant yet, but this is an active investigation. I'll text you my contact info. Can I use this number to send texts?"

"Of course. It's my work cell." Nelson hung up the phone. Thinking aloud, he said, "Wow, guess I need to put this on the ranger blackboard notes, to watch for Bradford." He drove back to the Mercedes. Although he hadn't thought of it before, he now wondered if there was a chance Bradford could be in the trunk. Nelson leaned over and sniffed the seams. If there was a body, even for just a little while, there would be a smell. It passed the whiff test, so it was unlikely that he was in the trunk and Nelson didn't want to get a warrant to search. Not yet.

Putting the mystery aside, Nelson's roster for the next day scheduled him for a routine patrol of the west coast. He was happy for the opportunity to run out to the Gulf, with nothing on the agenda but checking the boundary. Buddy and a couple of junior rangers were already at the service basin dock so they helped him cast off. Buddy said, "Boss man, I know this has to be great for you - no crisis and beautiful weather. And you won't have to fly a desk, pushing paper while the weather's so nice."

Teasing, Buddy asked, "You going to take a fishing pole?" knowing Nelson was mostly a by-the-book kind of ranger.

"Not today, Buddy. And, if I did, you wouldn't know it. I'm working." Nelson smiled and motored out of the service area basin to the Buttonwood Canal.

The Buttonwood Canal and Coot Bay now was cut off from Florida Bay by a water control structure that prevented the fresh water from spilling out into the bay. In the past, the canal had been an open drain on the freshwater system and a pipeline for saltwater intrusion. Park biologists, working with the Everglades restoration program, devised a plan to better emulate the natural flow of fresh water into the bay by adding a water control structure. The structure was an obstacle that cut off easy transit from the service area basin to the bay, but the ecological need outweighed the inconvenience of not having quick access to Florida Bay.

An hour and 20 miles later, he was entering the Shark River. Keeping an eye out for the hermit houseboat, he wanted to catch up with Thompson. It had been a month since he rescued the kayakers.

There was not much boat activity that day. A couple of flats boats worked the shore with fishermen angling to land a tarpon on fly rods. Nelson waved as he passed by, giving them a wide pass so he didn't rock their boats. Out on the Gulf, he turned north to round Shark River Island and started winding through the braided creeks of Ponce de Leon Bay. The Park was gloriously free of boats. Flocks of ducks were his main companions.

His route was plotted to go to the river outlets: Harney River, Broad River, Rodgers River, Lostman's River and Chatham River. Near Duck Rock he saw the houseboat.

Thompson was on deck as Nelson approached. Grumbling, he asked, "What's it this time? I haven't been here 30 days yet!"

"Not here to hassle you, Mr. Thompson. It's just a courtesy call to thank you for your help with the rescue." Knowing he would be rebuffed as usual, he asked, "Can I come aboard?"

"Not without a warrant." It was the same answer every time. Thompson was dependably consistent.

"I have something for you. Actually, two things," he said as he handed a bag up to the old man. It was a bottle of bourbon, a premium brand. "There's more. This came to my office with a note asking me to pass it along to you," he said as he handed the old man an envelope.

Thompson opened it and unfolded a card, reading out loud,

"Dear Sir, I don't know your name and I hope this gets to you. I want to express my deep appreciation for helping my husband, Cameron, and me get to safety when we were in a desperate situation. While our honeymoon turned out to be a terrifying nightmare, you were so kind to save us and the injured men. I am forever grateful you were there in our time of need.

Sincerely, (Mrs.) Ashley Clark-Greene"

"Well, ain't that nice. A thank you note from the young bride." Thompson tried to be nonplussed by the note, but he couldn't hide that it meant something to him. He put it back in the envelope and tucked it away in his camper.

"Now, Nelson, is there anything else?"

"I thought you might be interested in what happened to the kids you saved." Thompson was curious.

"Well, after you brought the two injured guys in and the weather settled down, I sent rangers out to Pavilion to bring in the two guys that stayed on the island, along with their canoes and gear and the honeymooners' gear and a kayak from the campsite. At the boat basin, when the couple met the guys left on the island, it was painful to watch how angry the couple was with their friends, the two in front of them and the two who were injured. All four guys and the husband had been friends for a long time. But the men pulling that immature prank strained that friendship to the breaking point. The newlyweds had a car in Flamingo that they had shuttled before they even started out from Everglades City on their honeymoon adventure. So, they loaded up their gear and kayaks and drove off, back to retrieve the rental car they left in Everglades City and then return to Atlanta to recuperate. The honeymooners were not in a mood to help their so-called friends."

Nelson went on, "The two injured men ended up in the hospital in Homestead. The one with the cut hand will need some more surgery to put him back together. The crocodile bite victim was worse off. He had internal bleeding, needed intravenous antibiotics and was out of it for several days. Likely your bourbon helped keep it from being worse than it was.

"The remaining two men were stranded in Flamingo. All four of them had started out in Everglades City, too, in two rented canoes. Their original plan was to harass the honeymooners for a night or two and then paddle back to their starting point. But, instead, because the prank was a monumental failure, they ended up at our dock in Flamingo, with a pile of their camping equipment and canoes that needed to be returned. And, they had no vehicle to get back to their cars in Everglades City."

Thompson snickered, "Served 'em right."

"We loaned the two stranded men a phone so they could call for an Uber to take them to Homestead where they could pick up their friend with the bad hand, rent a U-Haul, drive back to Flamingo to gather their gear and the canoes, and eventually take their stuff back to Everglades City and retrieve their cars. It took them an entire day just to do this. Then they still had to return the U-Haul.

"All in all, it turned out OK, but there's going to be a lot of hurt to heal for those folks, both physically and emotionally."

Thompson was pleased that it worked out. Despite believing that his hermit life had been disrupted by the event, a bad outcome would have made him feel that his efforts to rescue the injured men in a wild storm had been fruitless.

"I've asked the other rangers to lighten up on your stays in the Park. You should still plan on moving out every so often, but the exact 30-day limit ought not be a problem for a while."

Thompson was relieved with this news, but he had already decided he would do what he wanted until he was told otherwise. He offered to Nelson, "I want to let you know about something curious I've been watching for some time. There are a couple guys who come down here almost weekly to fish."

"That's not so unusual. It's a popular place."

"No, these guys are up to something, not just fishing. They stop at the boundary signs that mark the Park area, and pull up some kind of trap, maybe a fish trap. I've looked for a float, but they must have the pull line sunk and attached to the post. Then they put out a trot-line in the mangroves and return at night to haul it in. Can't see what they catch, but it must work or they wouldn't be back so regular."

"When do they come? Any particular day of the week?" Nelson queried.

"Mostly middle of the week, either a Wednesday or Thursday. Hell, I don't know. Days of the week are not important to me. What day is it anyway?" Thompson had shared all that he wanted to.

Nelson thanked him and started to push off from Thompson's houseboat. "I'll be heading back to Flamingo now. Oh, I almost forgot, here's your Golden Eagle Pass to federal fee areas, a cruising permit, and your Florida senior saltwater fishing license. You passed the Park test with flying colors! Now, I think you are completely legal."

Thompson took the handful of paperwork and plastic cards. He was grateful for Nelson's help, but didn't want to be too effusive. He responded simply, "Much obliged."

Nelson enjoyed the return ride to Flamingo, as he thought about what, if anything, to do about Thompson's report of the fishermen. It was the golden hour; a pleasant late afternoon, with the sun showering a warm tint on the mangrove shoreline. The olive-green forest brightened to glow in contrast with a darkening intense blue eastern sky. Behind him the sun was low on the horizon tinting the sky orange, partially blocked by purple clouds.

Nelson got back in time to turn his attention to the possibility that Ronald Bradford was in his park. His car was still there, but it had only been a day since he last checked on it. He drove by it again to see if there was anything he missed. The only new observation was a decal for a parking garage in Manhattan.

Back in his office, Nelson searched the Internet again for information on Bradford. Google turned up little that was new or useful. Bradford's Linkedin account revealed his ivy-league pedigree and past affiliations with other financial associates. Nelson thought, "This is not my investigation. My responsibility is the Park and whether he is here and safe. The NYPD's issues are not really my concern."

The next morning, he decided to glue a notice tag on the windshield of the Mercedes. The neon green tag stated the car would be towed and impounded if it was not removed within 30 days. He added his cell phone number to the tag with a Sharpie. Now all he could do was wait.

Following the passing of a recent low pressure system, the usual heat and humidity were reclaiming the weather. The bugs would be increasing. Yet, for a few more days, Flamingo would be pleasant for the visitors and campers. Nelson's time would be spent on paperwork and work schedules for the district. He regretted being inside when the weather was decent.

SIX

Ronald Bradford, III did not know what to do. His business had crashed and he was out of his own money, as well as his clients' money that he had been using to keep his business going. Not that long ago, he would add new clients and use their funds to cover his expenses and pay fictional dividends to existing investors. He thought so long as he could keep adding clients, he might be able to coast long enough for some real investment to pay off.

Receptions and events he attended with his wife were fertile fields to recruit new clients. The social events were rife with moneyed people who donated to charitable purposes. Being introduced by his wife was instant cred, because she frequented every event. She was even acquainted with the top tier donors. He hoped one day to score an introduction to one of those super-wealthy donors. That could solve his problems. He knew he could get back on track if he had enough resources to plug the leaks in his collapsing enterprise. The scam he invested in was the first domino to fall in the cascade he was experiencing now.

After the money was gone, so was his wife. Ronald knew she only stuck with him for the glamour of his business. But she wasn't up for sticking with him through tough times. Taking their daughter, she went running back to her parents in Barrington. Her family was wealthy and a safe refuge from the turmoil in which Ronald had become embroiled. When she left, she told him that she hoped he would get back to his normal, self-absorbed self and they could resume the equilibrium of their separate lives together.

His situation was desperate. He sat alone in his office. There was no way out. No scheme he could imagine would boost him out of the quagmire. He could not face his clients. His wife was gone. It was time to change the channel, to run to where he couldn't be found.

It was a cold gray winter in New York. While Internet searching he caught an advertisement of Florida tourism venues showing greens and blues and sunshine. The slogans like "Visit Florida – our beaches are waiting!", "Hike, fish, swim, camp, paddle!", and "Escape to Paradise!" caught his attention.

Ronald thought, "Maybe I can hide out until this blows over. For damn sure, there is nothing left here. I'll go to Florida and live off the land." It didn't matter that his only outdoor experience had been a cushy guided hunting experience on a South Georgia quail plantation. He had enjoyed the trip that had been sponsored by an investment fund soliciting representatives to push their product.

The hunting wasn't so much fun. It was a little intimidating to be handed a loaded shotgun by a man accompanying each guest. Dogs pointed up the birds. Then, once the birds flushed, he was supposed to aim and shoot. He was horrible at it. He was worried more about shooting somebody or even himself. The experienced black attendants were used to the inexperienced novice hunters and kindly assisted. When he finally shot one quail and it was retrieved by a dog, Ronald was done.

Walking in the pine woods was enjoyable. Being out in nature was a new experience for him. Sure, he'd been in Central Park jogging on the paved walkways, but this was different. It was a tall forest with a carpet of knee-high green ferns, miles away from civilization. He watched in awe as a whitetail deer bolted from the brush and disappeared into the forest shadows. Ronald was intrigued and wondered about living a rural, even wilderness life.

He enjoyed the evening gatherings in the austere old lodge when he could talk money with the other prospective finance advisors. The more the bourbon flowed the more tongues wagged. They were all braggarts and he was aspiring to be the top dog. The sponsor's sales pitch was compelling, too good to be true with a guaranteed return on investment and generous commissions. Seeing an opportunity for great riches, he was seduced by greed. He bought into the scam. He went all in, now to his deep regret.

With most of his credit cards maxed out and only a few thousand dollars in his secret petty cash bank bag, Ronald schemed his plan. He was off to Florida.

Ronald picked up some clothes at his home, got in his Mercedes and started driving. Once on the road, after he exited New York City's traffic, he could turn his attention to the details of his plan.

As he drove, he thought, "If I'm going to disappear, I need to be careful about doing things that would leave a trail for someone to track me." He reasoned that traveling on the toll roads was not a good idea, because the toll system would record his license plate and charge his Easy Pass transponder. Stopping at the first service plaza he came to in New Jersey, he paid cash for gas and purchased a *Rand McNally Road Atlas*. Sitting in the parking lot, he plotted his route south. He did not want to use his cell phone, knowing he could be tracked by cell towers so he purchased a burner phone at the service plaza gift shop. He decided he was mostly going to take US 1, not the interstate highway, all the way to Florida.

Since he'd already telegraphed his path by getting on the Jersey Turnpike, he decided to exit and detour taking another interstate highway west. The map showed a big natural area along the route, the Great Swamp National Wildlife Refuge near Basking Ridge. If he used his credit card at a store there, he could purchase camping gear to use up the small amount left on the card's credit limit. If the purchases were discovered by checking his card activity, maybe anyone looking for him would think he was camping in the swamp.

An REI store was nearby. There was so much merchandise in the store and he really had no idea what he might need. After wandering around awhile, feeling overwhelmed, he decided to ask for help. All he had in his cart was a Patagonia winter coat.

The salesperson was helpful, loading Ronald's cart up with a pop-up tent, back pack, frame, sleeping bag, air mattress, nesting cookware, trail knife, dried trail meals, long underwear, trail stove, and more. There was so much stuff, he needed an extra shopping cart. Tallying the purchases, the register showed $4,587.

Ronald handed his card to the clerk. It was declined. He pulled out another. It was declined. Finally, the Visa that he rarely used worked. It had a $5,000 credit limit, so Ronald decided to max it out with a pair of boots. Happy with such a large sale, the REI associate helped him out to his car to load the bounty into his trunk.

From now on, he would travel the back roads to US 1 and continue on south to Florida. As it was now night and Ronald was hungry, he decided to stop at a McDonald's, peeved that he shared his name with the mascot. In school, it had been a constant source of teasing.

He figured he could nap for a couple of hours in a Walmart parking lot and then resume driving straight through to Florida. He dreamt of the Sunshine State until someone rapping on the driver's window startled him awake. It was a security guard making his rounds. It was now dawn; Ronald had slept longer than intended.

Twenty-four hours later, Ronald saw his first Florida sign: "Welcome to the Sunshine State, Ron DeSantis, Governor." The sign had been altered to read "DeSatin." Obviously, the governor was not popular with everyone.

Glad to be in Florida, and in warmer temperatures, he only had 500 miles to go to reach his destination, the Everglades. During the many hours of driving alone, he had refined his plan. He would go to the end of the road, remove the New York plates and park his car. Then, he would hike out to a place where he could hide out. Although he thought he had enough supplies to support himself for a long time, he wasn't thinking clearly about how he would transport it all to a remote campsite.

Driving US 1 with a second wind of adrenaline, Ronald passed through little towns and traffic-snarled suburbs. It was slow going. Florida seemed to be an endless strip of chain stores and defunct shopping malls, traffic lights, and stop-and-go gridlock. A few stretches were open roads through fields and forests. Real estate signs promised some parcels would be suitable for development. If he still had the money, these real estate opportunities would have tempted him to invest. New developments were sprouting up on the outskirts of the small towns, promising wonderful retirement living. Indeed, these places would be paradise for the aging baby boomers living up north in a land of congestion, crime, and snow.

The 500-mile trip down was not taking the 10 hours his burner cell phone predicted. Five hours after entering the state, he was barely south of Daytona Beach. The remaining 340 miles would be too far for him to make without stopping. He was tired. Contemplating staying in a cheap hotel, he decided it would be too risky. Presenting his ID to get a room could lead to his being tracked.

The longer he drove, the more concerned he was that he was being followed. Periodically, he checked his rearview mirror for familiar vehicles. If he had been seeing a car behind him for a while, he slowed to let it pass. If the car didn't pass he would turn in a block or two so he could be certain he wasn't being stalked by anyone.

Ronald stopped at another fast-food joint to eat and check his atlas. Maybe he could get to Titusville and find a place to stay the night – either a hotel parking lot or maybe a Walmart. Then he saw a marquee for a truck stop in Mims, just a little north of Titusville. Talking to himself, he said aloud, "That will work."

He pulled around to the large lot and parked next to large trailers waiting to be picked up, in a place where he wouldn't be visible or bothered. The next morning, he woke to see that his parking scheme had worked. He regretted that he hadn't thought of sleeping at truck stops on the way down.

Later in the day, he arrived at Everglades National Park. In the visitor center he wandered through displays about wildlife and sat to watch a film about the park. Ronald collected brochures and a general leaflet and he purchased a trail guide in the bookstore. Sitting in his car, he studied the literature intently. It was hot, even in winter, so he started the car to get air conditioning.

Along the road to Flamingo, there were a number of hiking trails, but it seemed most of them were short and not set up for camping. Long Pine Key campground wasn't far. He would check it out. He could see that another campground was at Flamingo at the end of the road. Beyond that was Florida Bay.

The Long Pine Key camping area was thick with pines and palmettos. It reminded him somewhat of the Georgia hunting plantation. The loop through the campground had dozens of sites, each with a driveway and a picnic table. Most sites were occupied with motorhomes or camping trailers. Only one space was being used by a tent camper. The campground was pleasant enough with a lake in the middle. Ronald stopped at the restroom building. Inside he found the toilets and a shower, with a sign hanging on the door saying "COLD WATER SHOWER."

The only problem Ronald saw with this campground was that the campsites were out in the open. They were too exposed to hide out for the long term. He drove down to Flamingo to scope out the facilities there.

The campground at Flamingo also had a couple of paved loops with a lot of empty campsites. There were a few tent campers and a couple of RVs. The restrooms were about the same, also with cold showers, and a notice on the door "NO POTABLE WATER – WASHING ONLY." The complex at Flamingo included a restaurant and boat launch and marina with a little store. There were no boats docked in the marina, but the parking lot had a number of vehicles with empty boat trailers. There were several cars and trucks parked with empty kayak racks. It seemed like a ghost town.

New glamping facilities nearby were booked with guests. A lodge was under construction, but not open yet. He determined that Flamingo would be a quiet place to hang out for at least a few days until he could figure out an alternative plan. Neither campground he visited was going to be a long-term place to hide.

Selecting a site that was as out-of-the-way as he could find, he backed his Mercedes into the spot adjacent to the picnic table and began to unload his purchases. When a Park cruiser pulled up and parked, Ronald was panicked. He slammed the trunk to conceal his gear. A young ranger opened his car door and got out, smiling "Hello there. Are you sure you want this site? It's a long way from the visitor center."

Ronald was relieved that this was a friendly visit, not a police stop. At least that's how the conversation was beginning.

"Yes, I like this site. It's going to be quiet here, without neighbors."

The Ranger said, "You're right about that, but you might get carried off by mosquitoes. But with low pressure recently passing through, it should be OK for the next couple days. It'll be cooler too. Can I collect your camp permit fee? How long will you be staying?"

Ronald said, "About a week. Can I pay you in cash?" The ranger handed him a fee envelope. He sat in his car as he filled out the envelope with a made-up name and address, using the Mercedes Benz USA address listed on the handbook in the glove box. As the ranger waited, he said, "I see you just got here and haven't set up your camp yet. Is there anything I can help you unload?"

"No thanks. I got it."

Before he left, the Park Ranger told Ronald that, since the weather had turned pleasant and the bugs would be down, the Park was holding a campfire program the next evening that he might enjoy. "It's been some time since we've been able to do it outside instead of in the visitor center auditorium."

Ronald exhaled when the ranger drove off. Now he could get back to sorting his purchases.

He had a lot of gear and he was not familiar with most of it. Unboxing the material, he was careful to collect the packaging so he could dispose of it in a dumpster. It took some time, but eventually he figured out how to set up the tent and move his gear inside.

He felt somebody was watching him, but it turned out that it was just a couple walking by on the road. The man had a flat tire on his bike and they were headed back to their campsite. They waved as they walked by. Ronald whispered to himself, "You have to quit being so jumpy. Nobody is following you. You are alone and safe – for now."

Deciding he'd try the stove, he read the instructions and discovered he had everything he needed except drinking water and fuel for the stove. Fortunately, the marina store had both of those items. Seeing a mosquito net hat, he grabbed one and tossed it on the counter, too. Returning to the campsite, he cooked a meal and retreated to his tent. Ronald had been operating on automatic, too tired to stay up, and too exhausted to sleep.

Yet he slept until nearly noon the next day. He made coffee in his mini-percolator on his mini camp stove, deciding that a granola bar would be just fine for his brunch. With the sun warming his back, he perused the trail guide booklet.

He read, "Cape Sable is unlike any other place in the park. The coastal prairie stretches for miles, bordered on the south with pristine beaches and a mangrove fringe on Lake Ingraham to the north.

"The Coastal Prairie Trail starts at the end of the Guy Bradley Trail. The Bradley Trail is a day hike to the memorial for the famed game warden. The Coastal Prairie Trail is for the most adventurous and experienced backpackers. The trail can be flooded. Camping is permitted only on the beach and fires can be made with only fallen dead wood, below the high tide line."

Ronald studied the trail map and thought that the route looked straightforward enough. Spurs from the main trail led to recommended campsites on the beaches. There was East Cape, Middle Cape and North Cape. A couple of features were noted, like straight canals leading to Lake Ingraham and a place called "Deadman's Hammock." This looked like the place where he could find solitude. He would become a flatland "mountain man."

As the sun set, he ambled over to the Flamingo complex. He had dinner at the Flamingo restaurant and stayed for the evening campfire program.

The rangers in charge of the evening's program, a man and a woman, lit a bonfire at the amphitheater. When it burned down to simmering flame they began. "Welcome adventurers! Congratulations! You've made it to the end of the road in the fabled Everglades." A large outdoor projection screen had been set up behind the fire.

"Let me introduce myself. I am Park Ranger Simon Cooper and this is my friend and coworker, Interpretive Naturalist, Anita Robertson. We will be sharing tales of the Everglades tonight. It's the first time we've hosted a campfire program since the hurricane hit this place hard. We're back and you are our test audience. Are you ready to hear stories of bugs and birds, life and death, paradise and hell?"

The audience of about 30, seated on benches, applauded politely.

Anita began with a story about mosquitoes, following the food chain that started in the primordial ooze and plant growth of producers. Then she projected a graphic of a pyramid of life, showing the volume of insect life that is supporting the top predators in a food chain, converting each organism to the biomass of mosquitoes. Her presentation went from microscopic zooplankton, to invertebrates, to vertebrates. The audience was amazed at how many mosquitoes an apex predator might represent.

She continued with a PowerPoint showing a diverse sample of plants and animals found in the park, explaining the differences between producers, consumers, predators, and prey. It was an entertaining biology lesson, concluding that the rule for survival is Eat or Be Eaten!

Ranger Cooper then announced, "Anita has shown you some of the natural inhabitants of the park and how important mosquitoes are. I want to remind you," he continued in a serious tone, "that all plants and animals in the park are protected, including the mosquitoes. Rangers will be patrolling to see who is killing mosquitoes."

This gave the audience pause, until Cooper laughed and said "You can only slap the ones that bite you!"

"Now," continued Cooper, "I want to tell you about some of the interesting human characters that have made this place home."

He started with the Calusa and Tequesta peoples, who were here when the Spanish first came to Florida in the 1500s. "They probably visited here for hunting and fishing, but there were more hospitable places for their settlements, like further up the coasts, or down in the Florida Keys.

"In more modern times, various schemes were tried and failed. Here on Cape Sable, a famous botanist Dr. Henry Perrine was going to develop a sisal plantation in the mid-1800s, until his plan was terminated when he was killed by a band of Seminoles raiding Indian Key in 1840.

"Then, dredges came to Cape Sable and put in a series of canals to drain the swamp. These scars are still evident today, a hundred years later. We've plugged some of them, because they aren't draining the land. Instead, they are siphoning off the freshwater and allowing salt water to take its place. Those early developers wanted to cash in on the land boom, like in Miami. The road you traveled down here on is built on the bed of the Ingraham Highway, from the 1920s. But the road turned out to be more of a road out of Flamingo than a road in. More people left than arrived!"

He continued to recount the history of Flamingo. "This community was a remote outpost, settled by hardy souls who made their living by fishing, making charcoal from the buttonwood trees, and hunting breeding wading birds during their nesting season. They harvested the birds' plumage for fashionable women's hats.

"It seems everything here was either dangerous, pesky, or hot and humid. Can you imagine living here without air conditioning or window screens? There were bugs, of course, but there were also alligators, crocodiles, sharks, the prickly pear cactus on the prairie, poisonwood, and the infamous manchineel, known as the 'Tree of Death.'" He laughed as he added, "Not much has changed in a hundred years!"

"The manchineel is the deadliest tree in the world and it grows right here and just a few other places in South Florida and the Keys. One tale says three men used the manchineel wood for a fire and were found dead. Don't worry, you are not likely to find it here in Flamingo. It's rare, even in the remote areas of the Park.

"Even with the denizens that were part of everyday life, this place was a paradise to some. Imagine, good fishing and hunting, sunny, breezes, and, for you northerners, no cold! At one time, Flamingo was a bustling community. In 1893, it had a church, a school, and a post office, even a rooming house! A dozen docks and boat houses were on the Bay. All of the homes were built on stilts, to survive the floods and hurricanes."

Cooper then recounted the story of wildlife warden, Guy Bradley. He had a wonderful collection of historic photos to project on the large screen, starting with a sepia-tone photo of Bradley, with a large mustache, and striped long-sleeve button-up Henley shirt. His face was rugged and furrowed.

"Like I mentioned earlier, ladies were using plumes of breeding wading birds for their hats. In the late 1800s and early 1900s, women thought the feathers would look better on them than on the birds." Cooper flipped through a few photos showing how ridiculous the fashionable ladies looked with stuffed bird chapeaus. The bizarre old photos sparked a few chuckles from the viewers.

"Some folks were outraged that the plumes came from birds slaughtered on their nests. You see, during nesting season, large congregations of wading birds gather in certain spots to make nests and hatch and care for their young. A plume hunter, like those here in Flamingo, could make a good living harvesting the birds and plucking their beautiful mating season feathers. Some have said that the feathers were even more valuable, by weight, than gold!

"The Audubon Society hired a warden to enforce the new law prohibiting plume hunting and stationed him here in Flamingo. He had been a plume hunter himself so he knew the 'glades as well as any hunter. Only one other warden was dedicated to enforcing the Bird Protection Act. Paul Kroegel was employed by the government, up near Vero Beach. Kroegel was stationed at the nation's first wildlife refuge, a nesting rookery called Pelican Island established in 1903. There were only two wardens for all of south Florida and so many rookeries to protect.

"One day, in 1905, Bradley was patrolling and tried to stop two men from shooting up a rookery. Instead, Bradley was shot by the men and did not survive. He is buried on Cape Sable. The men were never held accountable for killing this deputized Monroe County law enforcement officer. The outrage over Bradley's death and the horrible practice of killing nesting birds attracted attention to the Everglades.

"But it took half a century for the vision of a park to be reality. Lots of folks worked and lobbied for many years to preserve this ecological treasure so you can explore its wilderness today.

"At one time, the population of Flamingo was nearly 100. By the time President Truman made this a National Park in 1947, the population had declined to just a dozen or so. Marjory Stoneman Douglas, author of the *River of Grass*, was on hand to cut the ribbon opening the park.

"Now, the population of Flamingo is booming again with campers, hikers, fishermen, kayakers, and all the rangers and concessionaires. Just imagine, for a minute, the time of Guy Bradley when this was a lost outpost at the end of the world. It was a paradise for some and a purgatory for others. We hope you take time to discover Everglades National Park for yourselves and let us know which one you think it is."

The audience applauded. Ronald thought it was an interesting interpretive program and the rangers were entertaining.

People wandered off back to their glamp-sites or RVs. Ronald found his way back to his tent. All along the way he was alert for predators like he had seen in Anita's slide show. It didn't matter that she had dismissed the possibility of being attacked by a panther as more remote than winning the Florida Lotto.

SEVEN

Ronald rose with the sun. He was motivated to get on his way, to leave the developed campground in Flamingo for the wild. After reading the trail guide, he was prepared to take the Coastal Prairie Trail. He could head out from his campsite and take the Guy Bradley Trail to hook up with the path out on Cape Sable. He would find a spot to set up a hide-out camp when he got to know the place.

Before he could leave, he still had to sort his gear and put it in his backpack. There was so much more than would fit. He could carry a separate bag for his food and hook a gallon of water to his belt. But, where would he put the tent? Or his sleeping bag?

"Once I get to where I'm going it won't matter if this stuff doesn't fit in the pack. I'll find a location in the wilderness where I can spread everything out." Was he asking or telling himself?

A sound startled him. Ronald jerked around, "Who's there?" It was only the wind rustling palmetto fronds. Nobody was near his campsite. He was nervous about embarking on the trail and self-conscious that his equipment wasn't fitting in the pack. He unpacked everything to cull unnecessary items from the essential ones.

He put the things he decided not to take in the trunk of the car. He removed the license plates and parked the car in the marina overflow lot, near where kayakers leave their vehicles. In one last stop at the marina store, he bought an over-cooked coffee and a couple of packaged snacks. Then he walked back to the campsite to take down the tent. Fortunately, it wrapped up small and fit into its own storage bag so he could tie it to his knapsack.

Resting the pack on the bench of a concrete picnic table, Ronald turned his back and put an arm through one of the straps. Leaning to the side, he hoisted the other side on his shoulder. Leaning forward to bear the full weight, he staggered a step forward. It was heavier than he anticipated. Ronald looked around to see if anyone might have noticed his misstep. He was still alone.

Pulling up the extra tote with his food, he slung it on his right shoulder. Now, finally he was off. Recalling the map in the Park brochure he knew he would find the trailhead at the far end of the campground. It would have a fork about a mile from the start that leads to the Coastal Prairie Trail.

His load was heavy. His goal was to get to the fork and the beginning of the wilderness Coastal Prairie Trail before resting. He made it to the junction of the trailhead and the campground and nearly collapsed, huffing. His gym fitness routine in the city hadn't prepared him for carrying a load on his back in a hot and humid place. After resting for a minute or two, he proceeded to the beginning of the trail into the back-country.

It being a winter cool spell, he had no idea how hot and humid, not to mention bug-infested, Cape Sable usually is. Ronald rested to catch his breath. He decided he needed to lighten his load so he walked off the trail to a spot he thought he could find again, and began dumping more gear, not the tent, not the sleeping bag, but some clothes, most cooking gear, and the food bag. Maybe this would be enough. He would try again to walk the trail with the lightened pack and then return for the stashed belongings after he made camp.

Back on the trail he thought someone was following him. He stepped off the trail into a palmetto thicket and waited a few minutes. No one appeared. He thought, "Well, maybe they saw me and stopped too."

The further he hiked the more the brushy forest thinned out. He emerged onto a vast low savanna, that stretched to the horizon before him. He saw only a few scattered buttonwood shrubs and, in the far distance, a line of low trees, probably mangroves. To the north, there was Lake Ingraham, to the south was Florida Bay and the beaches.

The trail became more difficult. The slippery white mud stuck to his boots, caking the soles with a soggy crust. The middle of the footpath was often covered with water, ranging from a skim to a couple of inches deep. Trying to walk on the vegetated edge was nearly impossible. The frilly looking plants covering the coastal prairie were a thick tangle of stems, snagging his pants legs and tripping him. Progress was slow and physically exhausting. He needed to stop as soon as he found a suitable spot. No place on this water-soaked plain was suitable to pitch a tent.

Little spur trails led off to the south and the beach. He decided the beach would be where he could make his camp and rest. He was tired.

As the afternoon sun descended, Ronald set up his tent on the soft beach sand above the high tide line, close to the forest edge. As he worked he was besieged by sand gnats, the ferocious "no-see-ums" that were so thick they were indeed visible. Ronald pulled on his mosquito net hat, glad that he had kept it instead of leaving it in the cache he left behind. Setting up his tent as fast as possible, he retreated inside, zipping up the screen opening to escape the relentless assault.

When darkness overtook the last glow of sunset, the bugs diminished. Ronald emerged from the tent to relieve himself and cook one of his prepackaged desiccated meals. He started his mini camp stove and poured the contents of the package into the pot once the water started to boil. As he ate, he thought, "I can do this!"

Then he saw movement in the brush. Was it his stalker or some wild animal? He shined his flashlight around the campsite. Seeing nothing, he gathered a few pieces of wood and built a fire near his tent. He reasoned that if it was a raccoon or a panther, it might be scared off by a fire.

He had a fitful night sleeping on the beach sand that shifted under his weight as he rolled back and forth, even under the tent floor. He worried about predators, bugs, snakes, and being discovered. Waking with the sunrise, he found that the fire was out and only warm ashes remained. The bugs were back in force. Putting on his mosquito hat and long-sleeved shirt, only his hands were exposed. Lamenting out loud, he said to his surroundings and the swarm of bugs, "Oh crap, the bug spray is back with my stashed gear." He rekindled the fire and stood in the smoke for relief from the insects.

Breaking camp, he moved on farther into the wilds of Cape Sable. There were a few points marked on his map: Clubhouse Beach, East Ingraham Canal, Cabbage Grove, Middle Cape Camp, and Deadman's Hammock. Ronald didn't want to be at a designated campsite, hoping to be off the path others might travel. He still had half of his water and some pills the clerk at the outdoor store assured him would treat river water, making it potable. Thirsty, he needed to be careful about using up his bottled supply.

As the day progressed, a sea breeze diminished the sand gnats. He studied the simple map and guessed he had walked only a few miles. He reasoned that he might make it to the Lake Ingraham Canal that day. Then he could return to his cache to collect the rest of his supplies.

Walking on the prairie trail was no easier on this second day. He had to stop often to scrape the marl mud off his boots. The white mud was a silty sediment broken down from the lime rock and saturated with salt. He could see that this was a tough place for plants to survive. He pushed on, noticing the low ground cover of dense thickets of salt-tolerant vegetation.

Step after step, he found a slow and steady rhythm, almost subconsciously walking. He was thirsty, but he took only a sip from his bottle. He was sweating out more than he was taking in. Not wanting to be eaten alive by the swarming mosquitoes, he stayed covered up. The mosquitoes were covering the net hanging from his hat. He was hungry, but did not want to stop because there was really no place to sit except for the water-soaked ground.

Finally, he could go no farther, so he headed for the shore again to camp for the night. He decided to have dinner when it was fully dark and the bugs were more tolerable. After his tent was set up, he pulled off his mud-clogged boots, dirty soggy pants, and long-sleeved shirt. He felt coolness bathe his body. He laid on his sleeping bag to rest, falling asleep quickly. In the middle of the night, he woke, startled by a sound. But he was not certain if he actually heard something or it was a dream.

It was dark, really dark, when he emerged from his tent. The breeze was blowing and it was cool, almost chilly. He started another driftwood fire, managing to spill half of the fuel he carried for his camp stove. But it didn't matter to him. What was important was having a fire. He paused to stare at the stars and assumed the large, colored, mist-like mass of stars was the Milky Way. He consumed his trail mix packet cold, mixed with a little seawater, and went back to his sleeping bag. He wanted to sleep as late in the morning as possible to avoid being bored while waiting in his tent for the morning buggy hours to pass.

The next morning, he rose and, not thinking, grabbed his water bottle, nearly draining it before he remembered it was all he had. Again, the fire was out, but the sun was up and the breeze was blowing. He made some warm coffee using a packet of instant in his cup and mixing it half with seawater added to his bottled water. It was salty, but he savored it as a treat. If he wasn't so bothered by bugs and the mud, this escape plan would be more tolerable.

Starting again, he decided to leave his camp set up on the beach and try to find a source of fresh water and a suitable place to set up a more permanent camp. Once he had a better campsite, he could return to the beginning of the trail for his stuff, or maybe not. He had what he needed and was getting by, so far, without the things he'd left behind. Ronald was still concerned he was being followed or watched.

Today the walking was a little better. Carrying a lighter weight day-pack helped and the trail surface was more firm and less muddy. But the trade-off was the increase in bugs. The mosquitoes were thick; a few were biting through his shirt. He was in a brushy forest, routing away from the beach. The breeze was blocked by the shrubbery, so the only wind blowing the bugs away was his own motion.

Ronald came to a fork in the trail. An old weathered sign pointed to Deadman's Hammock, with an official NPS sign posting it was closed to unauthorized entry. The trail appeared overgrown and disused. This would be perfect for making a camp that other people might not find. He took the trail less traveled.

The hammock was not far. The ground seemed a little higher, maybe by a foot or two. A little elevation in the Everglades can make a big difference in the vegetation. The trees were a little different from the black mangrove forest he had been walking in.

A cooler breeze came up, the precursor to an afternoon squall. The sky was darkening to the west. He was getting desperate for a water source. Maybe he could find water nearby or dig a hole for a well. He thought he might set up a longer-term encampment here, just a little off the abandoned pathway.

The wind picked up quickly and the tree canopy began rustling. Leaves were blowing in advance of a sudden deluge. He remembered that one shouldn't get under a tree in a lightning storm, but he dismissed that advice because he wanted more shelter from the rain.

It rained heavy for 30 minutes, then lightened to a soft shower. Even under the trees he got soaked. Mosquitoes came out again and were biting more through his wet clothes. Once the rain slowed to a drizzle, it was suitable to hike back to his beach camp. He welcomed the cool temperature after the squall. He only wished he had a container to put out during the storm to collect rainwater. He licked the water tricking down his face and from his hands.

Before he got back to his beach camp, his skin was itching. He scratched his bug bites. The places where his skin touched the openings in his clothes were starting to burn, like a sunburn. His neck collar, wrists, and waistband were irritated. Back at the tent, he duffed his wet clothes and waded out to swim off the beach. He still wore his net hat to protect his head while he was submerged in the water from the neck down. He kept his boots on to keep his feet from being cut by shells. He thought the salt water might comfort his skin, but it only stung. His throat was getting harsh and painful. Thirsty, he started sipping sea water. It was salty, but cooling and thirst-quenching. At first it was a sip, then he went on to drink, lowering his head to the water surface to take in a mouthful at a time, until his belly ached.

He entered the tent to lay on his sleeping bag. His stomach hurt. His throat was flaming and swollen, his lips were swollen and his skin was covered with a pox of mosquito bites and burning with little pustules. He could only breathe through his nose. Miserable, he begged for sleep to a God he didn't believe in. His mind was in a fog.

He woke again with the dawn. The pustules had turned into a blistering rash and his mouth and throat were thick from inflammation. He had soiled his sleeping bag with a foul diarrhea. Through his mental fog, he knew he would need help to survive, or at least feel better. Emerging from the tent, the sand gnats were of little bother in comparison to his other afflictions.

Leaving everything at his camp, he started walking back on the beach, back toward Flamingo. He would just take the beach rather than the trail.

He heard a voice that startled him. "Hey, looks like you are in trouble." The voice was familiar but he couldn't place it.

Through blurred eyes he saw a man's figure following behind him. Ronald made a guttural sound, "Who are you? Have you been following me? What do you want? Can you help me? Please?" His speech was hardly intelligible.

The man said, "I'm Sidney. But you can just call me Sid."

Then he was gone. Looking around, Ronald saw nobody on the beach in either direction. He picked up a piece of driftwood to use as a walking stick or a weapon against the sadistic prankster who was following him and then disappearing.

He pressed on. The sun in the east was bright. The least bit of sunlight set his erupting skin lesions on fire. Stumbling on, his breathing was labored and his legs felt like noodles as he wobbled on the sand.

He heard the voice again, "What were you thinking? You think you could run away from your troubles, rather than face the consequences, like a man?"

Sid was sitting on a log ahead of him on the beach with the sun backlighting his form.

"Please help me!" Ronald struggled to speak loud and clear.

Sid replied, "I think you are going to have to help yourself. You got yourself into this mess and you can get yourself out of it. Just have a little faith! Man up!"

Sid vanished again. Ronald's vision was so impaired he couldn't tell if Sid walked off or just disappeared. Ronald kept moving. He would take a few steps and then pause, resuming after a few seconds.

He heard his wife call out, "Ron, Ron! What are you doing here?"

She couldn't be here. He knew he must be hallucinating, but she was so real, dressed in her wedding gown and carrying a small suitcase.

"I'm staying at my parent's house with our daughter. You've been behaving so crazy for the past year. I couldn't take it anymore."

Sid was back. "You could have helped him out with money from your trust fund but you were more committed to donating to all the non-profit organizations than your own husband's needs."

She was gone. Sid was sitting on top of a dead tree snag, beside a black vulture. "Hey, why do you think she should have helped you, when you didn't let her in on your troubles? She had no idea you were so deep in debt until she saw the overdue bills and foreclosure notices."

Ronald looked away, only to see a blur of boats coming toward him. A dozen or more of his finance clients were paddling to the beach. His mind was racing. "Could it be Mr. and Mrs. Hightower and Tom and Karen Morgan?" The others he didn't know.

Sid said, "They are coming after you! The Hightowers lost everything and they are too old to start over. The Morgans are down all the money they had saved to buy a vacation house. The others are out too. They have found you. You better run away!"

Ronald was desperate. He ran toward them for help. He was waving his arms with the stick high over his head. "I'm sorry, please help! I will repay your losses. Just help me please!"

This burst of energy drained all that Ronald had left. He fell to his knees on the beach. The people left quickly. Sid told Ronald, "They are leaving you. Can you blame them?"

Ronald replied, "But they were so greedy! They were happy so long as they were getting my checks. If they only waited, I could have turned it around."

Sid agreed, "You're right. They were happy with the dividends. They knew the risk. It's not your fault. They were gambling … and lost." Sid was standing on the beach. "You need to get back up on your feet and get moving again. You are running out of time."

Ronald leaned on his stick and took a few steps. Everything hurt and he felt very ill. "I've got to make it back to Flamingo. I don't know if I can keep going."

Then, his mother Rita and his father, Ronald D. Bradford, Jr. MD, were standing over him. His mother cried, "Oh my, Ronnie. This is terrible, you are so sick. Let me help you. I can make it all better." Dr. Bradford disagreed, "My diagnosis is that he's dehydrated, sick from drinking sea water, and suffering from some kind of very toxic irritant."

Sid was back, "Your mom was always there for you and your dad never was. He was always away at his office or the hospital. Don't listen to him. He never had time for you when you were a child. You know they are both long dead, so how are they going to do anything for you now?"

Ronald wondered to himself, "Am I dying?"

Sid answered, "No, Ronald, you are not dead yet, but you can't get out of this unless you keep moving and get help. You've always wiggled out of any bad problems. All the pranks, the petty thefts, the cheating, the DUI's. You can get out of this too."

Ronald wasn't so sure. This time he was in real trouble, not like the social entanglements and excesses of his self-absorbed lifestyle. This time, his mother could not save him with his father's money.

Sid reaffirmed, "Yes, you can, but it's time for you to face up to your own character. Who you really are compared to who you have pretended to be. Did you wonder why you had a lot of failures with women before you met Cindy? When they saw you for your pretentious selfishness, they all moved on."

Ronald knew Sid was right, but the pain of his maladies was a more immediate concern. Ronald stumbled forward, then fell. This time he could not get up. He rolled over on to his back and stared up to the sky through blurred eyes.

Standing over him was Cindy, in a cocktail dress, holding his daughter. The sequined dress twinkled. She looked ready for a party. The little girl was in her pjs, "Daddy, please come with us back home." Cindy added, "Yes, Ron, come home. I'm angry, but we can work it out. My father can help with the financial troubles."

Sid chimed in. "See Ronald, you were lucky to find a woman who could look past your failings. But maybe she hasn't. Your call. This is your nightmare, so you get to decide how it ends. Are you listening to me? Ronald? Ronald?"

"What? This is hopeless! I am so weak and sick." Ronald closed his eyes for a minute. When he opened them, there was a man standing over him.

"Howdy, rambler. Did you reckon you could get away? I'm takin' you in for hunting birds." Through the milky fog covering his eyes Ronald saw it was Guy Bradley, still wearing the striped shirt, still with the broad mustache and steely stare he had in the photo at the campfire program.

"I'm hurt. I'm a camper, not a plume hunter. I need help!" Ronald could barely see through his clouded eyes. The sun was so bright. He could barely breathe. His skin was on fire, but he was cold.

Bradley loaded him into his boat and raised the sail. "Don't worry. We're going to head back to Flamingo, and get you to a hospital."

"Where did you come from? You're dead a hundred years. I don't understand, but it doesn't matter now. Nothing does."

Sid was in the boat too. "Good luck, you've got a long road ahead of you, if you make it. Like I told you, it's your nightmare."

EIGHT

The group of kayakers raced away from the East Cape Beach. There was no question that they would not be camping on their much-anticipated Sierra Club weekend outing. Seeing a crazed nude man on the beach, moving erratically with incoherent speech, and chasing them with a spear instantly changed their plans. The naked man was covered with sand, only wearing a mosquito net hat and hiking boots. This is not what the intrepid adventurers had anticipated. He was obviously hysterical. Most of them worried he could be dangerous.

The group paddled fast back toward Flamingo. When they were a few hundred yards off the beach, they all gathered for a minute to formulate a plan. They needed to report this and get the demented man apprehended before he hurt someone or himself. Three stronger solo kayakers would go ahead, trying to get within cell phone range to notify the Park rangers. If they couldn't reach the park by cell phone, they would get to the ranger station at Flamingo in person, as fast as possible. The rest of the group, in tandem kayaks, a few single sit-on-top kayaks, and a couple of canoes, would stay together and paddle back at a moderate pace.

While on their way, the three solo paddlers stopped occasionally to check their phones for cell service. There were no signal bars the first time, but a little closer to Flamingo, they were successful.

"Hello, I am Mark Goring, with the Sierra Club group that left Flamingo this morning to overnight camp on Cape Sable. I need to report a..." Mark didn't know how to characterize what he saw – a lost man? a crazy person? an assault? Well, no, not exactly.

"I need to report an incident we just experienced near East Cape. There is a naked man who appears to be very disturbed running along the beach and retreating into the brush."

"This is the Flamingo sub-station. I'm Ranger Buddy Smith. Is anyone hurt or in immediate danger? Can you provide more information, like a GPS location and a description of the person?"

Mark said "Hold please and I'll ask the friends I'm with to check their GPS units for lat and lon coordinates."

While his friends checked, he continued, "When we approached the beach ... there are 21 in our group ... this guy, without any clothes, only a mosquito net over his head and hiking boots, started running toward us shaking a long stick over his head. We couldn't understand what he was saying. He was acting very strange, kind of stumbling drunk.

"Wait a minute, I've got the numbers for our location. This is where we are now. But, the guy on the beach is even further west of our current location, on the beach near East Cape Sable." Then he repeated the lat-lon coordinates to be sure the ranger got them. Ranger Smith said, "Thanks. We need to look into this. Is your group safe?"

"Three of us are closer to Flamingo, the other 18 are behind us. We will meet up at the marina and figure out an alternate camping plan. This was upsetting to most of the folks in our group. Nobody's hurt, only disappointed that we won't be out on Cape Sable. I think the guy really needs help!"

Ranger Smith alerted Bob Nelson. They developed a plan to search the trail and East Cape by both land and by water. Nelson would take Ranger Fuentes on a patrol boat to the beach, while Smith would partner with Ranger Cooper to hike the trail.

Smith drove as far as he could on the trail and then took the footpath, carrying a first aid kit and reserve water supply. He called on the Everglades National Park radio, "Ranger One we are at the trail and proceeding west, what is your position? Over."

Nelson responded, "We are just leaving the Flamingo channel and will be heading toward East Cape soon. Please check in if you find something. Over."

Nelson sped up the boat and turned to follow the coastline. Fuentes grasped a rail with one hand and held her binoculars with the other. It was unlikely the sick man would be in the mangrove fringe near the campgrounds, but Ranger Fuentes kept a sharp eye. Ranger Nelson thought it might be a good idea to contact the Coast Guard to alert them to the search. Grabbing the marine VHF, he hailed the USCG Marathon on Channel 16 to update them, "Pon, Pon. Pon, Pon. U.S. Coast Guard Marathon, U.S. Coast Guard Marathon, USCG Marathon. This is Everglades National Park, Flamingo."

The U.S. Coast Guard answered. "USCG Marathon to the vessel calling. Switch to 22 Alpha."

Once on the alternate radio channel, the Coast Guard radio dispatcher said, "What's up, Everglades?"

"This is Ranger Nelson with the National Park. We've had a credible report of a lost hiker on East Cape who is in some kind of trouble, acting erratically. Two rangers are presently engaged in a search of the nearby trail and we are running by water along the beach. I wanted to alert you in case you have any aircraft nearby. Over."

"Stand by."

In a minute Nelson heard, "Everglades Park, this is USCG Marathon. I checked and we don't have anything in the air right now. Do you need assistance?"

Nelson responded, "USCG Marathon, no, we have a search underway, but I may be back in touch if we need help. Just wanted to give you a 'heads up' in case we need assistance with this. Over."

"Roger. We'll stand by on Channel 16. USCG Marathon out."

USCG Marathon then broadcast a marine advisory for boaters in the vicinity of East Cape Sable to keep a sharp eye for a stranded hiker acting erratically on the beach at Cape Sable, ending with, "Do not approach. Report any sightings to USCG Marathon."

Nelson slowed the patrol boat when he saw the flotilla of canoes and kayaks on their way back to the marina. Nelson decided to check with them, intercepting the group at idle speed. "How are y'all doing?" Several in the group looked a little unsettled. A few of the older people were happy to take a break from paddling to speak to the rangers.

One of the sit-on-top kayakers asked, "Have you heard from the three of our group that paddled ahead? Did they tell you about the crazy guy on the beach?"

"Yes, we got the report. Your friends are fine and we appreciate your help. We are on our way to look for him. I bet this wasn't what you expected for your camping trip! Sorry this has spoiled your expedition." The kayakers didn't have anything more to add, except that the man seemed to be headed into the woods the last time they saw him.

Fuentes and Nelson thanked them and resumed a faster pace. When they were getting close to East Cape, near the trail location, Nelson slowed and Fuentes scanned the beach with her binoculars.

"I think I see something!" Pointing to the beach, Fuentes said, "About 10 o'clock – midway up on the beach."

Nelson couldn't quite see without binoculars, but pointed the boat to the spot Fuentes observed. As they got a little closer, the rangers could see it was a man, laying face up on the sand. Nelson trimmed the outboard motor to draw less, pulling up carefully to beach the boat. Mud from the shallow bottom was being stirred up by the motor prop.

Nelson told Fuentes to call the land-side team and report they found someone, probably the target. Fuentes called on the park radio, "Ranger Smith, Ranger Smith. This is Fuentes and Nelson. We think we have something."

Buddy replied, "I was just about to call you! We found a stash of camping supplies hidden a few yards off the Coastal Prairie Trail. There's a bunch of useless stuff and a dry bag full of camp meals. What is your 20?"

Fuentes said, "On East Cape, not too far west of East Cape Canal. Stand by. We will let you know when we get to the body. Over." Rangers Smith and Cooper slowed the pace of their search along the trail.

The rangers jumped off the bow of the boat, bringing the first aid kit with them. Nelson quickly dug the anchor into the sand. Approaching the figure lying on the sand, they could see it was a naked male. They couldn't quickly discern if he was breathing or see his face behind the veil of the mosquito net hat. Pulling on latex gloves, they lifted the guy's shoulders to remove the headgear.

When they touched him, Ronald convulsed with a spasm, his eyes wide open, but glazed with a bizarre frosting and puffy eyelids. His body was covered with oozing blisters. His lips were swollen and blood red. His whole body was covered with a pox of red pustules. His breathing was shallow and he was shivering.

Nelson took off his Park Ranger coat to cover the guy's private parts that he didn't want to see. Fuentes gently poured bottled water over some of the most sand encrusted areas of his body. Nelson said, "Let's get a blood pressure, heart rate, and body temperature," as he pulled the instruments out of the first aid case. Ronald made a jerky movement when the blood pressure cuff was wrapped on his blistered arm.

Ronald was mumbling, softly and incoherently. "I'm hurt. I'm a camper, not a plume hunter. I need help!" He wasn't looking at Nelson, nor did he seem to even notice the two rangers. The guy appeared to be delusional and having a conversation with somebody.

Ranger Nelson reassured him, "Don't worry. We're going to head back to Flamingo and get you to a hospital."

Looking straight at Nelson, he said, "Where did you come from? You're dead a hundred years. I'm not a plume hunter! I don't understand, but it doesn't matter now. Nothing does."

Ranger Nelson contacted the USCG while Fuentes called to update Smith and Cooper, advising the two rangers that they had found the person the kayakers had reported. She instructed Cooper and Smith to return to the station.

Nelson advised the USCG of the situation. "We found the missing person on East Cape. He is not in good shape. I believe he's showing signs of shock. We have taken his vitals and have done as much as we can with our limited kit. Can you transport? He will need an emergency medical facility."

USCG Marathon answered, "Stand by."

In a minute, The Coast Guard dispatcher was back, asking "What is your location?" Nelson replied with the coordinates and received the response to stand by. It was five minutes before a hail came on the boat's VHF radio.

"Everglades Park, this is USCG Marathon. We contacted Monroe Emergency Response and they do not have a med-evac copter available. We can have a chopper in the air in five and estimate 23 miles to your location. Maybe about 20 minutes ETA. I have passed along the vitals to Marathon Community Hospital and they will be ready."

Nelson replied, "Thanks. This guy is in pretty bad shape. Obviously, time is of the essence. We will prepare a landing site and light a couple of day flares when we hear your aircraft."

The dispatcher responded, "We will have a Monroe County EMT on board with our crew. Good luck with your patient."

Twenty minutes later, the helicopter landed, blowing a maelstrom of sand that blasted Nelson and Fuentes despite the landing site being about a hundred yards away. The Coast Guard corpsmen jumped from the copter and sprang into action. With the EMT's help, they had Ronald on a stretcher and on board quickly. In a spur of the moment decision, Nelson determined he should accompany the patient to Marathon, to provide whatever information might be useful. Fuentes would take the boat back to Flamingo.

It had been several hours since the first report of the crazy man on East Cape. Now he was on a flight heading to treatment and still hanging on. It looked bad to Nelson, but his medical training was only rudimentary instruction, long ago, in the Park Service's Ranger Academy. This incident was the second medical emergency at Everglades in two months. These rescues were personally stressful.

During the twenty-minute helicopter ride, Bob Nelson started to put two and two together. He figured out that the naked camper must be the owner of the abandoned car in the Flamingo parking lot. He searched his memory, finally recalling the guy's name was Ronald Bradford and he was from New York. He'd have to have his computer to get the rest of the details but at least the guy had a possible name for now. He remembered that he did have the name and number for the detective investigating Ronald on his cell phone. He would provide the hospital with the detective's number as a contact for more information.

Landing at the hospital, the victim was rushed to the emergency room. Nelson thanked the Coast Guard crew before they departed. He spoke with the admitting staff to fill out what he knew about the man being treated.

A nurse came out of the ER in her scrubs, asking the desk for the park ranger who accompanied the patient. Nelson was in the waiting room. Pulling down her mask, she introduced herself, "I'm Suzanne, an ER nurse. The physicians are still working on him. The doctor wanted me to ask you about what happened to the patient."

Nelson told her the story, "Midday, we got a report of a man, naked and acting strangely, way out on East Cape Sable. We found him delirious and mostly unresponsive, laying on the beach. The USCG facilitated rescue and transport here."

Suzanne nodded, "It seems he was lucky you found him when you did. He's got a lot going on." She was making notes.

"Any idea of what he got into? His skin is very erupted."

Nelson said, "To me, it looks like he's gotten into a poisonous plant, like poison ivy, only much worse. I don't have any direct experience, only anecdotal stories, about manchineel poisoning. Based on where he was found and the severity of the rash, I'd guess it's manchineel."

From the look on her face, he could tell she wasn't familiar with the tree. Dropping into his park naturalist role, he explained, "Manchineel is a rare tree found in the park and tropical Caribbean. It's called the Tree of Death because it is reportedly the most toxic plant. It has poisonous bark and leaves. It's tiny apple-like fruit is poisonous and supposedly causes rapid death if consumed. Wildlife seems immune, but there are stories of people dying from breathing the smoke from manchineel wood being burned in a campfire."

Suzanne was surprised and a little skeptical.

Nelson continued. "This plant is hard to find in most areas of Everglades Park, but there is a grove of these trees out on Cape Sable. It's a place called 'Deadman's Hammock' and is closed to the public to avoid exposing our visitors to such a poisonous plant. Bradford, that's the patient's name, might have wandered there and been exposed. From the way he looks and his symptoms, it fits with what I've heard. But, again, I'm no expert on this."

Suzanne smiled a thank you and departed quickly back to the ER.

The team attending to Ronald was still trying to stabilize him. He was hooked up to fluids, being administered anti-inflammatory drugs, and on oxygen. Blood samples were sent to the hospital lab for analysis. The doctor wanted to go slowly until he could diagnose the problem. Nelson's information about manchineel was useful.

One doctor pulled up a quick search through the *Merck Manual PDR* on a computer, while asking a Physician Assistant to call the National Poison Control Center for guidance.

Sid was back. Ronald saw him there floating over his bed in a crowd of people, people from his past, his wife, childhood friends, clients, in-laws, his secretary. They were all poking him and speaking in a language he did not understand. Sid said, "OK, now you are in trouble! The cops will be here soon to take you away and lock you up."

Ronald's beleaguered body winced and spasmed. "Oh, no, I can't. I can't go to prison. I have a lot of ideas on how to make a big score in the market."

Sid chided, "Money is the least of your worries. How can you think about money at a time like this? Why don't you focus on what's important in life. You don't seem to care about anyone but yourself and you're not even true to anything but your own greed."

Bradford didn't want to hear it. "Go away! You're not helping! Why can't I see your face? I see everybody else? Dammit, who are you? And what makes you the authority on me? Get the hell out of here!"

Sid was gone, vanishing as quickly as he arrived.

A loud alarm pierced the ER. The lead doctor snapped, "He's coded. Get the defibrillator." In a moment, he stood at the bedside and barked. "Clear!" The team backed away, saying "Clear" as the paddles sent an electric pulse into Ronald's chest. It worked.

"That was close. With the inflammation in his throat, we need to get a surgical airway established. He's not getting enough oxygen with just the cannula tube. I want to check on his labs and see if I can figure out a treatment plan."

The physician found Nelson still in the waiting room. "Your victim just passed, but we were able to bring him back quickly. Is there anything more you can tell me about the poison?"

Nelson replied, "I told the nurse pretty much all I know about the manchineel tree. I can try to contact the Park Biologist, Carol Godfrey, to see if she has real science instead of the anecdotes I'm familiar with."

"Thank you. Please contact her. We're also in touch with the CDC Poison Control Center, but this is a troubling case that we have no experience with. If you reach her, please pass along our nurse station's number. I know it's well past your closing time. We're trying our best, but we're in the dark about this."

Carol Godfrey, the Park biologist, reached the doctor by calling the nursing station directly. When he came to the phone, she confirmed what Nelson had already told him, adding, "This tree is so poisonous that rain dripping through the leaves could leach the toxin onto the skin if someone was standing under it. And, if the rainwater was consumed, the toxin would get into the mouth and throat. I understand from Bob that the patient is having difficulty breathing. Call me if I can do anything more. I gave my number to the nurse."

Nelson called Buddy Smith to update him, adding, "Hey, I'm going to stay here in Marathon for tonight. I think I'll hang around the hospital a little longer to see if Bradford makes it. He's already coded once."

Smith commiserated, "It's been a long day for you and you are in Marathon without a vehicle."

Then, in an attempt to lighten the mood, he said, "Why don't you grab a pole and go night-fishing off the Seven Mile Bridge?"

"Ha! It would be a good distraction from this mess. It's one of my least favorite things to do – hang out in hospitals."

After waiting for news for another hour, Nelson called Island Taxi to pick him up and take him over to a nearby hotel, chancing that during tourist season they would have a room. They did and Nelson was relieved to have a shower. His late dinner was the finest snacks from the limited selection at the hotel lobby store.

Just as he dozed off, his cell phone rang. The nurse, Suzanne, was on the line. "Ranger Nelson? We spoke earlier about patient Ronald Bradford. I wanted to update you on his condition."

Nelson was anxious to hear.

"We have moved him to ICU. He is stable, but his condition is serious. He's not out of the woods yet. He's been cleaned up and the superficial dermatitis had been debrided and is being treated. More serious are the out-of-normal ranges in his labs, indicating there is some internal organ involvement."

Nelson asked, "So, for a non-medical person, what's the prognosis?"

Suzanne paused, "We are cautiously optimistic. It all depends on the efficacy of the treatment. He's in good hands with our ICU crew. I'll update you if anything changes. Is this a good number to reach you?"

"Yes, it will work, unless I'm in one of the dead spots in the Park. Thank you for all you are doing to help this guy out. When he recovers, I want to learn his story, if he even knows it. Good night."

He texted Buddy: "The guy we found on the beach is in serious but stable condition at Marathon Community Hospital. I want to get back to the Park. Can someone pick me up at Faro Blanco in the morning?"

Texting back, Buddy assured Nelson he would get there in the morning. It is a 125-mile drive from Flamingo in the Everglades to Marathon in the Florida Keys, although, as the egret flies, it's only about 30 miles. Buddy contemplated taking the park boat, but decided it would just be easier to go in a park vehicle.

Buddy departed at 8 AM for the drive up to Florida City and then down US1 to Marathon. The Keys were usually a pleasure to transit, but it was always a little sad too because on each trip one could see the incremental encroachment of banal American urbanism and corporate developments capitalizing on the Keys' unique character. It's talked about as "Progress", but it's supplanting the authentic with the artificial, at the expense of the natural assets. The essential character of the place was being displaced by the accommodations for people wanting to see the Keys in their natural state.

Nelson's cell phone rang at 9. "I'm at Jewfish Creek and should be there in a couple hours to pick you up. Any news on Bradford's condition?"

Nelson hadn't heard from the hospital, but he planned to call in a few minutes. "Thanks for coming to get me. I hope Bradford is improving. To be honest, I was worn out from yesterday and I just got up. See you soon. Oh, you know where Faro Blanco is?"

"Yep, the new upscale place built where the historic lodge was, the old icon of sportfishing, with the lighthouse. Hope you caught some fish in your dreams!"

Nelson checked with the hospital on Bradford's condition. The response was, "Serious, but stable. No change. Are you family?"

"No, I'm the Ranger who brought him in yesterday. I'll stop by a little later to speak with your doctor and administrative staff."

He had just hung up when his phone chimed. He could see it was the New York Detective Ramos. "Hello Detective. I suppose you got my message. I'm in Marathon, Florida. Ronald Bradford is in the hospital here, in serious but stable condition."

"Yes, I know. I've coordinated with the Monroe County Sheriff's Department to keep an eye on him. It's important for us to talk to him. In fact, with him running off to Florida, we're concerned he might be a flight risk before, or if, he's charged with anything."

"I don't think you have to worry about him going anywhere soon." Nelson added, "He's in pretty bad shape in the ICU, at least when I left him late last night."

Nelson had a little empathy for the guy he'd rescued and who was so pathetic. His New York crimes didn't seem to be violent, although they were still crimes. Saving his life was the Park's interest in Bradford. His other troubles were out of Nelson's jurisdiction.

Nelson asked Detective Ramos, "Have you informed his family about his situation?" Ramos replied that he had. Nelson really didn't want to be further entangled in the New York crimes, hoping his involvement was nearing the end. He had only to deal with the abandoned Mercedes and follow up on what Ronald might have left in the park. And, of course, there was paperwork to complete to record the actions of the NPS in the search and rescue. For now, there was no Park violation to consider.

Nelson waited in the Faro Blanco lobby for Ranger Smith to arrive. When he did, they drove to the hospital for a final check before heading back to Flamingo.

Meeting with the resident physician outside the ICU, they exchanged pleasantries and discussed the unusual circumstances of Bradford's problems. The doctor said, "We were stumped by this case. It looks like he's got a decent chance now, but it will be some time before we know how he responds to treatment. I think we got him in time, but this one is for the books! Do you want to see him?"

Nelson paused, "Yeah, sure. I'm curious about how he's doing."

"OK. Wait just a few minutes. By the way, the Sheriff's department has him handcuffed to the bed and it's really hampering the nursing staff's ability to care for him. Do you think you can do anything about that. I can swear he's in no condition to go anywhere."

Nelson didn't know what he could do. Detective Ramos was worried about flight, but then as of an hour ago, he hadn't been charged with anything. There was no reason to handcuff an invalid. The nurses didn't need the additional hassle to get him uncuffed every time they had to treat his wounds or change his bedding.

Standing at his bedside, it was pretty clear to Nelson that Bradford was seriously ill. There were many monitors, IVs, and bandages. And, an arm was chained to the bed rail. It didn't seem to be necessary to Nelson.

A deputy was seated outside the ICU, reading a newspaper. Nelson introduced himself and asked, "Why is the patient, Bradford, cuffed?" The deputy shrugged, "Just the instructions from the duty officer." Nelson asked if the deputy could get the duty officer on the phone.

During the conversation Nelson approached the Sheriff's department as a fellow law enforcement officer. "I'm a federal law enforcement ranger with Everglades National Park. I brought in a very sick man, Ronald Bradford, yesterday for emergency treatment here in Marathon. Now I see he's handcuffed to the bed and the nurses are having problems treating his condition. He's in no shape to go anywhere. The doctors told me he will be out of it for days. Has he been charged with anything?"

The Sheriff's Department bristled a bit and their response was terse. "No, there is no warrant for his arrest. We are only restraining him as a favor to the NYPD. They are worried he might get away."

"Well, if he's not under arrest, why don't you do me and the nurses a favor and lose the cuffs. Your deputy can watch the door to be sure the patient doesn't get away in his hospital gown." Nelson was smug, but firm. "I'd hate for a civil rights violation to spoil the chance for a conviction."

After a pause, he heard an exasperated, "OK, let me speak to the deputy." After the call, the deputy sneered and went into the ICU. He came out dangling cuffs from his forefinger, with a frown on his face.

Ranger Smith, who had been waiting in the hall, asked Nelson, "What was that all about?"

"Tell you later. Let's hit the road. We are done here and there are mosquitoes we need to feed back home."

NINE

On the drive back to Flamingo, the two rangers discussed the rescue and speculated about Bradford. They each wondered why he ended up nearly dead on the beach and had theories about what had happened to him. How did he get across the East Cape Canal? Did he go to Deadman's Hammock or encounter the manchineel someplace else? Why was he naked?

It was a conundrum. Nelson hoped the puzzle would be solved, completing the picture of who this man was. For now, he needed to figure out what to do about the Mercedes he tow-tagged in the parking lot. Since the guy was already in so much trouble, he really didn't want to add to his problems with an expensive tow to an impound lot in Homestead. But, on second thought, would one more problem really make a difference for someone who already had an overwhelming hole to dig out of.

Buddy Smith told Nelson he brought back the gear he and Ranger Cooper found abandoned on the trail. "What do we do about that stuff?"

Nelson said, "If I had a key to the car, I'd put it in there. But I guess we'll just add it to the lost and found if there's nothing really personal or identifiable. I need, or we need, to go out to the Cape to check for what he might have left there. It might help answer some questions.

"Let's take a trip out there while it's fresh. We don't have to walk out. We can start where we found him and see if we can backtrack his route. I really don't want to spend the day at a desk doing reports."

As soon as they got back to Flamingo, the two rangers jumped in the park patrol boat in the Flamingo marina and headed to East Cape Sable. Landing on the beach where they found Bradford, they cleaned up some litter left behind during the hurried rescue. Footprints on the beach led to a campsite. The tent was up and a soiled sleeping bag and crumbled clothes were inside. It was foul-smelling. "This stinks!" they said, in unison. Pulling on latex gloves, the rangers quickly stuffed the tent contents into a large contractor's trash bag, sealing it tightly. They bagged the other gear laying around the campsite separately.

"Seems we're on the clean-up crew. I don't feel much like 'Everglades CSI – Crime Scene Investigators.' Let's move on. I bet he went to Deadman's."

They discovered that, indeed, he had. Although it had rained, the rangers could see evidence that someone had been there, beyond the Closed Area sign. Ranger Smith said, "We need to be careful here or we can wind up like him. There are a lot of manchineels in this hammock."

Nelson responded, "Buddy, you've been at the park a long time. Do you ever recall something like this before? I heard the stories, but frankly, they seemed a little fantastic to me. I guess the reputation was not so exaggerated."

Buddy grunted, "Nope. Nothing like this. Maybe someone got a skin rash, but nothing incapacitating."

Finding an energy bar wrapper, like others that Buddy and Cooper had found on the trail, confirmed that Bradford had made his way to the hammock. That's where he had been exposed to manchineel, but it didn't explain why Bradford was out there in the first place. Given that he had troubles in New York, they speculated he might have been on the run, but why run to the Everglades?

Retracing the path out, they returned to the beach, loaded the trash bags into the boat and headed back. Buddy suggested, "Let's go check out Sandy Key before we head back. It's a nice day and we've got time." It seemed like a good idea. Sandy Key is only five or six miles out of the way and being on a boat, on the bay, was better than a day in the office behind a desk and computer.

Ranger Nelson changed his course slightly to head to Sandy Key and the adjacent Carl Ross Key. Both of the small islands are the outermost islands in Florida Bay, at the border of the vast shallow tidal flats and the Gulf of Mexico. It was their favorite place to fish, particularly at night. When the water flowed in and out of the grass flats with the change of the tides, all manner of fish funneled through the cut between the islands. Sharks, redfish, rays, sea trout, even snapper and grouper could be seen, and caught, in the deeper water of the natural channel. Years ago, before a 2005 hurricane, the islands were larger and the cut was a narrow opening. After the storm, half of the keys were washed away and reshaped. Buddy had been there when the keys were whole and lamented on how good the fishing had been. He'd even seen evidence of the tarpaper shacks dating back to the 1920s that were remnants of a charcoal-making camp on Carl Ross Key. Buddy commented, "This place must have been a really spectacular rookery when John James Audubon visited the area and created his famous roseate spoonbill painting in the 1830s. The keys have been hit hard by hurricanes and I now wonder how long they can survive climate change and sea level rise."

Nelson chided him with a sarcastic snip, "What are you talkin' about. Ain't no such thing! The water is at the same level on my boat as it's always been. If it was higher, we'd be sinking!" He was mocking the kind of nonsensical thinking of the science deniers. Buddy winked at him.

After surveying the keys and checking the posted signs around the remaining rookery, they departed with a promise to return to go fishing there again before the keys were fully washed away.

Back at Flamingo, Nelson called the Marathon Community Hospital to see how Bradford was doing. It had been a little over 48 hours since he'd brought Bradford to the hospital. He asked the switchboard to connect him to Suzanne in the ER, if she was available. "Hello, Suzanne. This is Ranger Nelson at Everglades National Park. Do you have a minute?

"I'm calling to check up on Ronald Bradford's condition. The switchboard gives me the HIPAA run-around because I'm not family or on his disclosure list. Can you tell me what's going on? That is, if you know."

Suzanne said, "Yes, I know how guarded the operator is about information. She's following protocol. Ronald is the buzz of the hospital! Everybody knows since it's such an unusual case. He's doing a little better, but he's still in serious condition in the ICU. He is very weak and doesn't seem lucid. His skin condition is horrible!"

"Thanks, good to hear he's hanging in there."

Continuing, Suzanne said, "Oh, you might be interested in this gossip. His wife came in a few hours ago on a private jet! She visited for only a few minutes. I don't know if she's staying in Marathon." Suzanne chuckled, "You also might like to know you are the hero of the ICU for getting the handcuffs taken off their patient. The deputy is still here, but the nurses are much happier to not have the restraints hampering their work. They know you are the one who got it done. Nobody thinks he can run away or hurt anyone, in his condition."

Nelson said he was happy he could help. "It seemed excessive for a sickly, non-violent offender. He isn't even under arrest! Thanks again for the update. I'll let the other folks involved in his rescue know. Bye now."

A few days passed without any more news from the hospital or any contact from the New York detective. Nelson's incident report was complete. The Mercedes was still in the parking lot, so Nelson thought he'd try to get in touch with Mrs. Bradford to see if she had a preference about what to do with it. After a bit of trouble, he tracked her down.

"Mrs. Bradford, I'm calling regarding a Mercedes registered to your husband and seemingly abandoned in the parking lot at Flamingo in the Everglades National Park. We are about to have it towed to Homestead, unless you can suggest an alternative way to get the car removed."

"Yes, it's my husband's car. He is in the hospital and can't get it. Where is it exactly?"

Nelson explained where Flamingo is, in relation to Marathon, and that it is really out of the way.

She asked, "Do you have an airport there? I have a jet that could land, but no key fob for his car."

"We only have a heliport pad here and I'm afraid we don't have a key either."

"Well, then it's fine to have it removed. Would you pass along my contact information to the tow truck driver? I'll make arrangements to have it picked up or maybe I'll just sell it." She was obviously frustrated with the situation, explaining, "My estranged husband is very ill. He seems to be involved in some kind of crime and I'm tied to him and his problems by marriage. I really don't know how to handle this."

"You have my sympathy ma'am. I am sorry to add complications. I hope your husband recovers. I know it must be tough."

Mrs. Bradford politely thanked Nelson and asked him to extend her thanks to whomever at the Park helped rescue her husband. "Everything was going perfectly until he became so obsessed with money and scheming to be a big-shot tycoon. We had a good life together and have a wonderful daughter. I just want Ronald back, to be the man I married."

It was more than Nelson needed to know, but helped satisfy his curiosity, although her private plane provoked more questions.

A few days later, it was time for the Ten Thousand Islands routine patrol. Nelson would be able to check in on the houseboat hermit. There was no telling where the hermit might be, but he hoped he would run into him. As usual, the run out to the Gulf was an enjoyable trip. Nelson stopped a couple of fishermen for boating permit certifications and fishing licenses. Everyone was pleasant and in compliance.

Nelson started his patrol up the coast toward the boundary the park shared with the wildlife refuge. There were a few kayakers camping on the island campsites. He could see large fishing boats and sailboats, in the deeper water outside the park boundary, making their way to and from the Keys. Along the shoreline there wasn't any activity.

Nelson didn't know if there were any boaters inside the mangroves, transiting the Wilderness Waterway. He couldn't check since the patrol boat drew too much water. But, he could go up the Little Shark River to Tarpon Bay and Rookery Branch. It was good water all the way to the Cane Patch campsite. Oddly enough, that's where he found Thompson. Actually, he found Thompson's houseboat, anchored. The pirogue and the old man were missing.

Cane Patch had once been a farm in the back-country. Located far enough upstream from the Gulf, fresh water flowed past the landing for the camping platform. A fisherman could catch largemouth bass and sunfish from the platform. The former farm site was on higher ground reclaimed from an Indian mound, perhaps one of the Calusa villages or seasonal subsistence sites. Nelson speculated that Thompson might be at the old homestead ruins.

He noticed Thompson's pirogue at the Cane Patch landing. Getting off his patrol boat, he followed the overgrown path to the ruins. He surprised Thompson, who was on his way out with a load of bananas. Nelson needled him, "Busted! Mr. Thompson, you know all plants and animals in the park are protected." He was kidding, to tease the old man.

The bananas Thompson was carrying were a vestige of the long-abandoned farmstead. Several fruit and vegetable plants were still surviving at the site. The NPS had determined they were not

119

invasive and made no effort to eliminate them. From time to time, Thompson harvested the sour oranges, key limes, bananas, and a sugar cane stalk or two from the residual volunteers. It was a nice trip up the river and there was always a reward of fruit at the end of the voyage.

Nelson helped him with the bananas, walking back to his pirogue. Thompson grumbled, "You ought not to poke me with your badge." Nelson just grinned.

Back at the houseboat, Nelson tried to engage Thompson in conversation, without much success until he asked about the suspicious boat Thompson had mentioned on their last visit.

"Yes, I've seen it regularly, doing the same thing. These two men on a lobster boat come late in the day. They pull a trap near a boundary marker and then head to the mangroves. A couple-few hours later, in the dark, I see them back at the same place and they seem to pull out big fish, maybe grouper, maybe jewfish. I don't know. I keep my distance and mind my own business."

Nelson said, "They're called goliath grouper now, not jewfish." Then, he asked, "Think they see you watching?"

"Can't imagine they don't, but guess they don't care. I'm not a ranger or game warden."

Nelson thanked Thompson for the tip. He asked if he'd been in the park more than 30 days, which peeved Thompson. "I've been leaving like you said. The refuge officer up the coast doesn't hassle me like you park people. Maybe I'll relocate up there!"

"No need sir, you're welcome here. I just need to keep you legal so the other rangers don't get too zealous. I consider you a real help in protecting the park. And, after your rescue of those kids, far as I'm concerned, you ought to be on the payroll. See you next time. Enjoy your bananas!"

Based on Thompson's tip, Nelson was off to check the boundary markers on the Gulf. Flying through the mangrove-lined rivers, he arrived at the open water and started checking boundary posts. At first he couldn't see anything suspicious. Then, using a boat pole, he reached down to check the depth at the post. He snagged and retrieved a sinker line attached to the post a couple of feet below the surface. Taking in the rope by hand, Nelson pulled and the boat followed the line toward something that was weighted on the bottom. Pulling harder, he dislodged a spiny lobster trap, bringing up a fair number of crabs and lobster.

This is what the men were doing at the boundary posts. It was not likely they would ever be caught since there was no reason for anyone to snag their pull line and there was no float. Nelson threw the trap back into the water. He sped to the next boundary marker and found the same thing.

"Hmm. Interesting," he thought. "There are a number of boundary posts, but really not enough to be viable for lobstering, even out of season or taking the shorts." He figured they must be up to something more. It had been a long day on the water, running up and down the west coast of the park, so he decided to go back to Flamingo and tackle the problem the next day.

When Nelson returned to the office in the morning he contacted the Florida Fish and Wildlife Conservation Commission and the manager of the Ten Thousand Islands National Wildlife Refuge to discuss what he had found. They agreed to meet in Everglades City three days later at the Park's western entrance office. Nelson asked Ranger Cooper to come along with him to the meeting.

Cooper was a new ranger, fresh out of his NPS training and federal law enforcement training course in Brunswick, Georgia. He seemed to like the law enforcement aspect of being a park ranger more than the public use programming part of the job.

When the group met at the Park's visitor center in Everglades City, Nelson relayed what he had learned from Thompson. The FWCC officers laughed. "You'd believe that old crank? He's likely the perp himself and feeding you a line to set you on a wild goose chase!"

"Wait, let me finish with what I know is fact. Besides, I believe Mr. Thompson saw something." He continued as the FWCC officers folded their arms and leaned back in their chairs. "First, Thompson told me about seeing this activity a couple months ago. He repeated the story when I visited him a few days ago and added the detail about how the men timed their operation.

"So, based on his observations, I checked the boundary markers – well, two of them anyway – and found the hidden traps. There were no floats and they were tied to the boundary sign posts, well underwater where they couldn't be seen from the surface. They were not tagged and the traps had no identification numbers on them." Turning to the FWCC representatives, he asked, "Aren't all Florida lobster traps supposed to have a permit number affixed to the trap?"

The FWCC men nodded. "Yes. ID and permit numbers."

"So, at the very least, these traps are illegal and out of season." Nelson showed around an iPhone photo of one of the traps with lobster in it.

The refuge manager brought up that the refuge didn't have any offshore boundary signs. The only signs they had out in the water were notices to prohibit landings on sensitive bird nesting and roosting islands. "We've never observed this kind of thing, but then, we've never looked. The only time we mess with any of our signs is when they need repair or replacement."

The group began discussing how they could catch the poachers in the act if this was an unlawful activity. One member of the group said, "Wouldn't it just be easier to check all the markers and retrieve the traps? That would foil their operation, even if we couldn't prosecute."

With more discussion, Nelson, with Cooper backing him up, advocated for a coordinated surveillance operation. "Thompson noticed there is a pattern to the visits, even though the potential poaching is taking place in a large remote area," he continued.

The Refuge Manager agreed, saying they could detail a law enforcement officer or two to try to catch the guys, at least for a couple of nights. The lead FWCC officer said, "I suppose we're up for a wild goose chase too. Maybe we could get lucky, but this is not as cut and dry as patrolling to check boating safety and fishing licenses."

Once all of the agencies were on board with the surveillance idea, they needed to form an operation plan. "According to Thompson, the activity occurs in mid-week, Tuesdays to Thursdays. Pulling the traps starts in the late afternoon and the visits to the mangroves are later, after dark."

FWCC offered, "Together we could stage a series of boats in the mangroves with one officer in each boat hiding under a camo tarp. If we all get in place around mid-day, we could wait to see if the poachers show up. We can space the boats out, adjacent to the park border boundary markers."

Cooper said, "We wouldn't need to be very far apart, so we can stay in radio contact to alert each other and call for assistance, if needed. Once the poacher is sighted, it'll probably take more than one boat and officer to apprehend them."

The Refuge Manager asked, "Can we hold off on deciding on the specific plans? I'd like our Refuge Law Enforcement Officer to be in on planning this. I don't have LE authority. He isn't too far away. Could we break for a half hour?"

They all agreed, deciding to go over to the Rod and Gun Club for a coffee break. On their way there, they cautioned each other not to discuss their purpose for being together or the upcoming planned surveillance while they were in the restaurant. Someone might overhear and the guys they were looking for might be local. Even the local police might not keep the group's plan confidential. In the past, from Goodland to Everglades City to Chokoloskee, the region had a nefarious reputation.

When Harry White, the Refuge's law enforcement officer, arrived they returned to the Park Service Visitor Center to resume their conversation. The refuge manager had brought Officer White up to speed over the phone while he was on the way to meet with the others.

Nelson unrolled a chart of the area. "This is where Thompson was on the occasion he observed the boat." Pointing to some marker symbols, he said, "These are our unlighted boundary markers."

Officer White pointed to the places where the refuge had signs installed in the water. "These are places closer to the Park and more suitable for traps. But, frankly, none of these places are prime habitat for spiny lobster. Maybe blue crab though."

"We could spread out here, here, and here," FWCC Officer Michelle Jones said, as she tapped on points on the chart that were about 6 to 8 miles apart at Harney River on the south, Lostman's in the middle, and Chatham River in the north. Her partner, Sgt. Wilson, added, "Then the secondary points would be south of Lostman's, at the Broad River, and south of the Harney River at the Shark River.

Refuge Officer White said, "We'll need tactical gear and night vision scopes. We should plan to run dark – no lights." The refuge manager added, "And insect repellent!" They all knew he was correct.

Ranger Nelson reviewed the plan, "Let's go over this again here. Then, we can do a Zoom meeting before we deploy, just to be sure we are all on the same page. Let's get whatever approvals we need from our agencies to do this joint operation."

The FWCC officers proposed, "Let's look ahead at the weather and select a tentative date." They all looked at their phones for a weather app, noting that eight to ten days out the weather was projected to be suitable.

"Final question, are we in for one, two, or three days?" Nelson waited for an answer. The men looked at each other, until Officer Jones said, "I think we can get approval for one day. Two would be the most I'd expect. Basing the investment on such a sketchy suspicion isn't likely to get a lot of traction with our boss." The refuge manager confirmed that two days for the operation would be agreeable to him.

Ranger Nelson concluded the meeting. "Well, thank you all for coming. I look forward to working with you on this. Although it might be a fishing expedition, we might just land some fish!" They shook hands and departed for their respective offices.

Before leaving, Rangers Nelson and Cooper stopped to check with the Everglades District Ranger, briefing him that they would be conducting a joint operation with FWCC and the Ten Thousand

Islands National Wildlife Refuge. The District Ranger asked, "Do you need help?"

Nelson countered, "No, only your support and, especially, confidentiality. We don't want any advance publicity that might tip off the suspects. We really don't have any suspects yet, only suspicions of poaching."

On the drive back to Flamingo, he phoned the Marathon hospital to checked on Ronald Bradford's condition. He asked for Suzanne, but she was off until her 7 to 3 shift the next day. But, the efficient operator told him there was no change, that Ronald was maybe a little better, but not worse, still listed as "serious" and still in the ICU. Nelson thanked the operator for the update and resolved to call Suzanne to get more information when she was back on duty.

TEN

It was a busy day for Flamingo. With visitation having run lower in previous years, it was good to see more people at the marina and campgrounds. The boat ramp was busy on the bay side of the water control structure and the launch ramp on the freshwater side was even more active.

Fishing was predicted to be good because a mild front was coming through, aligning with the tide. Boat trailers were filling the parking lot. Nelson asked Ranger Alondra Fuentes to watch over the ramps, saying "Alondra, it's better to head off problems at the ramp than respond to problems out on the water." Ranger Fuentes casually surveyed the activity with an eye out for boats that might be of particular concern, such as those being overloaded or under equipped. Nothing stood out.

She noticed two older gentlemen stopping at the marina store, purchasing gas for a 5-gallon tank and a bag of ice. Their boat was an old aluminum skiff with an antique-looking outboard motor. Their fishing rods were hanging over the boat's gunwales. Fuentes could see they had a couple of life vests. Nothing was really out of the ordinary. They appeared to be in their mid-80s.

The only thing odd was they didn't launch their boat at either ramp, but instead drove off.

This piqued her interest, so she decided to follow them because there wasn't another boat ramp along the park road to Flamingo. They turned left on Bear Lake Road, just south of the Buttonwood Canal bridge. She waited a few minutes to let them get a head start on the unpaved road leading to the launch site of the Bear Lake Canoe Trail.

She caught up to them as they were about to launch their skiff. Approaching the two men, she called out, "Hello gentlemen. How are you doing?"

"Fine," replied the elder man, Arthur. Don, his companion, said respectfully, "Yes, fine, and how are you?"

Fuentes asked, "Do you plan on launching here? You know motors are prohibited in this part of the Park. Only canoes and kayaks or electric trolling motors are allowed."

The two older men looked at each other, their disappointment palpable. "We've been coming here for 50 years. But, it's been a long time since we've been here. We just wanted to go fishing on Lake Ingraham on Cape Sable."

Fuentes hated being the bad guy. These two certainly couldn't row the trail, even if they had a suitable boat. One of the old men said, "It's been our ambition to go fishing on our own like we used to do. But I guess we need to pack up and head back to Miami."

Fuentes said, "Wait a minute and I'll see what I can do." She walked away and called Nelson on her cell phone to explain the predicament of these two old men. "Bob, I really hate to bust their dreams. They are like my grandfathers."

Nelson thought a minute, "How about we give them a special use permit, if they promise not to go any further than the end of the

128

canal into Bear Lake. I can't see how that would hurt much. Are there any canoers out there?"

Fuentes answered, "No, they are the only ones here. If anyone was going to paddle this trail, they probably would have started much earlier."

Nelson said, "Write it down on the permit as a 'legacy/accessibility purpose exception.' I'll sign it when you get back. I'd also suggest you paddle out in a couple hours to check on them and to make sure they are OK."

Relieved she could help these guys out, she explained to them the special permission they were being granted and the limitations. "Don't go fast and make a wake," she cautioned. Don responded, "Don't worry, honey. The days for us to go fast are long gone."

Arthur and Don were delighted they would be able to go fishing in one of their old haunts, even if they didn't make it all the way to Lake Ingraham. It wasn't the swan song fishing trip they dreamed of, but at least they could revisit the memories of past days. Being in their mid-80s, it wasn't likely they would be physically able to do this alone again, even if they could cajole their families into acquiescing to their desires.

They promised to comply with the terms. Ranger Fuentes helped them launch their aluminum skiff at the primitive ramp. After Arthur parked, they boarded and puttered down the canal toward Bear Lake.

Don said, "Skipper, we are off to go fishing again, just like the old days!"

"That's right Cap! Like old times." Arthur said. "We've had a lot of good times out here. I wish we could have made it to Lake Ingraham. Reckon we probably wouldn't have had time, anyway."

"Doesn't matter Skipper. At least we're fishing. It can only be better if we catch some black drum."

Don smiled. They were both happy and grateful the young Ranger lady had made an accommodation for them. Otherwise, the trip would have been a bust.

The canal was straight, shaded by an overarching canopy of tree limbs. The dark water reflected the umbrella-like canopy like a mirror. The old outboard hummed. Don, a retired airline mechanic, had spent the past month reworking the old Johnson outboard so it would run tip-top.

At the end of the canal, they emerged from the vegetated tunnel into the open water of Bear Lake. They proceeded a couple hundred yards, killed the engine, and dropped the anchor.

"Hey Skipper, we need to get fishin'!"

They both set up their rigs and cast their lines out to the inky dark water. Both were thrilled to be there, but kept quiet so they didn't scare the fish away.

"Cap, I think I got a bite!"

"Skipper, that a bug or a fish?"

Arthur definitely had something on the line. It was fighting hard, pulling forward every time he pulled back and reeled in more line. The fish vigorously resisted being extracted from its habitat. Back and forth, the struggle between angler and fish went on for five minutes. "Skipper, you getting' tired, old man? Need some help?"

Arthur joked back, "You think you're any better? I've got one on the line and you don't. I about got him. Get the net!"

Don dipped the net in the dark water. The fish was thrashing just under the surface. Don scooped it up. It was heavy, maybe eight or ten pounds. Once the fish was out of the water, Don laughed.

"Well Skipper, you caught a bowfin – a mudfish – a choupique – grinnel! No matter what you call it, it's damn ugly! You are the winner!"

This slimy eel-like fish with a menacing row of needle-like teeth in a wide mouth was about as useless a catch as a fisherman could hook. "Skipper, do I need to take him off the hook for you?"

"No Cap, I can do it myself. You want to talk or fish?"

The old friends sat for a couple of hours. Their conversations were a mixture of banter about fishing prowess and reminiscing about the old days in the Everglades, even before the Park was established. They whiled away the time, replacing baits stripped off by pinfish. About the time they decided it was time to go, they each hooked a fish; not big ones, but still keepers. Both fish were the black drums they were hoping to catch.

Just as they were pulling anchor, they heard a woman's voice, "Hey there guys. How's it going?" It was Ranger Fuentes paddling up in a park kayak.

"We're doing great! We each caught a fish, but Cap here has a tiny one. Do you want to check his?" asked Arthur.

"No, they are both legal. Skipper only wants to stir up trouble! We are ready to get back. Thank you again for helping us out! It's been a great day."

Fuentes watched them leave and head back down the tunneled canal toward the launch. She smiled thinking she would catch up in a few minutes to help these two nice old guys load up their boat. When they got home, they would both be dog-tired but with memories for the future, recaptured from the past.

Meeting Nelson later, he asked Fuentes, "How'd it go with the old guys?"

She replied, "Fine. It was a good feeling to help them out by bending the rules a little bit. They really seemed to have a great day, you know, being out on the water and fishing."

"No harm, no foul," Nelson said. "Connecting people with nature is what it's all about. It's the people's park. Not to get sentimental, but those two old guys owned it before we were here and another generation will own it after we're gone. Let's just not make a habit of it!"

Returning from the field, Ranger Buddy Smith walked into the office saying, "Today's been a busy one. There were so many folks fishing, and, so far, no problems on my end. Anything going on here?"

Ranger Cooper was at his desk. "Looks pretty good. Lots of float plans have checked out and the parking lot is clearing. Keep your fingers crossed there's no fool still out there." They all agreed and departed for their regular end-of-the-day patrols.

While he was out and about, doing his daily checks, Nelson received a call from the NYPD. Detective Ramos was on the line to check in with him about Ronald Bradford. Nelson didn't have any updates for him regarding Bradford's visit to the Park. "We found some of his gear and his campsite. He didn't have anything prohibited. His car has been towed to an impound lot in Homestead, per his spouse's instructions."

The detective said, "That's pretty much what I already knew. The hospital still has him in the ICU, but say he's improving enough to be moved to a private room soon. They want a psyche evaluation, based on his history and some of the rantings he had while he's been coming back to his senses."

Nelson said, "We won't ever know what was inside Bradford's head. For whatever reason, he made some very bad choices that about ended him. The Everglades can be great, but it can be dangerous if you don't know what you're doing."

The detective agreed, "You know that sounds a lot like New York City. Thanks for your help with Bradford. I may be calling you again, pending how our investigation goes."

Nelson hung up and wondered what would happen to Bradford once he recovered. It's frustrating to be in on part of a story and not know how it turns out; disappointing to be intensely invested in someone's life for a little while, then never see them again.

More pressing was the plan to conduct surveillance on the poachers Thompson had reported. So far, the Refuge law enforcement officer, Officer White, was approved to participate for two days. The Refuge was ready. The Park Service would have two small boats with a person in each and two back-up officers standing by on the larger patrol boat at the Little Shark River anchorage. Whether FWCC would participate was still pending, but it was looking promising.

Nelson already planned to have Cooper in one boat and him in another. Cooper wasn't very experienced, but he was well-trained. Rangers Smith and Fuentes would staff the back-up boat. They would be able to relay messages with the powerful Park radio antenna on the larger boat.

Nelson reviewed ENP's part of the plan and equipment, double checking to be sure everything was operable and that the camouflage covers would be suitable to disguise the boats in the mangroves. He planned what armaments and body armor were appropriate.

Since this was not a drug operation, but a fishing and poaching issue, he did not anticipate that a SWAT team was necessary. It would be surveillance, with the chance of making an arrest if they discovered a crime. Additionally, there was not even any evidence of unlawful activity more than the illegal lobster poaching. As he was finishing the final touches to the plan, the FWCC called to inform Nelson that they were approved for two days, two officers, and two boats.

Nelson decided he wanted to make a run out to find Thompson before the three agencies started the joint operation. He trusted that Thompson was not involved in any way in whatever fishing scheme was going on, so Nelson thought it safe to let him in on the plan.

Nelson approached the houseboat, anchored in one of Thompson's typical haunts, in Ponce de Leon Bay, north of the Shark River. Thompson was waiting for him on deck. "It's you again, so soon after you caught me at Cane Patch?"

Nelson answered, "Yes, but this is a just courtesy call. I'm here to let you know about something we've got in the works to catch the poachers. Can I come aboard?"

"Nothin's changed since the last time. You stay on your boat and I'll stay on mine. I'll get you coffee. Just wait there."

Thompson retreated to his trailer, returning in a few minutes with two cups of coffee and then seated himself on his aft deck. "Whatcha got?"

Nelson told him, "We are conducting a secret surveillance in a few days to watch the coast for the boat that you said was up to something suspicious. The state game wardens and the wildlife refuge officer are working with a few of us in the Park to hide out in the mangroves and watch for what the men are up to."

Thompson asked, "So what does that have to do with me? You gonna chase me off again?"

"No, you just go about your business, as usual. We shouldn't be bothering you, but please don't light us up with your Q-Beam. We want to be camouflaged in the mangroves.

"I do want to ask you a favor though. I'd like to give you a two-way radio to call if you have any trouble or if you see the guys. They might be on the VHF marine radio, so I don't want you to use VHF to call about anything to do with them." Nelson handed him a walkie-talkie. "This will communicate with just me if I might be within its range."

Thompson looked at it and keyed the mike. Nelson's unit squealed. "Good, we're on the same channel. In case they might use this kind of radio, I'd like you to use code words for locations." Nelson then handed Thompson a sketched map with people's names on the geographic locations.

"Just hold on Ranger man. I ain't agreed to helpin' you just yet." Thompson looked at the map. The names were "Sam" for Little Shark River entrance, "Bill" for the Broad River, and "Larry" for the Lostman's River.

Nelson explained further, "The code would be: Call the name and ask, 'do you hear me' if the boat is arriving at the location. If the boat is leaving the location, call the code name of the location and say 'I can't hear you.' If the boat is stopped in the mangroves, use the name of the place and ask 'are the bugs bad?'

"If I get the message, I will come back with the answer 'I'm having trouble hearing you!'"

Thompson looked at the sketched map, the two-way radio, and Nelson. "So you want me to be a look-out spy?"

Nelson nodded, "Yes sir. It would be a help to have another set of eyes. It's a big space for us to cover with only seven of us."

Thompson said, "I suppose I can help you, but you might need to come back with another bottle of bourbon, no, make it rum. Even if I don't see anything."

They went over the code again, confirming the new names for the places on the coast. "Do you have any idea where you might be next week?"

"I plan on staying right where I am, unless y'all run me off!"

"Thanks, I really appreciate your help. I'd like to catch these guys if they are poaching. The DEA has mostly stopped the drugs coming in, so I'm glad we are back to chasing illegal fishing."

Thompson snickered, "You think you've stopped the drugs? I still see strange things out here, but not on a regular basis. Like the guys on the lobster boat. Strange things."

Nelson exclaimed, "Really?" thinking to himself, "I don't need to know that. It's above my pay grade."

Casting off from the houseboat, he added, "Oh and I almost forgot, if you need help or want us to come over to your houseboat, just call for Sally, or any girl's name for that matter. That would tell me that one of us should get to you ASAP. See you later. Keep your head down!"

"Always have, always will."

Nelson was very pleased he had given Thompson advance notice of the operation and even happier that he would have another set of eyes on the coast. He sped back to Flamingo to check the weather forecast again. Nelson had high hopes this effort would pay off. He would have a Zoom meeting with the interagency team the next day to confirm the operation. He also

136

wanted to get his Park Service team together so they were all on the same page.

Finally, the day of the operation arrived. Other rangers would cover the normal duties at Flamingo. Fuentes and Smith boarded the larger park boat. Cooper was ready in the patrol center-console and Nelson took the olive-green aluminum bass boat. They were all ready to go.

The larger boat would stay overnight in the basin at the Little Shark River. Cooper would be undercover in the mangroves with his boat under a green tarp and camo net. Nelson would have a camo net over his skiff, hidden in the mangroves too.

Up in Everglades City, the other partners were ready with their boats. The FWCC had their gray center-console boats. The Refuge had an aluminum jon boat. All had camo nets to hide under while positioned close to the mangroves.

SANIBEL

NAPLES

MARCO
ISLAND

EVERGLADES CITY

Chatham River

Lostmans River

Rodgers River

Broad River

Harney River

Shark River

Gulf of Mexico

CAPE SABLE

ELEVEN

On the day planned for the joint surveillance operation, the weather was clear and hot. The seas were calm and there was only a slight breeze, just enough to ripple the water's surface. The plan was a go. The boats all departed mid-morning to get to their positions. They had set a 14:00 check-in time for a radio call on the handheld radios supplied by the National Park Service. This allowed enough time for the officers to get to their undercover locations and be set up.

At the north end of the stakeout line, the refuge officer was first to call on his radio, "Office White from the Refuge to FWCC Officer Jones, do you copy?

Jones replied, "Affirmative, roger. FWCC Sergeant Milton, do you copy also?"

The FWCC Sergeant Milton replied, "Loud and clear." Continuing the chain, he called, "Ranger Nelson, do you copy?"

There was no answer.

Sergeant Milton called again, "This is Sergeant Milton. NPS Rangers, Nelson, Cooper, do you copy?"

Cooper answered, "FWCC, I copy loud and clear."

Nelson then replied, "Ranger Cooper, I copy you, but did not receive any other transmission. Please repeat."

Cooper transmitted, "All stations, please respond to confirm transmission and location. Nelson seems to be receiving only me."

The Refuge Officer replied, "Refuge LE White in position at Chatham River."

FWCC Officer Jones replied, "Jones, in position at Lostman's, receiving loud and clear.

The FWCC Sergeant responded, "Sgt. Milton, standing by in position at Broad River, loud and clear.

Ranger Cooper stated, "NPS Officer Cooper, at Harney River, received 3 calls, loud and clear."

Ranger Nelson responded, "Ranger Nelson here, only heard you Cooper. Did not receive White, Jones, or Milton. I'm in position north of Shark River."

Fuentes and Smith on the patrol cruiser announced, "Fuentes and Smith at Little Shark River anchorage. Received Rangers Cooper and Nelson loud and clear. No other transmission received."

Ranger Nelson added, "Fuentes and Smith. Got you loud and clear."

Cooper seemed to be able to reach everyone, but the southern end of the coast was out of communication with the FWCC officers and Refuge officer on the northern end.

Nelson transmitted, "Please switch to NPS Channel B."

Cooper replied a confirmation, "Channel B."

Nelson and Cooper adapted the plan to keep all of the officers in touch. They decided they would use Channel 83 on the marine VHF radio as a back-up radio, if the new radio plan worked. To check that everyone could hear each other, Nelson would call on 83, using the cover name "Faro Blanco Fishing Club." They would all pretend to be in a Florida Bay fishing tournament. Nelson asked Cooper to inform the others on the Park-supplied radio.

"All stations, because we cannot all hear one another, we have an alternate communication plan. Please be advised to stand by for a transmission from Ranger Nelson on marine VHF channel 8-3, repeat 8-3. He will be identifying as 'Faro Blanco Fishing Tournament coordinator.' Please reply to him if you hear him. Count off 1 to 6. Refuge, you be one."

Nelson broadcast on VHF 83, "All tournament fishermen, good luck. Monitor 83 for any updates in addition to your normal radio. Good luck, gentlemen and lady. Out." The back-up plan worked. All boats could hear one another, from Little Shark River to Chatham River.

Back on the federal park radio frequency, Cooper updated all of the officers to use VHF 83 as a last resort alternative, especially if the situation called for everyone in the operation to know. "Everyone should dual monitor 83 and the park radio frequency because Nelson and the Park Patrol Cruiser are out of range to those of you north of my position."

With this snag addressed, Nelson hoped there wouldn't be any other glitches to complicate their undercover stakeout plan. The six boats were spread over 22 miles of coast, with incalculable miles of riverlets and creeks in the labyrinth of mangrove islands. With so much territory to cover, the odds of catching poachers in action were against them, but the locations were prime fishing spots and, with Thompson's observations that they were in the area previously, there might just be a chance.

Now they all would pass the time and wait. Anxiousness battled with boredom. The Refuge officer pulled out his binoculars to watch for birds, making a day list while he still had light. Under the mosquito net, it was warm. The breeze was blocked by the camo net and he was backed up into the mangroves, under some overhanging limbs. A bundle of spaghetti-like, long -tentacle roots stretched from the water to high over his head. He was well-hidden in his bird blind.

Officer White quickly spotted brown pelicans, cormorants, and gulls. He couldn't identify the gulls at a distance. Looking into the mangroves, he saw fluttering. He made phishing sounds and a couple of squeaks to draw the birds in closer. Several fluttered to see the source of the noise that imitated the sounds songbirds make to communicate in their secret language. Two redstarts were in the canopy, along with the ubiquitous yellow-rumped warbler and, back further in the canopy, there was a black-whiskered vireo. He thought, "Not a bad start to my list." As the hours passed, he built his list to 23 species. The best bird he saw was a common loon, a migratory bird, that was further south than usual. It was a rare sighting. No birders would accept the sighting without photographic proof.

Solitary time doing nothing in nature could be excruciatingly boring, or exhilarating, or restful. It depends on a person's interest and attitude. Since the officers were to be sparse in radio communication, each officer waited, either patiently watching the clock or watching nature. Only the two northern-most officers had intermittent cell service. The signal varied in and out depending on how they held their phones. Officer Jones pondered how this part of Florida was about as remote a wilderness as one could find in the eastern U.S. Maybe the Smokies were wilder. But, in the mountains, you could transit on foot. Here, without a boat, you were sunk.

Nelson broke the silence, calling on VHF channel 83. "Faro

Blanco Tournament Anglers, Faro Blanco Anglers. Tournament director here. Anybody got any luck yet?"

It was quiet on the Gulf with a gentle breeze from the east. The waters were only rippled on the surface. All of the "anglers" responded to the check in with "No bites yet!" and other chatter that maintained the ruse. Nelson replied, "OK, just checking. Looks like you are all trying. Good luck, call me on the 68 if you catch anything." They all knew that channel 68 was the code for the park radio frequency. Nelson then hailed Fuentes and Smith anchored in the Little Shark River on the park service radio. "Y'all got any company there? I saw some sailboats heading north. Were they anchored in the cove? I couldn't make out where they came from."

Fuentes transmitted, "We had one sailboat depart a couple hours ago. I think they turned south. Two boats came in to anchor here. We checked with them and told them about the rules for the cruising test and fee policy for boaters. Hope that was OK."

"There's also a trawler with a Looper couple on it. They started in Miami last year and have made their way on the Great Loop up the east coast, across the Great Lakes and down the Mississippi, 6000 miles by water."

Nelson replied, "Good initiative, to see who they are. I suppose Cooper is copying this. We are getting close to the time Thompson said the boat arrives at the boundary to pull their traps. The plan is to watch to see what they are doing after that and track them into the night. I expect they won't be down at the cove, but y'all are our back-up."

Cooper radioed, "Roger, I heard your instructions. I'll stand by on this channel and monitor VHF 83."

In the late afternoon, the sun descended as it began to sink into the Gulf of Mexico. Yellow skies transitioned to orange, to red, highlighted with bright pink tufts on the underside of the deep purple-shadowed cumulus clouds. In the pastel afterglow, Refuge Officer Jones noticed a small commercial fishing boat motoring south, fairly well outside the Park boundary. Radioing on the park frequency, "I think we might have the boat we are looking for heading south, offshore, about two miles from my position. From what I can tell, it's got a small cabin and open back deck, with a full cover. A stack out the top is spewing a little smoke."

Before long the Fish and Wildlife officers confirmed the sighting. "The boat is barely visible, we are running out of light and I don't see running lights. It seems to be headed south toward Cape Sable."

It was a good bet this was the boat they were on the stakeout to catch. It had been a question of whether the boat was out of somewhere in the Keys or up towards Cape Romano. About an hour after the first sighting, Ranger Cooper saw a boat light up at the park boundary, near the location of an unlighted boundary marker. Using his binoculars, he could see two figures moving on the back deck under the bright lights on the boat. Occasionally light hit the reflective boundary sign, lighting it up like a beacon.

"All stations, this is Ranger Cooper. I have suspects in sight of Harney River at the boundary marker. I cannot tell what they are doing, but the boat is illuminated by their deck lights. Two POB. Repeat, sighted two persons on board."

Nelson responded, "Good! Stand by, maintain your position and observe. They're probably pulling one of the traps. Watch what they do next. Cooper, please relay information to the boats north of you. They may need to intercept the perps on their return to home port, wherever that is."

The boat was only at the marker for a few minutes. "Nelson, the boat has left the boundary sign and is heading down your way. Do you copy?"

"Copy that, Cooper." Nelson waited, attentively listening for the sound of an engine. In the darkness, he heard the boat before he saw it coming directly toward him. It had no running lights. The engine noise stopped, but the hum of a gas-powered generator was constant. Nelson looked through night-vision binoculars to observe the boat. Two men were moving to the back. Suddenly, the deck lights flashed on, overwhelming his vision for a moment. Now, Nelson switched to his regular binoculars for a clearer image.

The boat was drifting a little, near the entrance of a creek off Ponce de Leon Bay. The men baited large hooks with whole mullets and spiny lobster, probably taken from their trap. The hooks were attached to what seemed to be like a trotline, a string of fishing line with baited hooks on short lines branching off at intervals. When they finished setting up their gear, one man threw a float over the side and lowered a concrete building block into the water. His cohort fed the baited line over the side as they drifted. Nelson counted ten baits. A second block was lowered into the water and one of the men threw another lobster pot float over the side. The lights went out. A moment later the engine rumbled on.

The boat moved away slowly at first, and then revved, heading north, disappearing around the corner of a mangrove island. "Cooper, heads-up. I think they are heading your way. They deployed something like a trotline here. Do you copy?"

Cooper responded, "Yes, understood. Targets have set a trotline near you in Ponce de Leon Bay and are headed north, possibly toward my position at Harney River. Over." Cooper hoped all the other officers heard his reply to Nelson and were updated on the status.

Fifteen minutes passed before Cooper heard the fishing boat approaching. The boat came so close to his location he could smell the exhaust and his boat rocked from the wake. The boat stopped less than 100 yards away. Cooper could make out their conversation. When their deck light came on, he could see the men clearly, even without binoculars.

"Butch, are you ready? Is the line baited?"

"Sure thing Harley, I did 'er on the way. It's ready to go. We at the GPS?"

"Nope, let me circle 'round to get closer. I want to hit the numbers before we set the line."

The engine rpm increased and their boat made a quick turn. They had turned the deck lights off, but Cooper could see the face of the man steering, dimly lit from the GPS plotter screen at the helm. He idled the engine and took it out of gear. Now they were drifting a mere 50 yards away from Cooper's position. He hoped no one would call on the radio because the poachers might hear it over their engine and generator.

The two men set their line, dropping a cement block and float to start. As they drifted, they fed out a line with baited hooks, then dropped another block and float. The line looked about 80 or 100 feet, with about 10 baited hooks.

One of the men started shining a spotlight to locate the floats, scanning the surrounding mangroves. When the light passed by Cooper's position, it twinkled through the openings in the camo net. The aluminum hull and stainless rails reflected the light. Cooper held his breath, frightened he might have been made. Fortunately, the men were talking to each other about having a beer.

"Hey Harley, how about another beer? Reckon we can hang out here before going back to the other line?"

Harley retrieved a beer from a cooler for Butch and got one for himself. Popping it open, he said, "Think we ought to move off a bit so the fish will have a little peace and quiet for their lobster dinner. Don't want them to be spooked by boat noise."

"OK, sounds good. We need to wait 'bout an hour. Let's go out to the marker and drift while we wait."

"You know it's a crap-shoot. We want enough time to hook something, but not chance taking too much time for a shark to take our catch."

"Right dat, Butch. We've lost some jewfish that way. Money right out of our pocket."

"Harley, think that's why this place is called Shark River?" He laughed through a belch. Then they were off to kill an hour.

After they were clearly out of range, Cooper could breathe again. They were so close he smelled their cigarettes and could clearly see their faces when their lights were on. He called to the team to relay what he had seen and heard.

"Stakeout team, stakeout team." With all the joint operation planning they had overlooked having a clever name for their surveillance. "This is Cooper. The boat was very close to me at the entrance of Harney River. There are two men. First names are Butch and Harley. Both are drinking but do not seem impaired. They set a 100-foot line in the channel with baited hooks about every ten feet, marked with lobster trap floats on each end. The line appeared to be stiff, maybe stainless wire.

"In about an hour, they will return to the other line they have set, near Nelson's position in Ponce de Leon Bay. Then, I assume they will return to this location to pull this line. Over."

Nelson replied "Good work, Cooper!" Others echoed congratulations. The refuge officer and FWCC officers asked Cooper for instructions. When Cooper radioed, Nelson replied for him to relay, "I think they can move out from under cover and position themselves to intercept the perps on their return to home port. There's no need to be in the blinds. We will have enough if we catch them here in the act."

The decision was made for the two FWCC officers to meet up and station themselves off Lostman's River. The boundary marker is lighted providing a good reference point. Refuge Officer White would stay at Chatham River in case the boat somehow made it through the net. White could track them back to wherever they came from and call the sheriff for assistance. For now, as the poachers waited, the officers waited.

Nelson used the time to check in with Thompson on the two-way walkie talkie radio.

"Hey, Thompson. This is Nelson. You on this channel?"

There was a quick reply, "Yes, I'm just sitting here in the dark, watching the stars go by."

"Thompson, I'm here fishing. I think I will go over to see how Sam is doing. I expect he will have a big fish biting in less than an hour. Stand by, OK?"

"You know I'm closer to Sam than you are, Nelson."

"Yes, I know. Just stand by and keep watching the stars. Maybe you will see the big fish!"

It was a silly exchange, but by being so stupid it probably wouldn't tip off the poachers in the unlikely event they used the same frequency of the walkie-talkie. Nelson wanted Thompson to be safe, wishing he could have been more direct with him. His houseboat was pretty close to where the poachers set their line.

Thompson pulled out his million-candle power spotlight. Shining the light along the surface of the water, in the distance maybe a few hundred yards away, he saw the floats marking the lines reflect back. He retreated to his trailer cabin to wait in the dark.

Nelson saw the glare Thompson's light made and wished he hadn't tried to shine up the floats. Nelson's position was about the same distance from the traps but in the opposite direction. Ten minutes later, the rumble of the lobster boat telegraphed its arrival. Instead of going directly to the fishing line they stopped at the houseboat.

"Hey! Hey, come out here!" Harley shouted. Alongside the houseboat, Butch banged on the aluminum pontoon with a boat pole. Then Butch yelled, "You ought to come out or I'll damn-sure pull you out."

Thompson emerged out of the trailer into the screened porch with his elbows down but his hands up. "What do you fellers want?"

Harley bullied him, "Old man, what were you looking at with your spotlight?"

Thompson replied, "Nothing special. Just wanted to see where the tide was. I saw you have a couple floats out there, but it ain't none of my business."

Harley and Butch looked at each other. Now they were drunk, not commode-hugging drunk, but well buzzed. In their impaired state, they reasoned that this guy was an old man on a derelict houseboat, probably no more of a friend of the law than they were, so they decided to just ignore him.

"You need to mind your own business, pops! If you know

what's good for you, you'll move on. Be gone by the time we finish fishing."

Thompson said, "You guys don't need to be bothering old folks. But I'll move outta here. Don't know what you're doin' and I don't care."

Butch pushed off the houseboat, while Harley eased up to the floats. Harley leaned out of the helm station to shine up the floats. Butch got the boat hook, retrieved a float and hauled up a section of the line. He wound it on the motorized winch and slowly began pulling. Harley turned on the deck lights, then dropped their anchor to keep them from drifting into shallow water or mangroves.

TWELVE

While the two poachers were engaged in their harvest, Thompson was starting his motor and pulling anchor. He wanted to be under power and not stuck at anchor if the two drunks returned with a change of heart. He called Nelson on the two-way.

"No need to call any girls just yet. I'm OK. Sam has the big fish on his line. I'm going to hang around a bit to watch what you catch. I think our other fishing friends are drunk."

Nelson said, "No need to stay. Why don't you move on out to another fishing spot. I'll catch up with you a little later. Sorry, I've got to go. I'm nearby and watching Sam too. Signing off."

Nelson observed the winch pull up the wire trotline. The first fish brought up was a good-sized grouper. One of the men gaffed and unhooked it, flopping it into a household chest freezer. Nelson realized that was what the noisy portable generator was being used for.

The second fish was a 3-foot tarpon. They cut it loose and it splashed into the inky depths.

Then came up the prize they were looking for, a sizable goliath grouper, maybe over 50 pounds. The men high-fived one another. "Hell yeah! That's what I like!" With a bang, the fish was pithed by a bullet to the head. It stopped thrashing. Butch hugged the big fish hanging from the winch boom. The two men struggled to get it into the freezer. The next hook was empty. Then, the poachers hauled in a couple of large snook and an even larger goliath. Another shot from the poacher's revolver meant two of these gentle giants were gone, never to grow to their full, near-800-pound size. Their catch exceeded the capacity of their chest freezer.

Thompson maneuvered his houseboat off the beam of the commercial fishing boat, still a few hundred yards away but now closer to Nelson's position. He called Nelson, "Why don't you come up on my starboard and hide behind me?"

Reluctantly Nelson decided to use the houseboat for cover. Moving quietly, without the motor, he came alongside Thompson's starboard, and tied up so that his Park jon boat was obscured from the poachers' view. The poachers were now a couple of hundred yards off *Épave's* port.

Nelson called both Fuentes and Cooper. "I'm ready to move in on these two guys as soon as you can get here. The poachers have landed several fish and two goliath. Advise your ETA. I'm tied up to Mr. Thompson's houseboat around the corner from Shark Point in Ponce de Leon Bay."

Harley yelled at Butch, "Hey! Pull the anchor and straighten up the fishing gear. Let's go get the other line up at Harney."

"I hope we can do as good there. These GPS numbers are sure paying off."

With the anchor up, Harley started to move on out of Ponce de Leon Bay to round Shark Point and head to the Harney River. Far on the horizon, a pulsating blue light was glowing in the humid atmosphere. It was Cooper on his way, coming fast. Harley idled his boat.

Butch blurted, "Hey, that's a warden out there! That old man must have ratted us out!"

"God damn it! I knew we should have just pushed him off his boat. If anybody ever found him it would look like just another boating accident." Harley was drunk and pissed.

Panicking, they quickly conferred about what they should do. Should they run for it or hide in the mangrove maze? Dumping their gear and freezer was an option. In the dark water, no one would find it and they could come back to get it, using GPS numbers. The glowing light was getting brighter on the outside of the point.

Cooper was running flat out through the darkness, 30 knots, trying to get there, fast. He called on the park radio to let the FWCC and Refuge Officer White know what was going on. "Ranger Cooper to team, I'm running to Ponce de Leon Bay. To help..."

The radio transmission ended abruptly.

Cooper had hit a shoal at full speed, grounding and cracking the transom of his boat. He was flung forward, his head hit the bow rail, and both bones in his right arm snapped. The pain in his side was sharp. It hurt when he breathed.

Cooper limped back to the console and found the dangling VHF mike. "This is Cooper. I've run hard aground." He coughed, sending a sharp pain in his side. "I'm not going to be able to help." He coughed again.

Fuentes asked, "Are you injured? You don't sound so good. Where are you?"

Not wanting to admit he was fallible, Cooper replied, "I am

hurt, but I can wait for help. I'm on a sandbar off of Shark Point. I cut it too close."

Cooper had been navigating by intuition instead of his GPS plotter. Now he saw he was in the middle of a tidal flat. If only he had followed his electronic chart and not tried to cut corners and follow the mangrove shore.

Nelson came on the radio. "Fuentes and Smith, it's more important to get to Cooper. We have enough on these perps. The officers to the north can intercept them and take them into custody. Get to Cooper."

"Affirmative, will do." Smith changed course to head to Shark Point. They would not be able to get close to Cooper's boat. If it was too shallow for the bay boat Cooper was in, it was way too shallow for the large park patrol boat. They would have to improvise when they got close and could assess the situation.

Fuentes called the other three officers on the marine VHF since the park radio wouldn't reach them. She was not cryptic, abandoning the ruse of the Faro Blanco Tournament. She apprised White, Jones, and Milton that they had an injured coworker at Shark Point and Nelson was at the scene with the suspects. I do not believe he will be engaging with them now. Nelson will let them escape for you to intercept. I believe it is time to alert local law enforcement to request assistance and a BOLO."

Sgt. Milton replied, "We'll set up a surveillance line to catch them and contact the Collier County Sheriff Department. White and Jones, let's get on the park frequency to coordinate. Good luck with your rescue of Cooper. Hope the young man is OK."

Fuentes then called Nelson to let him know the FWCC and refuge officers would be set to intercept the poacher's boat. There was no answer on the park radio so she tried on VHF 83. There was only silence.

Thompson had maneuvered his boat, with Nelson's boat tied alongside, to turn around at the head of one of the tidal creeks flowing from the Shark River. Nelson told Thompson, "The plan has changed. Cooper is injured off Shark Point. Now I don't have any back-up coming. We need to give them a clear path to escape. There are officers lying in wait to catch them at Lostman's River."

Thompson nodded as he increased his speed to pass by the poachers who were still busy securing their catch so they could make a run for it. The giant goliath groupers were difficult for them to handle. Seeing the houseboat passing by, one of the men was spooked.

Butch grabbed a semi-automatic assault rifle and fired. A hail of bullets strafed the aluminum storage shed on the aft end of the houseboat. Wood splintered and debris exploded from the penetrating slugs. The engine banged to a stop. It had been hit; the houseboat was dead in the water, no longer maneuverable, but still drifting toward the poachers.

Harley yelled "What the hell are you doing?"

Butch replied, "That old man called the cops. We need to get rid of him."

"Dammit, Butch. If we did get rid of him, we wouldn't do it with a gun. We'll take him offshore to sink his boat and let him drown." Harley pushed the gun down and Butch slung the strap over his shoulder. "Grab his boat and we'll tow him and his junk boat out. Get on board the houseboat and tie the old man up. Maybe we can get out of here before the cops get here."

The momentum from the now-dead motor pushed the houseboat toward the poacher's boat. When it was close enough,

Butch jumped on board and moved to overtake Thompson.

In the darkness, the blue light was still flashing, but not moving. The poachers could see the lights of another boat heading north. They doused all of the lights on their boat and the houseboat. Once the houseboat was tied to theirs, Harley started the engine and plotted a course to go well behind the boat they could see that was moving north.

Butch hollered, "Harley, there's a Park boat tied to the other side of this houseboat! It's empty."

Harley said, "Get the old guy. Shoot him if the cop doesn't come out. Cut the park boat loose."

Butch roughly manhandled the old man, held his assault rifle to his head and shouted, "If you don't want this old man to die, you will come out from wherever you're hiding!"

With that he lowered the rifle and shot the old man in his foot, through his white rubber boots. The bullet passed through and exited through the deck. Thompson collapsed and held his knee. Falling back against the side of the trailer, he knocked over a chair on the way down.

Harley, at the wheel, was trying to control the unwieldy raft-up of his boat with the houseboat.

Butch yelled again, "The next one is in his head!"

Nelson came out of the trailer, his hands up, holding his semi-automatic pistol, pointed up.

"Throw it down." With that instruction, Nelson tossed his gun overboard. There was no sense in giving this guy another weapon; his service pistol, in particular.

Butch left the old man crumpled in the corner of his screened porch, leaning against the trailer.

Nelson was secured, with his own handcuffs, to the bottom rail of the steering tower.

"I gotta piss!" Butch shouted to Harley. The response was, "Go off the back of the houseboat. I'll watch them." Butch walked through the storage shed and turned to unzip.

Before he could react, he heard "Chunk-clunk, BANG." The report amplified and echoed through the shed. Butch quickly turned around. Even in the darkness, Thompson and Nelson saw the astonished look on his face. "He shot me in the ass!" he screamed.

As he reached back to grab his backside, the rifle strap slipped from his shoulder. While trying to catch it, he lost his balance and fell into the black water.

Harley slowed to a stop. Because the heavy houseboat was tied to the fishing boat, it took a long time and some distance to come to a stop. Harley could hear Butch yelling for help but he couldn't see his partner. Butch was hanging on to an empty gas cylinder he had taken overboard with him. Harley put the boat into reverse. He turned on the deck light to see if he could tell where Butch was.

Harley shouted over to the houseboat, "That was dumb as shit, old man! I've got a gun too." Thompson helped Nelson wiggle into the cover of the trailer so he would be less exposed.

Thompson whispered, "Here's the shotgun."

It was a short-barreled 12-gauge with a pistol grip. Nelson hadn't seen one before, but he knew it was a barely legal Mossberg pump shotgun. It was a sawed-off shotgun, but the barrel length technically made it legal.

Thompson continued, "When I give you the signal, pump the shotgun to make a sound. I'm going to the side window."

Thompson crawled forward into his camper home.

Nelson saw Thompson moving things out of the way and lifting a seat top and extracting a wooden box. He carefully opened the box to remove a long-barreled revolver. He looked over at Nelson, then peered back through the window to see Harley at the helm of his boat trying to get back to Butch.

Harley would bump the boat in reverse, then bring it back to neutral and run to the transom to check Butch's location. Then he'd get back to the helm to adjust the heading. Without the unwieldy houseboat attached Harley would be expert at piloting his boat.

From inside the trailer, Thompson looked back and signaled Nelson, who was still hampered by the cuffs, to pump the action of the shotgun. "Chunk-clunk." The sound is as recognizable as a diamondback's rattle. Harley turned to look and "POP!" Dropping his revolver, Harley immediately grabbed his face, which was splattered with blood, and hurting like hell, like he'd been hit in the nose with a hammer.

Thompson quickly moved back to Nelson, then to the shed, returning with bolt cutters. He clipped the handcuffs that shackled the ranger. Nelson regained an upright posture, a little dazed by the turn of events. It had all happened so fast. But he didn't have time to ponder the experience. Nelson jumped over to the commercial boat and took it out of gear. Retrieving Harley's revolver, he went to the back of the boat where he saw that Thompson had climbed his steering platform and was spotlighting Butch floating in the water. The old man was spry!

Thompson yelled down, "Nelson, you better tell that fat moron to get out of the water or the bull sharks will smell the blood and eat his ass!"

When Butch heard this, he sprinted to the boat, leaving his gas cannister to drift away. There was no way Nelson was going to make it easy for him to get out of the water. He let the heavy suspect struggle to shimmy aboard. Tumbling flat on the deck, the big guy was laid out beside the biggest goliath grouper.

Thompson came back down the ladder and held the shotgun on the two buffoon criminals. Nelson told Butch to remove his hands from his face so he could see the damage. His nose was shot clear through. Blood was still oozing from his wound, but the steady stream that stained the front of his shirt had subsided. Nelson bound his hands with a zip tie and gave him a rag. "Keep pressure on it and sit down over here." Then Nelson strapped Harley's ankles.

Nelson told the heavy man, who was shot in the butt, to roll over. He used zip ties to bind his hands behind his back and tie his ankles. Now he was immobilized, laying in a tangle of wire and hooks in pools of slippery slime from the illegally-taken fish.

With the rustlers subdued, Nelson and Thompson could both breathe a little easier. Thompson was nonchalant. "How about some coffee?"

Nelson thought to himself, "How could he be so nonplussed after such a violent encounter with these two rednecks that were intent on killing us?" To Thompson, Nelson said, "Guess so. But let me call this in first."

Nelson got to the helm of the commercial boat, checked the position on the Garmin GPS, and picked up the VHF radio mike.

"Faro Blanco Fishing Team, Faro Blanco Fishing Team, Faro Blanco Fishing Team. This is Everglades National Park Ranger Bob Nelson, channel 8 – 3, please respond."

Fuentes was the first to answer, "Bob, we've been worried.

You have been out of communication for a couple hours. Did you hear our hails? Are you OK?"

Before Nelson could respond, the FWCC Sergeant radioed, "This is Milton. I'm positioned with White and Jones. Do you require assistance?"

Nelson said, "The two poachers are subdued and on their boat. Both are injured with non-life-threatening injuries. I am with Mr. Thompson on his houseboat, north of Shark River, about 2 miles southeast of Shark Point. I do not have my Park radio or boat.

"Sgt. Milton, we could use your help to transport these guys. And, I would like to get a park radio so the communication isn't so public. What is the status of Ranger Cooper?"

Fuentes responded. "We have him. He's got a broken arm and a bump on his head. I think he may have broken ribs, too. We were able to wade over to help float his boat off the bar at high tide. Smith and I think we should get him back to Flamingo ASAP, if you have your situation under control. Over."

Nelson said, "Please take Cooper. I'll be fine until the fish and wildlife folks gets here. When you are in radio contact range, please inform the Superintendent and NPS Regional LE Office of the situation. Oh, and we need to prepare a place to lock these guys up. And, they will require some medical assistance."

"Coffee's ready," Thompson announced, bringing a steaming mug to Nelson. "Let's sit at the table and rest a spell." He righted the chair he had knocked over when the fat guy put a bullet through his boot.

They sat at the small table in the screened area. "Think the bugs are getting to those guys you got tied up?"

"I'll keep an eye on them and make sure they don't hurt any of the mosquitoes. But they are probably too drunk to care."

Neither man had much sympathy for the guys who had just tried to kill them.

They just sat in silence, waiting and watching. Lights illuminated the deck of the commercial boat. The houseboat was dark. They both were pondering how lucky they were to have made it.

Thompson broke the silence. "You know, they shot up my boat. I can patch the bullet holes on the shed, but I'm worried about what they did to my new Suzuki. It was a lot of money. I don't know how I'll get back without it. Figure I'll have to get a new one if it can't be fixed."

Nelson asked, "Where would you want to be towed? Flamingo doesn't have any mechanics. You got your engine in Marco, but Marathon would be closer."

"I think Marathon. By the time word gets out that I helped the feds apprehend these two rednecks, I don't think I'd be welcome by some of the folks in Everglades City. There's still a lot of resentment over the drug busts in the 1990s and that was thirty years ago."

Help arrived more quickly than expected. Within a couple hours the two FWCC officers materialized out of the darkness. It was about midnight. Nelson tied their boats to the stern of the houseboat.

The Fish and Wildlife officers came aboard. Nelson introduced them to the houseboat hermit. "This is Mr. Thompson. He saved my life from those two who are over on the other boat. I couldn't have done this without him."

The officers recognized the old man, but had never engaged with him out on the water. They always figured he was a problem for the park or the refuge to handle, not their problem. They had pretty much ignored him and his unusual boat.

Nelson conferred with the FWCC officers to discuss how and where to take the men. Bringing them to their feet, the FWCC officers held the poachers upright. Nelson repeated the statement that they were under arrest for unlawful taking, violation of park rules on possession and discharge of a firearm, and operating a motor vessel while under the influence. Other charges would be pending.

"You have the right to remain silent. You have the right to an attorney. If you cannot afford an attorney, one will be appointed for you. Anything you say can be used as evidence against you in a court of law. Do you understand these rights?" With the FWCC officers being present, Nelson had witnesses to the arrest and Miranda statement. The officers fit Harley and Butch with personal flotation devices, administered a breathalyzer test and secured them with handcuffs in place of the zip ties.

Nelson and the FWCC officers decided the two poachers should go to Flamingo. Then an Assistant U.S. Attorney and the Florida State's Attorney office could sort out where they should be booked, in Miami-Dade County or Monroe County where the violations had occurred. The men were loaded into the FWCC boats. Refuge Officer White arrived in time for him to join the flotilla procession around Cape Sable, back to Flamingo.

As the three boats motored off, Nelson would wait with Thompson to safeguard the scene and wait for crime scene investigators to arrive. Then the poachers' boat could be towed and impounded. It would be easier to clear the scene in the light of day. Nelson had a lot of questions and a whole night to learn the answers.

THIRTEEN

The running lights on the boats transporting the men who had been taken into custody disappeared on the horizon. Thompson and Nelson settled back at the table in the screened enclosure.

Nelson expressed his heart-felt thanks. "Thompson, I know you saved my life. What you did was astounding. I can't thank you enough. You kept your wits and stopped those two guys from killing both of us. Hell, I don't know how you did it. I could hug you!"

"Don't get all sappy on me. I just did what I had to do."

Nelson protested, "Take the compliment. Without you, I'd be dead and those idiots would be on their way back to Everglades City instead of on the road to jail."

Thompson demurred, "Would you like a shot of that good bourbon you brought me? Or maybe a little rum. I think we should toast our good luck."

Nelson said, "Sure, I'm off the clock now. I'm just waiting for the crime scene folks and the tow boat to get here. I think we should."

"Damn, there are more cops coming?" Thompson was aware there would be more to this incident, but he didn't have to like it. His desire was to just get on with repairing his outboard and putting this night behind him. He opened the bourbon, poured a generous amount in two glasses, and passed one to Nelson saying, "To life well lived."

Nelson raised his glass and said, "To you!"

After the first round of bourbon, the second round was rum, neat. Thompson made another generous pour. Nelson said, "Easy man, I need to stay sober.

"I've got a lot of questions about how you pulled off subduing the poachers. Where did you get the shotgun? How did that shot in the foot miss? You looked like your leg was hurting when he shot your boot."

Thompson was a little more relaxed, from either the rum or the fatigue that follows the high of emotional trauma. For whatever reason, he was more open and talkative than ever before. In fact, he had not even mentioned his usual prohibition of Nelson boarding his boat without a warrant.

"Well, Nelson, I'll show you why it didn't bother me when he shot my foot." Thompson rolled up his pantleg and removed his rubber white boot. The bottom of his leg was a prosthetic, with a hole in the foot. "It hurt when the shockwave hit my knee joint. But it was temporary and not nearly as painful as my arthritis."

Nelson was shocked. He had never noticed any gimp in Thompson's gait, but then he'd never seen him walk anywhere, only standing on his boat. Obviously, Thompson was well acclimated to his artificial leg.

"As for the shotgun, it's got a holster under the table. I bought that when I moved onto my houseboat. It made more sense than some high-caliber weapon. A big high-caliber gun could put a hole in the boat if I missed my target. The shotgun is pretty forgiving on the aim and the recognizable sound is pretty intimidating. I only keep light birdshot loads. I promised myself a long time ago, I wouldn't be killing any more.

"I figured the fat guy could survive a shot in the butt. He has plenty of cushioning."

Nelson took note and was even more curious. What did Thompson mean by 'any more'? He asked, "But what about shooting the nose off the other guy?"

"Well," he paused, getting into his reply with a drawn-out "well." Back a long time ago, I was pretty good at pistol target shooting. I got the target pistol I keep in the box as a prize in a marksmanship competition. I keep in practice helping you parkies get rid of exotics like iguanas and pythons. Don't want to brag, but I'm a pretty fair shot at up to 10 yards. Suppose you'll give me a citation for that!"

"You hit the guy in the nose. What if you had missed?"

"Well, I suppose I would have tried again, unless the shot hit him through the ear. Then I guess I wouldn't need a second shot." Thompson grinned, showing his confidence that he wouldn't have missed his target. "He had a big nose."

Nelson said, "There must be a lot more to your story. Can you tell me how you got so well trained?"

Thompson snapped, "No! I can't talk about my past. It's dark and secret." When he saw how much Nelson wanted to know, and feeling the effects of the drinks, he relented and started his story.

"Well..." Again, he began with a drawn out "well" as he exhaled a sigh. "I can tell you that when I was young and gullible, I was recruited to be involved in some very bad things by our government; the same one you work for. One off-book operation went very badly. I lost my leg and was pretty messed up. I was the only survivor of my team. When I recovered, I had a special private meeting with the highest politician who thanked me for my service and gave me a medal."

"Wow, that's amazing!"

"Well… it wasn't long before I saw that same politician shaking hands with the person my team and I were sent to target. That op cost seven dead men and one leg and there he was, smiling on TV, shaking hands with someone so vile that the U.S. had decided the world was better off without him. Turned me sour for years."

Nelson was without words.

"After a lot of medical rehab, I was placed in a federal job, with no qualifications or education for the job I was assigned and nothing to do. I flew that desk for a 20-year career. I was contacted regularly by my handler to be sure I was keeping the secret. They changed my name and removed me from all contact with friends and family. It was hell. I finally found peace reading the Bible and wandering in nature." Then he smiled as he concluded with, "Until the Park police kept hassling me to move my houseboat."

Nelson was astounded, but it explained how the old guy was so capable and crafty.

"Of course, now you know more than anyone besides me and the new wet-behind-the-ears intelligence officer that still checks up on me. That is, if he can find me. I hope you will keep tight lipped on this."

Nelson knew he would, out of respect for Thompson, and knowing Thompson had the skills to take him out if he ever spilled the beans. "Trust me, Thompson. Your story is safe with me. I am forever indebted for what you did tonight."

Their conversation lingered on, mostly small talk, for a couple hours more until they fell asleep in their chairs. Nelson had his head on his folded arms, resting on the table, when he was awakened just after daybreak by the sound of outboard motors. Several boats with the Monroe County Sheriff and the U.S. Coast Guard transporting FBI agents and a crime scene investigation unit were approaching. They brought donuts.

One of the Coasties introduced himself, "I'm Lieutenant Shaffer. I was in on the rescue of the crazy guy wandering naked on Cape Sable." He sniped at Nelson, "Looks like you're making a habit of this! But we're here to help. As you know, the USCG's motto is *"Semper Paratus* - Always ready."

Nelson was impressed with how fast a team had been put together and then made it to their remote location. He knew that the FBI and CSI units would have had to come all the way from Miami. Assaulting federal law enforcement officers required FBI investigation. Monroe County would handle the state violations and leave the poaching crimes to the Fish and Wildlife Conservation Commission. It was a beehive of activity. A little later Fuentes and Smith returned to the scene with FWCC investigators.

For the next hours, investigators were busy fingerprinting surfaces and taking photographs of everything. They gave Thompson a warrant to search his boat because it was a crime scene. He scowled at the paper.

"So that's a fine reward for helping," Thompson commented.

Nelson was horrified that his friend would be a victim instead of a bonafide hero. Nelson pulled the lead FBI agent aside and asked him to lighten up on the old guy. He explained, "He was key to nobody getting killed, including me!"

The FBI bagged and tagged the Mossberg shotgun and the prized vintage Model 41 Smith and Wesson target pistol. The 22-revolver the poachers used to dispatch the goliath grouper was put into another evidence bag. One boat was dragging the area for the semi-automatic assault rifle, but there was no chance it would ever be found. Thompson was livid his guns were taken, with no assurances that he would get them back. Nelson knew he would have mounds of paperwork to do to explain what happened to his service pistol.

While the FBI and crime scene technicians were investigating the scene, Nelson remembered the second trotline up near the Harney River. He felt a pang of sadness as he thought about the fish on the line, realizing they were probably dead, for no good reason. He suggested to the FWCC people who were looking for his Park boat that they should check and retrieve the other line.

The Coast Guardsmen called for a tow for Thompson's houseboat. The Sheriff deputy would tow and impound the commercial boat.

Nelson decided to go to Marathon with Thompson to help him get settled into a boatyard or even a hotel if he couldn't stay on his houseboat in the boatyard. On the long tow to Marathon, they both straightened up the boat, after the mess left from the crime scene inspectors and the gun shots. Thompson resented the intrusion, but appreciated the help.

Nelson phoned to Ranger Smith when he got to Marathon. "Can you pick me up at the Marathon Boat Yard? I'm here with Thompson. I think he's settled as much as he can be under the circumstances."

Smith said, "This is like déjà vu. Maybe we should open a field office in Marathon for you."

Nelson wasn't in the mood to joke. Thompson was in a situation he didn't deserve, upset that his guns were taken, and facing unknown costs for his engine repair. "Please come get me. Let me know when I can expect you. Oh, and how is Cooper?"

"Cooper is going to be fine. He's in a hospital in Homestead. His ribs are only bruised, no concussion and he has a cast on his arm. He's banged up and will be out of commission for a while."

"Glad to hear he'll be fine. I'll be waiting here for somebody to take me back to Flamingo." Nelson didn't relish the thought of writing incident reports and enduring more debriefing on this operation. He just wanted a shower and his own bed.

Finally, his ride arrived. He had to firmly ask his driver not to get into a discussion about the operation. Before leaving, he asked Thompson to please keep him apprised of the repairs. It was a quiet and awkward trip back.

After taking the rest of the day off, when Nelson returned to work the next day he was still tired. His first call was to the boatyard to check on Thompson. The manager told him the engine was toast. It could be rebuilt but would cost more than a new motor. Nelson asked to speak to Thompson.

The service manager said, "I'll have to fetch him. He's out in the yard. Can he call you back?"

"Sure, this number will go straight to my phone, not through a bevy of options. Bye."

For the rest of the day, he was doing reports and on conference calls with the Park Service Regional Office. How many times would he have to go over this? His fellow rangers were also besieged with questions. The Park Service attorney set up appointments for affidavits.

Life went on at the Park with no respite from the extraordinary experience they had all just faced. There were campgrounds to patrol, boat ramps to monitor, visitor questions to answer, interpretive programs to deliver. Fuentes, Smith, and Cooper had a lot to catch up on about their experience, not to mention Nelson needed to confer with the other agencies' officers involved in the operation.

Checking with the boatyard daily, he was never able to speak directly with Thompson, only getting reports from the service manager. A new motor was on order and would be installed the following week. Nelson decided he'd pay for a new outboard himself, if there wasn't another way to cover the cost for Thompson. Surely, there must be some kind of victim compensation fund. Since his phone calls weren't being returned, he decided he needed to go down to Marathon and catch Thompson in person. It would be a few days before he could take off from work to drive to Marathon.

When his boat was finished, Thompson was surprised to see a new Suzuki 50 was hanging on the stern. "Just like my old one. Now I need to settle up with you," Thompson told the service manager.

"No sir. Your bill is paid in full, by someone who wants to be anonymous."

Thompson didn't argue because the deed was done. He appreciated that he wouldn't have to do a complicated transfer of funds with the bank in Marco, but he was self-respecting enough to resent someone else paying his way.

"OK, I'll find out who paid for this fine new motor and pay them back. Thanks for getting the motor put on."

Nelson arrived at the boatyard only to learn that Thompson had just left. He raced down to the end of the Boot Key channel, only to see the houseboat motoring out toward the Seven Mile Bridge. Talking to himself, "Damn, I drove down here for nothing. That old man will be heading back to the Park or maybe up to Ten Thousand Islands National Wildlife Refuge."

Nelson wanted to catch up with Thompson to help with anything he could as well as to update him on the case against the two poachers. He also wanted to caution Thompson to be careful since the poachers might have friends who could have it out for him.

But since he was there in Marathon he thought he might as well have lunch before driving the couple hours back to Flamingo. Ironically, he ordered a grouper sandwich and looked out on the bay. He wondered if his grouper was legal or even authentically grouper. It could be farm-raised Asian pangas. Who would know what the filet really was underneath the fried crust.

On the drive home, Nelson was fixated on how Thompson must feel after all he'd been through and the way he'd been treated by the FBI agents. Nelson felt certain it would all be straightened out and Thompson would get due recognition, along with his guns. It would just be a matter of time.

He said, out loud, to himself, "What a waste of a day off and a long drive for lunch."

There had been a brief report on the national news media about the poachers and a shoot-out in the Everglades. The news story was probably a result of the operation having to use the unsecured VHF channel for communication and being overheard. The news report even mentioned that an old man living on his houseboat lost his outboard motor. It didn't draw much attention; it was just a newsy, human-interest-story media filler. On CNN, there was an AP photo taken in the boatyard of Thompson's shot-up houseboat, but not much else.

The following morning, Ranger Alondra Fuentes came into Nelson's office.

"Hey, Bob. You got a minute?" Nervously, she began to explain. "Ahhh. Umm. I am still not quite over the way the stake out turned out. I need to talk about it. I'm so mixed up about what happened. It's so far out of my experience. It was scary and dangerous. I'm not sure I'm cut out for this."

Nelson consoled her. "Believe you me, that was way outside of everybody else's experience, too. It was kind of like the war stories we heard at FLETC. Trust me, I'm still bothered that we could have been killed over illegal fishing. I know Cooper is hurt and shaken up, and even Smith, who's been a ranger a long time, never had something like this happen in his career.

"You know, this was a traumatic event. And all the follow-up questions and FBI investigation only adds to the stress. We'll all be looking over our shoulders for a while."

Fuentes responded, "Glad I'm not the only one a little confused about what happened. It was scary!"

"It's the same for all of us, but it worked out. It will just take time. Hopefully we can get back to normal soon. You know, get back to walking in the woods and picking up little birds to place back in their nests." Nelson smiled, kidding her about the public perception of a ranger's job with the National Park Service.

Fuentes was second guessing her career choice. "When I was a kid, that's what I thought working in national parks was – helping nature out. After a few years into this, I'm realizing that every problem that exists in an urban environment can happen out here in nature. When I signed on with the NPS, I wanted to work in an environmental job, not so much in extreme law enforcement. I'm not sure this is right for me."

Nelson sympathized, "You know, before I transferred here to Everglades I was at Fort Jefferson. It was an idyllic paradise - the tropical waters, the historic fort, and people who were thrilled at the juxtaposition of a huge brick fort in the middle of a coral reef. But, for all the rewards, there was a price."

Ranger Fuentes looked puzzled.

Nelson continued, "I got burned out. Almost every day, and even into the night, I was called to help handle Cuban refugees that arrived in the Dry Tortugas. The Cubans pieced together homemade craft or stole fishing boats to make the 90-plus mile crossing of the Florida Straits. They came in quest of freedom and a better future. Some paid enormous sums to traffickers to bring them to the U.S. Sometimes the traffickers left their human cargo on nearby Loggerhead Key as castaways. While many survived their escape, crossing the open water between Cuba and Florida, unknown numbers did not. A few washed ashore wearing life vests or were found dead or dying in their derelict boats.

"It became overwhelming. None of it was what I ever imagined I would be doing as a ranger. The immigration situation caused me very mixed emotions. I had sympathy for the people so desperate to escape life under a communist government and tacit admiration for their courage to risk the perilous sea passage. But I couldn't handle the number of uninvited arrivals. I resented that the park operations were being disrupted by the constant patrols and internment of detainees at the fort. Although Fort Jefferson had been used as a prison in the 1800s, it seemed an insult to use a historic relic for a contemporary jail, even if only temporarily."

Her uncertainty about her career resonated with Nelson, though he had not ever discussed his own career crisis before.

He continued, "Dealing with the waves of human immigrants at Dry Tortugas is what brought me to the Everglades. I hoped I could get back to the job I wanted. But, shoot outs with poachers isn't part of it."

Alondra said, "Wow. I didn't know that. It must have been really hard to deal with."

"I can empathize, Alondra. It's a dilemma that each of us has to face. For me, I try to focus on the moments when I'm most connected with nature and find reward when the visitors are engaged. We get to experience places so few will see." He paused. "Does this help?"

She nodded yes. "I really liked helping those old guys get out to Bear Lake and it was wonderful for me to paddle the canal. Thanks for taking the time to talk with me."

Nelson was moved by Fuentes's questioning. It helped him clarify some of his own feelings. But, he didn't have the time to reflect much. Smith came to his office door and interrupted.

"Nelson, we just had a call from a researcher from a university marine lab that the FWCC referred to us. He wants to know the location of the goliath groupers that were taken. Can I give him the lat-lon numbers or is that privileged?"

"What's his interest?"

"He tracks the data on goliath grouper and has been researching them for years all over the state and even down in Brazil. He says he wants to see if he can match the location to his records."

"Wow, censusing individual fish! I suppose there's no harm in giving him the location, but don't give any details about the case. Hey, just a thought – how about we take a day off and go fishing?"

Smith replied, "Just what we need. Let's look at the tide and the weather. How about Sandy Key?"

"Yep, just what I was thinking. I want to fish that channel."

When the designated fishing day arrived the Flamingo marina concessionaire was happy to give the two rangers a rental boat for the day. The rangers got ice, snacks, bait and gas and were off for the ten-mile trip out to Sandy Key. The day was beautiful, with bright sunshine and a cool breeze.

Arriving just past the peak high tide, they beached the boat to offload their ice chest and beach chairs. Then they pushed the boat off to set an anchor in deeper water. Neither wanted to be left high and dry when the tide went out.

The water started running out of the vast tidal flats, slowly at first and then turning into a torrent, with mini-rapids rippling on the surface. They set their fishing lines with bottom weights and a rig that kept their bait off the bottom. Leaving their rods in holders placed in the sand, they waded to the edge of the water and cast top lures. Nelson would cast out to the far side of the channel and retrieve his lure with jerking action, across the stream. Smith's technique was a little different. He'd cast up into the middle of the current and then reel in against the flow.

They had some excitement hooking rays and lemon sharks. Each put up a good fight, momentarily buoying their hopes that they had a big redfish on the line, only to be disappointed with a fish they didn't want. After a few hours it was dead low tide and the channel was at its lowest level.

Nelson looked to the east over the exposed grass beds stretching as far as the eye could see. There were birds everywhere:

shorebirds on the muddy flats, wading birds searching the seagrass for food, and a few osprey hovering over the remaining pools of water hunting for the trapped schools of mullet and sea trout. High overhead, a bald eagle soared. A shimmer of heat waves animated the distant vista. Far off, mangrove keys seemed to float over the horizon like mirages. Both rangers, being birders as well as fishermen, took a break at low tide to watch the birds.

Smith asked, "So how many species you got?"

Nelson said, "34, how about you?"

Smith said, "29."

Birders often fall into a sublime competition on the number of species they can see, kind of like the competition of anglers, claiming bragging rights for superlatives; first fish, biggest fish, most fish. Each birder likes to share sightings, both to help others, but also to exhibit their proficiency.

"I'll catch up with you! What's the most special bird you've seen today?"

Nelson replied, "A Wurdemann's heron, when I walked to the other side of the Key."

"Hey, I'd like to see him. Think he's still there?"

"Don't know. Let's go see. There were a huge number of spoonbills congregating over there too."

The Rangers trudged through the soft sand, then up and over the vegetated part of the island. The past couple of hurricanes had reshaped Sandy Key and Carl Ross Key, diminishing their acreage by more than half their former size. Nature was striving to reclaim the islands. The old designated campsite on Carl Ross and Sandy Key was closed to all entry during nesting season.

Approaching the opposite shore, there it was, standing tall at the water's edge. The two-toned Wurdemann's heron was about

4 feet tall from feet to bill. Birding circles were debating if this was really a separate species or a color morph of the great white heron, the pride of Florida Bay. The range of this largest of the American wading birds is mostly restricted to Florida Bay and the Keys. "Listers" seek them out as Florida specialties to add to their life lists.

"Cool, I always like seeing them and I'm calling them a separate species until the ornithologists settle their debate. Hey, that's a big group of roseate spoonbills. Nice to see them doing well."

"Okay, let's get back to fishing. The tide's turned by now and we can try our luck with what might be returning to the flats."

On the walk back, they saw a red-bellied woodpecker and a couple of redstarts. Smith grumbled, "You just want to quit birding so I don't catch up with your tally."

Nelson chuckled. "Tops in birding, tops in fishin'. What can I say?"

They fished the returning tide and caught a few trout, but none of them were within the legal slot size limit. Still, it was a good day. Each caught a keeper redfish, a few sea trout, and a decent sized pompano. Wading back to their rental boat, they were happy to have a day away from the recent tumult of successive extraordinary incidents. It was a great distraction, but only a temporary respite.

Even off-duty, they were Rangers. On the way back to Flamingo, they came on a boater tied to a navigation aid. He stood in his boat, waving his arms back and forth and yelling, "I'm out of gas! Can you guys tow me in?"

Smith said to Nelson, before they were within earshot of the stranded boater, "What do you say? Should we leave him here and call Sea Tow? He would have to pay a few hundred bucks for going further than his fuel supply. Oh, hell, I know what'll happen. We'll tow him in and reject the twenty bucks he thinks will settle things up."

Nelson approached the boater, "Do you have a line we can use to tow you?"

Of course he didn't, so the rangers rigged their anchor rode to make a bridle. Now, having to go slow, they wouldn't be back until after sunset, which was not a nice thank you to the marina that had loaned them a boat for the day.

On the way in, Nelson lamented, "Yep, the Coasties' motto is 'Always Ready.' The Park Ranger motto should be 'Always On.'"

FOURTEEN

It had been a week or so since Thompson left Marathon. Nelson guessed he'd be back somewhere along the coast at one of his usual anchorages. He decided that today would be a good day to patrol from Shark River up to the northern boundary with the Refuge to locate the houseboat and check up on Thompson.

Thompson was anchored at Duck Rock, off Pavilion Key and the adjacent unnamed islands. He heard Nelson coming and waited on deck. When Nelson pulled up alongside, he greeted Thompson with a smile, "Long time, no see! Can I come aboard?"

"Not without a warrant." After a long pause, he said, "Well... I reckon it's OK, if this is a just a social call." Try as he might, in spite of his gruff disposition, the old man wasn't able to disguise his pleasure at seeing Nelson.

It seemed like things were back to normal. At least as normal as things could be after their joint encounter with being assaulted and nearly killed. Their shared experience had forged a bond between them. After the night they spent sipping rum while waiting for help, Nelson now knew more about Thompson's amazing backstory than anyone else.

Thompson put the coffee on. The men sat at the table waiting on the percolator to brew.

"Nelson, the coffee will be ready directly. What's on your mind?"

"I just wanted to catch up with you. Thought you might be interested in getting an update. A lot has happened since I left you in Marathon. I see a new motor hanging on the stern."

"Yep, I'm sure happy to have one back. This one even has a power tilt lift, so I don't have to scrape barnacles off the lower unit and prop. How much did you pay for this motor? I want to pay you back. I don't like bein' beholdin' to anyone. I can pay my own way."

Nelson was puzzled by the question. He answered, "I didn't pay for the motor. Who told you I paid for it?"

Thompson answered, "The yard manager told me my bill was paid by someone who wants to remain anonymous. I'll find out who it was – even if it was you." He didn't want to argue so he held up his hand to stop the conversation when Nelson began to insist it wasn't him. Changing the subject, he asked, "What is the story on those two deplorables?"

Nelson thought that was an interesting term, not really knowing Thompson's political persuasion. He answered, "The two men were from Everglades City; ne'er-do-wells who weren't too successful at commercial fishing. The boat they were on belonged to another man who claims to not know what they were up to."

"They are sitting in jail in Key West, without bond. A slew of state and federal charges has been filed against them. The guy steering the boat, the one with the handgun, was on probation for a felony, but I don't know what it was."

Thompson interjected, "Probably being really ugly and smelling bad."

Nelson laughed, continuing, "The FBI investigated the assault on us. I think they are ready to release your guns. I've been pestering them about that. The Monroe County Assistant DA has cleared you for shooting the guys, as justifiable self-defense. The state wildlife folks and federal attorney are still trying to sort out the poaching and goliath grouper charges."

"Well," Thompson said, with his characteristic long pause, "I hope they throw the book at them. They shot up my boat and killed my motor. But, I guess there's no law against taking a month of living away from an old man."

Nelson agreed. "There's always civil court to settle that score, but judging the depravity of the perps, they probably don't have a pot to piss in."

"You might also like to know about the kids you rescued out on Pavilion," pointing over to the island campsite, "They were in contact with our office after they saw a report on CNN about our episode with the poachers. They recognized your houseboat from a picture on the TV news. They wanted to know if you were OK."

"That couple and her friends had a lot to deal with. What a mistake their prank turned out to be. It wound up being a real test of friendship," remarked Thompson.

"Yeah, let me tell you about another crazy rescue just after that. A New York City fellow was on the run from trouble over a fake investment scam he invented. Apparently, he decided to hide out by camping on Cape Sable. He had no idea what he was doing and got tied up with manchineel. He almost died. He went crazy, seeing the ghost of Guy Bradley. Talk about troubles, he and his wife have a difficult road back, not counting his legal problems.

"Come to think about it, it's all been crazy these last few months. Nothing like what I want to deal with. The Ranger job is getting more like being either a cop or an EMT. Both are noble and necessary, but not what I signed up for. I transferred here from Dry Tortugas because I was burned out from dealing with immigrants crossing from Cuba in tiny overloaded boats, not to mention the search, rescue, and recovery calls all hours of the day and night."

Thompson mused, "You can be out here in the wilderness but society catches up with you. Even when I'm out here seeking peace and quiet, minding my own business, troubles find me. You can run, but you can't hide."

They sat for a bit longer, watching the pelicans crash dive into the water, scooping up a meal of fish. Sailboats cruised by offshore and a couple guide boats with fly fishermen were casting the edge of the mangroves for tarpon or snook. Time passed and it was pleasant even if they were not deep in conversation.

Thompson asked, "Isn't it time for you to head back?" A polite way of inviting Nelson to leave him alone.

"Yep, thanks for the coffee. I'll be back if I find out anything else. You gonna be here for a while?"

"Well, ain't quite decided where to go. Think I might head up to Everglades City and hitch a ride into Marco to do some banking. I'm up on provisions with what I got in Marathon."

"OK, I'll keep an eye out for you. 'Til next time." Nelson was off, through the backwater route to Flamingo.

Hanging up his hat for the day, Nelson retreated to his apartment in the government housing located in the service area at Flamingo. It was a simple accommodation, a one-bedroom studio apartment, sparsely furnished. Nelson had yet to make the place his own. Most of his personal belongings were still in a storage facility in Homestead. Luckily, he hadn't moved his belongings to Key West when he got the job at Ft. Jefferson. The hurricane last year would have put all his stuff under water.

Nelson sat at his kitchen counter and looked around his domain. It was depressingly austere, with nothing on the walls, only empty picture hangers. Had he really been at Everglades eight months? He had been so wrapped up in the job, learning the landscape, and living day to day that he hadn't even given any thought to making himself at home.

He turned on his iPod and Bluetoothed his music to a portable speaker. Hitting shuffle, what came on first was a song by a Florida State Park Ranger, *Memory of Florida Bay*. The tempo and the lyrics hit him just right.

> *"Who would ever have thought the Bay would be thirsty...to drink from the river of grass."*

He started thinking, "Yes, the memories of Florida Bay are what I'm seeking, not what I've been involved in for the last year. The Everglades is still special, even if there are so many perils facing the survival of the ecosystem. How wild it must have been when the park was established, or long ago when the Calusa and Tequesta people were the only inhabitants!"

Nelson didn't have long to enjoy the shot of bourbon he just poured. His cell phone rang, "Hey boss. Sorry to bother you, but I think we need you over at the visitor center."

"What's up?"

"There's a very agitated couple here. Apparently their dog is missing and they are getting hysterical."

Nelson pulled on his uniform shirt and grabbed his Ranger hat from its specially-designed rack that kept the brim of his campaign hat flat. He jumped in his personal vehicle and raced over to the central visitor complex.

Entering the building he could hear screaming echoing through the hall. "What the hell are you doing standing here when you could be out there looking for our dog?" A woman's voice shrieked, "You don't seem to understand! Mr. Bojangles is a national champion show dog worth thousands of dollars. He could be lost or even kidnapped."

Entering the lobby, Ranger Nelson smiled to introduce himself, "I'm the supervisory ranger here. Can you tell me about your missing dog. We all want to help get him back for you."

The couple calmed down a little, but through their hyperventilating, they explained, "Our Afghan hound is a champion show dog, only two years old. He's our child. He's got a royal lineage. We have a dog show in Homestead in two days. He can't be upset or scarred up for the show."

"Where did you have him last?"

"We were walking around the marina and let him off the leash for just a minute. He ran off toward the other side of the building. He was chasing a squirrel. Why can't you keep the squirrels under control so they don't pester dogs?"

Nelson recognized their concern for their dog was overwhelming any common sense.

"Okay, Smith and Fuentes, can you go over to the boat ramp and help look. Call the marina too and ask them to keep an eye out."

He turned to the couple, "If you go over there to help, there will be more eyes looking."

The two distraught dog parents were about to leave when the marina manager hailed on the park radio. "Nelson, this is the marina. I think I see the dog. Gator got him. He's on a log across the canal. It's a big one."

The couple howled with heartbreak. They were inconsolable. Then they returned to berating the rangers and the park for having such a dangerous place for dogs. "We are going to sue you for all you got." The man pounded the desk, "What's your name?" It even seemed like he was ready to be violent, shaking in anger.

It had been a long day for Nelson. It took all of his self-control not to argue with the couple or tell them they were being unreasonable and irrational. He thought to himself, "Blame us when you let your dog get away, despite the posting 'All Dogs Must be Leashed.'"

Nelson put on his law enforcement persona, "Sir, you must calm down or face consequences of failure to cooperate with law enforcement officers. I am sorry about your dog. We can help you recover his body."

The couple stepped back, fuming at the park, in deep despair that their cherished pet was killed by an alligator. As the couple was leaving the building, the woman said, "You haven't heard the last of this. I am best friends with the sister of the owner of the landscape company that takes care of U.S. Senator Scott's secretary's lawn."

Nelson politely said, "Thank you" as he thought to himself "Now that will make a federal employee tremble!"

Tongues were wagging for an hour after the dog episode. They all regretted that the dog had died. Alligators are a fact of life in the park, hence Rangers actively warn people with dogs to keep them on a leash and away from the water. Fishermen cleaning fish and throwing carcasses to birds is a mistaken kindness because feeding contributes to drawing the gators to the marina. Even with a posted threat of fines for not properly disposing of cleaning waste many don't follow the rules.

Fuentes said, "It's so sad that they lost their dog, but that's no excuse for their behavior. I can understand how they wouldn't be gator-aware, but if that dog was so special, why were they letting him run free?"

Smith complained, "Reminding visitors about the simple rules isn't my favorite thing to do. Most resent it and I'm not sure that they don't just go back to doing the same thing as soon as I leave."

Nelson wanted to put an end to the grousing, "I know how you two feel. We've all been there. We just need to not take it personally. It's simply part of the job. Let's be thankful they're gone. All we can do is wait to see if we get a complaint letter from Senator Scott's office."

Nelson returned to his apartment, just wanting to relax. He chugged the shot of bourbon he had left and poured another. Leaning back on his GSA-supplied couch, he put his feet up on the coffee table and hit play again on his iPod. The song he started before being interrupted resumed,

"Does anyone remember Florida Bay like it used to be? Showers of shrimp in the wake of the bow and an egret in every tree."

His thoughts turned to egrets in the mangroves, ospreys soaring, shrimp, and the astonishing sunsets. These were all things he really loved about the park, not the demise of show dogs, avoidable injuries, gun fights with poachers, poisoned psychotics, desperate refugees, and all of the similar extraordinary situations. He recalled Thompson's advice from earlier in the day, "You can be out here in the wilderness but society catches up with you." Nelson exhaled, sipped his drink, closed his eyes and promised himself tomorrow would be a new day.

FIFTEEN

First thing in the morning, the phone was ringing. The NYPD detective was on the line asking for copies of any reports that Nelson had filed regarding Ronald Bradford. He immediately referred the detective to the legal section in the Park Service's Regional Office in Atlanta. He said he would be happy to help, but release of reports was above his level of authority.

Curious, Nelson asked, "So where is Bradford now? I left him in the hospital in the Florida Keys and haven't had any information since."

"Psychiatric ward here in New York. Charges are pending, but the prosecutor doesn't want to proceed until she has a better idea of his mental state. Physically, he looks like he's getting over a bad burn. Was he in a fire?"

Nelson told the detective about the manchineel tree. "Bradford seems to have been a lucky victim of poison. While I can't release our reports, I guess I can tell you that his wife authorized us to make arrangements to tow his Mercedes that was parked in our lot. It was taken to an impound lot in Homestead, but I'm not sure if it's still there."

The detective thanked Nelson. "I don't know where this case is going. But I want to get all the facts for the Assistant DA."

The NYPD had just hung up when the phone rang again. This time, it was an FWCC investigator. "Ranger Nelson, I'm with the state, looking into the case against two men, Brian "Butch" Bouchier and Harley Davis Ryder. Yeah, I know, the name is real and I'm thinking his parents must have been bikers. Well, anyway, these two are presently in the Monroe County jail. I'm working on the case to provide background on their poaching activity. This is separate from the federal offenses."

Nelson asked, "Can I call you back? I want to confer with the Park Service's senior LE officer regarding our reports."

Nelson decided to drive up to the headquarters near Homestead to have a conference call with the FWCC investigator. He and the park service officer relayed everything they had on the case and forwarded photos electronically. "More information might be available from the FBI and crime scene team. The park has deferred to the FBI and federal prosecutor's office."

The FWCC investigator said, "You might be interested in what we found. The two poachers had previously been chartered by a university professor to transport researchers to several locations along the Southwest Florida coast. The scientists surveyed various sites for goliath grouper. When they found one, they marked the GPS location, made measurements and then tagged and released the fish.

"The print out of a marine chart with GPS numbers that was found on the boat corresponds to the sites where the researchers found goliaths. We confirmed the data with the lead scientist, who is the foremost expert on the biology and ecology of groupers, especially goliath. He did not suspect the charter boat guys were tracking the locations, but obviously they banked the numbers so they could return. One of the fish found on the poacher's boats had been tagged by the marine lab."

Nelson replied, "And they poached the bait for their lines at the park boundary."

"Yes, we've got that on the list of state offenses as well. It's quite a list of violations! A real bonus is the clues we got on where they were selling illegal fish. A number of restaurants have been implicated. DNA tests are pending on samples taken at the suspected restaurants. Maybe one of the defendants will cooperate for leniency and then the people buying the fish can be charged as well."

"Thanks for this update. We were curious about the back story on the poachers. Good work on finding out why they were at those specific locations."

The Senior Law Enforcement Ranger was pleased to hear the report from the FWCC, but upset that all the efforts of the Park and the scientists aimed at protecting the species had been compromised. "You know Bob, we do what we can to protect the Park and conservation policy is based on science. When the science is stolen to enable this kind of exploitation, it's damn aggravating!

"You know what's more disgusting is the politicians working against conservation to pander to special interests. It's an insidious assault every time the legislature meets in Tallahassee. We can't protect the Park from the politicians."

Nelson replied, "I don't think anyone could have guessed that the charter boat crew would betray the trust of the university researchers. To avoid the potential problem, it seems like we should support research directly, with our own boats and people.

Thanks for sitting in on the call. I didn't want to go outside Park Service protocol."

Nelson had more good news from a phone call he received while driving back to Flamingo. The FBI cleared the return of Thompson's guns. Someone in the Miami field office would work out logistics to get the firearms back to the Park so they could be given back to Thompson.

Nelson was already thinking he wanted to check on where Thompson might be. Now he had an excuse, figuring he could deliver the guns the next time he and Thompson rendezvoused. The rangers patrolling the west coast had promised to keep him apprised of the houseboat's position.

SIXTEEN

Thompson pulled anchor, bound for Everglades City. He had enough provisions, but there was banking to do and his post office box to check. Everglades City was only 25 miles away, but he decided not to push it and take two days to get there, stopping at Rabbit Key along the way. From there it is only a few miles through a narrow channel to get to Everglades City. Because his houseboat is hard to control, he preferred to dock at slack tide when the river current is the only factor that complicates steering.

Arriving at the Rod and Gun Club, a new worker was at the dock to help him tie up *Épave*. Thompson hoped he could stay a week, giving him enough time to patch the bullet holes in the shed, buy paint, and do his banking business. He needed to get cash to pay for the new outboard. He was not content to let somebody else pay his bills. He still suspected Nelson had interfered in his affairs.

Maggie at the Rod and Gun Club said that Thompson could stay a week, even two, if he liked. As usual, the resort wasn't busy. He walked to the post office to pick up any mail in his post office box. When he got to the door, he saw the postmistress flip the lock and turn the sign to "Closed". She walked away even while

Thompson rapped on the door. He heard a faint, "Sorry. Closed for lunch."

Figuring he would need to kill time until the post office reopened, Thompson returned to the bar to get a Coke. When he passed through the door, the normal bar din quieted. All eyes were on him. He pulled out a bar stool and sat down. The bartender seemed to be ignoring him, although Thompson wasn't sure. He was used to being last in line for service, so he was patient. He'd rather let little slights pass. Eventually, Thompson spoke up, politely asking, "Sir, can I order a Coca Cola on ice?"

He got a gruff answer. "No. We're out." It was clearly a lie.

"OK, how about any soda pop? Doesn't matter. Whatever you have."

The barkeeper mumbled, "Sorry mister. We don't have anything for you," pointing to a tattered and weathered sign taped to the mirror behind a stack of liquor bottles. The sign said "We reserve the right to refuse service to anyone!"

Thompson couldn't recall ever being denied ordering at the bar or anyplace in Everglades City for that matter. He tipped his cap and left the bar. He decided to stroll around town to wait for the post office to reopen. The streets were as vacant and quiet as ever, maybe even quieter. Thompson could see people in the houses, glimpsing shadowy figures behind screened windows when curtains moved.

Back at the post office, Thompson found it closed when it should be open, especially since the area where the PO boxes were located had never been closed before. Someone was inside but not unlocking the door. Only when a young mother with two kids in tow banged on the door did the postmistress come from behind her desk to unlock the front door. She smiled sheepishly,

"I'm sorry, I didn't see you there." That was another lie. Thompson wondered, "What's going on?"

He retrieved his mail and left the building without his usual "thanks" to the post office employee. There was nothing of particular interest hiding in the junk advertisements. In the quick sort he did while standing in the post office he found only a U.S. government check that he would cash as usual at the City Grocery.

The manager greeted him and, when presented with the check, said, "Sorry, we can't cash this. We don't have enough in our till."

Thompson understood. Sometimes he would have to wait a couple days for the store to have enough money to cash his check. "Thanks. Expect I'll be around at the Rod and Gun Club dock for a few days. I can come back."

The manager, who had always been friendly in the past, stiffened and replied, "Don't think we are going to be cashing your government checks anymore."

Thompson was puzzled. "Why?"

Brusquely, "Change of policy. You can shop here, but cash only."

Although peeved, Thompson reasoned he could do his banking when he went up to Marco.

Returning to his boat, he stopped at the Club desk and told Maggie about his troubles. She arranged for a new employee to take him in the Club truck to Marco Island, the closest place with a bank.

At the bank, he cashed his check and transferred enough funds to cover the cost of his new engine. He arranged with the bank manager to be able to do an electronic funds transfer when Thompson figured out who it should go to, whoever paid for his motor. Strange how the world had changed from cash to checks to credit cards and now wireless banking. This was a new technological environment that he knew nothing about and had no interest in learning.

The Rod and Gun Club truck came by the bank and waited at the curb. Thompson slid into the shotgun seat. "Get your errands done for the Club?"

"Yes sir. Now I can take you back, if you are finished, unless you have something else to do."

"Nope, back to Everglades City is fine. Thank you for driving me here." Thompson handed him a ten. The driver acknowledged the tip.

Back at the Club, Thompson used the lobby phone to call the Marathon boatyard to find out who had paid his bill so he could repay them. He spoke with the service manager who balked at revealing the identity of the donor. Thompson persisted, "I am not accustomed to having anyone pay my bills but me. If you can't tell me who paid for this engine, I'll darn sure bring it back and you can take it off the boat and refund their money!"

Thinking there was no use in arguing with an old man who was ranting, the service manager offered a compromise. "How about I call the folks that paid for your new motor and tell them they need to contact you. Or, I will ask their permission to give you their address and phone number. I do not want to be in between you and someone who is trying to do you a big favor. My business is boats, not secrets!"

Thompson agreed. "OK, I'll see if that works. But, if I don't hear from them in two weeks, I will be back in Marathon. You can give them my mail address. I don't have a phone. But they can leave a message here at the Everglades City Rod and Gun Club, 239-555-6971." With that he hung up.

Maggie caught him on his way out to his houseboat. "Mr. Thompson, I'm afraid I made a mistake. You can't stay here for the two weeks. I won't have a space for you. Maybe tonight and tomorrow night, but you will need to leave after that."

Thompson was in a funk from the rejections of the day. He'd not had any recent experiences with being rejected and he could not think of what might be causing the discriminatory treatment by the post office, bar, or store and now the Club. It seemed to add up to everyone in the community working against him. Thompson was exasperated. "What the hell is going on? I've never had any problems here before."

Maggie said in a whisper, "Let me go out to your houseboat with you."

When they exited the lodge, Thompson saw it immediately and stopped in his tracks. The side of his boat was vandalized with bright red spray paint. "SNICH BEWARE" was emblazoned on the side of his metal shed.

Maggie placed her hand on his shoulder, almost tearfully, and said, "Mr. Thompson, I'm so sorry somebody did this. It's not how most of us feel, but many are blaming you for the two men getting caught fishing in Everglades Park. Feelings run deep and family loyalties are causing a few idiots not to think straight. This is not who we are in Everglades City."

Thompson was hurt that he was targeted for hate. The two men were criminals, violent criminals, who were willing to kill him and others over fish.

Maggie said, "I think we should call the police to report this," as she gestured at the graffiti. Thompson protested but eventually agreed there should be a report.

The officer responding to Maggie's call took photos of the misspelled graffiti, joking, "Looks like whoever did this isn't going to win the Collier County spelling bee." He seemed dismissive of the spray paint, partly because the houseboat was such an ugly patchwork mosaic of materials. "This looks like a case of vandalism, probably just kids doing a prank, maybe on a dare."

Maggie argued, "This looks like a threat to me." She continued, "You know damn well that the two men sitting in the jail in Key West are from this area and some of their friends and family blame this man for them getting caught. I don't know the whole story, but Thompson could have been killed!"

The officer frowned. "Yes ma'am. I've taken the report. I'll ask the watch commander to provide a little more attention to your dock." Turning to Thompson, he asked, "How long do you plan on being here?"

Maggie answered for him, "I think he will be leaving day after tomorrow. I'm so embarrassed for our city. We should be better than this."

The police officer left. Thompson touched the paint, seeing if it would rub off of the metal siding. The paint only smeared, so it needed to be painted over. "Maggie, I want to go to the hardware store tomorrow morning and get a gallon of paint and a brush. I can cover the hate but I know the hatred won't go away."

Maggie said, "I'll get you the paint and I think our new maintenance man, who is not from here, will be able to help you. I can't tell you how sorry I am for this happening here at my place. I want you to have dinner at the lodge tonight – on me and order anything you want."

After two coats of house paint, the graffiti was covered. The bullet holes had been taped over with duct tape and the ripped screens were patched. Thompson would be ready to go the next morning. He was feeling a little vulnerable at the dock. The FBI still had his guns and, being tied to the land, anybody might come on his boat while he was sleeping. That night, he woke frequently and checked for intruders.

With the dawn, he cast off into a golden sunrise. The flat calm water reflected an intense orange outlined by the deep green mangrove shoreline. As the sun crept higher into the sky, the blaze of light streamed across the bay. He was careful to stay in the tight shallow channel out to the Gulf. Mentally he flipped a coin on where to go, north to the refuge to anchor at Dismal Key or Panther Key, or back south toward the Park. Tails it was, back to the Park, near Pavilion Key. He felt he would be safer at anchor, with good visibility to approaching traffic. Maybe whoever had it out for him might be a little less inclined to return to the place where their buds had been captured.

Thompson's nerves calmed a little after a few days back in his familiar haunts. He resumed his routine of fishing and reading. Life was peaceful, but he was still perturbed that his solitary life was complicated by unwanted attention from unknown miscreants.

Thompson studied old chart books and cruising guides from his heap of books. He had an old copy of a *Guide to Florida's Big Bend*. It was 30 years out of date, but told of a lonely wild coast. Perhaps this would be a suitable place to move to. The Everglades and Ten Thousand Islands were seeming to be less hospitable, with increased traffic and bizarre situations that found him in the back-country spaces he'd been ambling for a decade. Marjory Stoneman

Douglas had coined the truism, "There are no other Everglades in the world." For Thompson this was heartfelt, but it was time to seek another refuge.

The more he studied the charts, the more possible it seemed that up near Cedar Key and the Suwanee River could be a better alternative for him. He'd never been north of Sanibel and he'd not been welcome there. The boat traffic speeding through the Intracoastal Waterway around Ft. Myers was very disturbing. Inconsiderate powerboats seemed intent on swamping his home with their huge boat wakes. It was worse than being out on the open Gulf of Mexico.

He tried to put aside the notion of moving for a while. But he was obsessed, convincing himself that a move north would be a better option than sticking around in Florida Bay and the Ten Thousand Islands. After another couple days cogitating, his mind was made up. He'd plan his journey north. This was not going to be a small undertaking for an old man in a slow houseboat. It would be a couple hundred miles through unfamiliar waters and a lot of urban coastline to transit.

A few days after he made the decision to move north, Ranger Nelson arrived. Pulling alongside the houseboat, Nelson asked his usual, "Permission to come aboard?" while Thompson secured the line to the houseboat's cleat. Thompson was uncharacteristically friendly, discarding his usual retort "Not without a warrant."

"Nelson, what do you know about my guns?"

"Funny you should ask," as he retrieved a cardboard box from the patrol boat. "I've got a present for you!" Inside, the short stock shotgun and 22 target pistol were carefully wrapped, still taped with evidence tags.

"Thanks, let me see how bad a condition they're in. I'm sure they'll need cleaning. Bet the FBI didn't do a damn thing to take care of them." Thompson was clearly pleased to have his firearms back, even if they were dirty. He inspected the guns carefully, checking that they were unloaded.

"Coffee's ready. I put it on when I saw you coming."

The two unlikely friends sat a while, without much conversation, when Thompson blurted, "Well...I've decided to move on. This place is getting too rambunctious and busy for me."

At first Nelson thought he meant moving on back up the coast to the Ten Thousand Islands. He said, "I'm sure the refuge isn't going to be any more peaceful. They get a lot of fishing boats up that way too."

"No, I'm going up to Cedar Key. I think I'll try up toward the Suwanee River area for a spell. From what I can tell, it looks pretty isolated, not a lot of people or towns."

Nelson was surprised that Thompson would wander so far. A slew of questions came next, not the least of which was how he'd pilot the houseboat to get there. Careful not to impugn his idea or abilities, Nelson asked, "So, when do you think you'll head off? Do you know how to get there? Have you found a place to stay? Do you want to check it out by land before you go?"

Thompson said, "Hey, slow down. Let me answer one question before you shoot another!"

Nelson realized his enthusiasm and concern was more like an interrogation than a conversation. "Sorry. What are you thinkin'?"

Thompson said he'd looked at some old charts and an old book about the Big Bend of Florida. "I figure I could watch the weather and head up the Intracoastal Waterway and, if it was nice and calm, I could go outside. Might take me a week to get there.

"I'm going to Marco first to have this old boat hauled out to deal with the bottom and prepare for the trip. Think I'll leave next week to head up there."

Nelson noticed the new paint on his shed. "Hey, did you decide to fix up the boat? I see some new paint on your shed."

"Well… some hoodlums spray-painted the side of my shed when I was up at Everglades City. Seems there are some hard feelings about me shooting the bastards when I got tangled up in your game warden work. The town made it pretty clear that I'm not welcome there. And, I don't trust that these yahoos are done with me."

Nelson regretted there wasn't anything he could do to undo the predicament that Thompson was in at Everglades City. It was a tight-knit, insular community. Even the Park staff stationed at the western entrance were considered to be outsiders.

"What can I do to help you out?"

"Nothing! Reckon I can do this myself. I'm not completely used up – not yet."

"I know. You are in better shape than most folks half your age, but it's a long way up to north Florida. I'd think help getting there might be useful."

Thompson knew in his heart that he could use the help. He was good at moving his boat around in wide areas, but a little apprehensive about tight spaces and unfamiliar routes. "Maybe. Let me think about it." He would have to ponder whether pride trumped practicality.

Their coffee session went on longer than usual with the discussion of the big news about the prospect of Thompson leaving. Nelson didn't know much about that area of Florida, only that it wasn't subtropical and the depths were particularly shallow.

It was a wild coast and had a reputation for drug smuggling. He resolved to research it when he got back to Flamingo.

Asking again, "When do you think you might leave out of Marco?"

"Well, I'm going there directly and will head north as soon as I get the boat prepared…and the weather looks good."

"OK, you've got my number. Will you promise to call when you get to Marco?"

"Okay! Yes sir, I will report in so you can keep track of me."

With that, Nelson was off, full of questions and concern about the old man undertaking such an enormous transition.

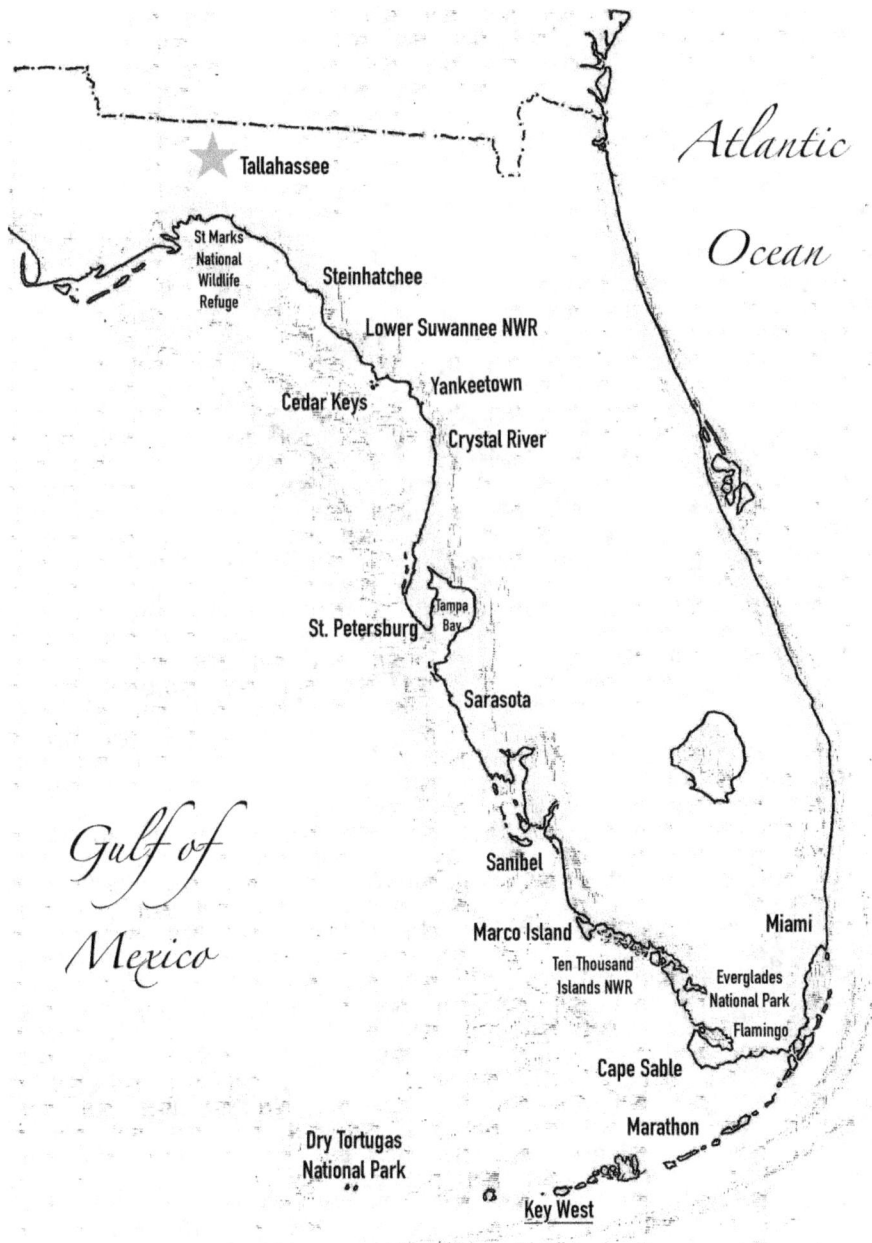

Atlantic Ocean

Gulf of Mexico

Tallahassee

St Marks National Wildlife Refuge

Steinhatchee

Lower Suwannee NWR

Cedar Keys

Yankeetown

Crystal River

Tampa Bay

St. Petersburg

Sarasota

Sanibel

Marco Island

Ten Thousand Islands NWR

Miami

Everglades National Park

Flamingo

Cape Sable

Dry Tortugas National Park

Marathon

Key West

SEVENTEEN

Nelson's cell phone rang. The caller ID showed a 239 area code. Usually it was spam, but he answered. "Hello, this is Bob, who is calling?"

"Nelson? Is that you? This is Thompson. I'm in Marco now. I promised I'd call. So now you know where I am. I'm using the boatyard's phone. Well… that's about it." There was a pause.

"Don't hang up. What's up with your plan and timeframe?"

"Well…I'm at the Marco Boatworks and Marina, getting the bottom scraped and painted. I haul out in two days and will launch after the weekend."

"So, then you will be on your way? Have you thought any more about taking me along with you?"

"Well…. I suppose it would be OK, if it's not too much bother. You could go along for a few days…if you wanted to. I guess you would have to take time off from work, so if you can't I'm fine on my own."

"I think I can get away. I don't have much to do if you aren't going to be squatting in the Park."

"Fine, I'll be out of your hair soon enough! I'm thinking of leaving first thing on Monday, if you want to come. Bring a sleeping bag. There's no bed!"

Nelson captured the number so he could call Thompson back before he left for Marco. With enough accrued leave, time off wouldn't be a problem. He only wished he had more than 5 days' notice to make arrangements and set up the ranger schedule.

Nelson researched the route up to Cedar Key from Marco. It seemed pretty straight forward. He guessed if they made 40 miles a day, it would take five or six days, maybe seven to get there. He planned to leave his car in Marco and try to rent a car in Cedar Key or somewhere nearby to return to pick it up. For now, what was important was packing for the trip, making sure he had the current charts on his iPad, and a way to charge his electronics. He packed a small duffel with convenience foods in case Thompson wasn't prepared with food. He figured he could get bottled water when they stopped for fuel along the way.

On Friday, he called the boatyard's number to confirm that Thompson was ready to go. The weather looked OK for Monday and Thompson was ready and anxious. Nelson arrived in Marco the next day and checked into a hotel near the marina. He wanted to start off fresh, not knowing what kind of shower arrangements were set up on the houseboat. He asked the dockmaster if he could leave his car for a week.

By Sunday afternoon, Thompson was tied up alongside the wharf at the boatyard. He had extra gas jugs that he had filled, along with other provisions for the trip, like motor oil and propane. He showed Nelson his old charts. Nelson was happy he had downloaded Navionics on his iPad so they would have up-to-date navigation.

Early Monday they cast off and took the inside channel behind Keewaydin Island to Naples. It was slow going, but easy enough. The navigation markers were easy to follow through the Rookery Bay National Estuarine Research Reserve. Thompson let Nelson take the wheel and coached him on how the houseboat could easily oversteer and was not responsive to quick adjustments. With some practice, Nelson got the hang of it.

The chart showed they would have to take Gordon Pass out from Naples into the open Gulf to run the coastline up to Sanibel. Overall, it was a 40+-mile trip and an ambitious start.

Traveling west to exit at Gordon Pass, they encountered rolling swells that subsided to calmer conditions when the houseboat arced north to hug the sandy beach. With an easterly breeze there was not a long fetch for waves to build, so the seas were only 1 to 2 feet. Both men were somewhat tepid about going outside, into the Gulf, off a high energy beach, but there was no other option from Naples to Ft. Myers. From Sanibel on, most of the route would be inside between barrier islands and the Florida mainland.

As the sun was setting, they passed by the famed Sanibel lighthouse on the southern point of the island and then went under the western span of the causeway. By looking at the chart program Nelson had on his iPad, he knew it had a 26-foot clearance. The air draft of the houseboat was 18 feet to the top of the tower helm.

It spooked both of them to go under the bridge as the light was fading. They worried that they might not clear. "Easy-peasy!" exclaimed Nelson as they exited under the span. "It's good to have this iPad for the navigation information." Then he put a dot on the map at the entrance to Tarpon Bay, just a couple miles away. The computer plotted a course and all they had to do was follow the track on the screen.

It was twilight when they dropped anchor, just off the channel, in a charted depth of 8 feet, which was plenty of water for the houseboat. As they were sitting down to dinner at nearly 8 PM, a flashing blue light approached. A law enforcement boat was coming toward them, fast.

It slowed, pulled alongside, and the boat's following wake rocked the houseboat.

The officer's spotlight poured over the boat from stem to stern, finally resting on Nelson and Thompson. They raised their hands to shield their eyes from the blinding light. The blue lights reflected on the surfaces around them. It was disorienting.

Nelson yelled, "Hey, can we help you? Can you give us a break from that spotlight?"

The officer lowered the light to aim at their feet. "I'm Refuge Officer Leigh Westenhart. Do you know you are anchored in a restricted zone of the Ding Darling National Wildlife Refuge? A call came in from one of the houses on the island." She pointed over to the mansions lining the shore to the south.

"No ma'am, we did not know. We were losing light and do not have navigation lights to run at night. This looked like a suitable place on our chart."

The officer looked at the derelict houseboat with skepticism. She didn't expect the boaters would be articulate. She asked for identification.

Thompson pulled his wallet from his back pocket, which made the officer a little nervous. She commanded, "Slowly! Please."

Nelson interjected, "I'm going to retrieve my wallet from my back pocket. I am Ranger Bob Nelson from Everglades National Park and this is my friend Mr. Thompson, the boat owner." It was a strange time for him not to recall Thompson's first name. "I can assure you his craft is legally registered and he has all required safety equipment. I'm helping him move this boat."

The refuge officer's voice changed to a more friendly tone and she lowered the light as she asked if they could turn on a deck light so she wouldn't have to spotlight them. Thompson quickly switched on the light in the screened porch, prompting Officer Westenhart to turn off her spotlight. She also eased her grip on her holstered sidearm.

Nelson thought, "I hope she's not that nervous. She's been exhibiting all the classic maneuvers from FLETC training." He whispered, "We need to be careful, Thompson. Stay calm and move slowly."

She approached the boat and reached for Thompson's ID and Nelson flipped open his wallet to reveal his badge. Now Leigh smiled.

"I got the call of a wrecked vessel at the entrance of Tarpon Bay. There's no overnight anchoring in the refuge waters and Tarpon Bay is Refuge. You are not in Tarpon Bay, so technically you are OK here, but real close to being across the line."

Nelson replied, "Thank you. We've been traveling all day, up from Marco, and would hate to have to move. This gentleman is a real hero. A couple months ago, he saved me from two poachers in Everglades National Park who tried to kill us. I'm helping him move up to Cedar Key, kind of for his own safety."

"I heard about the poachers and the gun fight from the Ten Thousand Islands guys. You were involved in that?

"I wouldn't have made you move at night. I was just being cautious and responding to the complaints we get from the neighbors. Some of them think the whole ocean belongs to them. Don't get me wrong, we love their help and support, but we're not really a "preserve-the-view private police force," as she gestured, making air quotation marks.

Ranger Nelson responded, "Yep, sometimes public support is a double-edged sword. Thank you. We will be on our way early in the morning."

"Good luck and safe travels." Leigh added "We have a national wildlife refuge up there in North Florida. In fact, there are a number of units: Cedar Key, Lower Suwanee, Crystal River, and further north, St. Marks. They're all nice areas." She handed back Thompson's ID and cast off, this time without the blue light.

Thompson and Nelson exhaled. What an end to their long day! After a supper of canned tuna and grits, they popped open the rum for a night cap. Thompson grumbled, "That lady refuge officer just wanted to hassle us. She must have been bored."

Nelson stood up for her, "No, she was just doing what she had to do. At night, on your own, it's daunting to do LE on land, and it's especially daunting on the water. I feel for her having to be so responsive to the neighbors. The wealthy ones can be connected to politicians."

"Enough said. I got no trust in the politicians." It was still a sore spot with Thompson.

Pulling anchor in the early morning, after coffee and oatmeal, they would try for another forty miles, maybe up to Lemon Bay around Englewood. Nelson plotted the route and reviewed it with Thompson. They left San Carlos Bay, traveling up through Pine Island Sound, passing some neat islands that were not connected with bridges. Their progress was slow; even sailboats were passing them. Marker to marker, they continued on the Intracoastal. Many of the markers had osprey nests built of stout twigs between the boards that displayed the marker numbers.

The large powerboats they encountered were a pain. The wakes of these yachts were so large they roundly upset the houseboat. Anything not secured was knocked over and spilled by the rocking action.

It didn't take long for the two intrepid mariners to learn how to steer into the wakes to minimize the yawing. Some of the yachts passing them reduced their speed to diminish the disruption to their smaller and slower boat, but most power boaters were self-absorbed and inconsiderate of the effect of their huge wakes.

After passing Cayo Costa State Park, they crossed the Boca Grande Pass and arrived at the north end of Gasparilla Sound. The chart showed a small opening between two old bridge spans. As they approached it looked even more intimidating. The hard-to-steer, wide, pontoon houseboat had to go between narrow concrete bollards that were the ruins of an old railroad bridge. A cross current was pushing the boat sideways and the forward motion was slow against the tide. Oncoming boats were crowding the tight space as well. Thompson frantically spun the wheel back and forth. The houseboat was always slow to respond and the current was wrestling the course away from the direction they needed to go. Fortunately, the boat squeaked through, only because an oncoming boater abandoned his attempt to go through at the same time, although he used a hand gesture to express his displeasure at having to wait.

They barely had time to discuss their relief at getting through the tight passage, when they approached a swing bridge. Nelson's navigation program revealed it was just too tight to go under without the steering station hitting the bottom of the span. This was the first bridge that they had to open. Instead of center spans lifting up, this bridge rotated on a center post. Now the problem was holding the houseboat in place outside of the bridge while the bridge opened. A sign on the bridge directed boaters to request an opening on VHF Channel 9 or by cell phone to the bridgetender.

Nelson asked, "Do you have a VHF radio?"

"No, never had much use for one. I get the weather on a weather radio I bought at Walmart. I never needed to talk to anybody."

"We need to call on the cell phone then. Can you read the phone number?"

Thompson got out binoculars. "It's not visible. The sign doesn't have the full number!"

"Okay. Now what do we do? I can't keep the boat pointed straight. We will need to turn around and hope the bridgetender sees us."

On the second pass around, close to the bridge, Nelson climbed up to the helm tower and waved his arms back and forth. He could see the bridgetender in the little building looking out of the window.

A moment later, he saw the bridgetender exit his cubicle and walk to the center of the bridge and enter a little booth. A horn blasted three toots and the bridge began to move, not up but sideways. It was pivoting from the center to open two lanes, one on each side of the span, for boat traffic. When it was open, Thompson throttled up to race through the opening. When they passed by the center, the tender shouted down with a bullhorn,

"Get a VHF radio! The next bridge is a dozen miles north. They may not see you!"

Nelson gave a thumbs up sign. He resolved to get a VHF radio as soon as possible. The Navionics app showed they would pass several marinas on their way, before the next bridge they would have to open. The first couple of marinas would be tricky to get into, but one looked like they could side-tie-up on a T-dock with an easier approach. Nelson called ahead to the number he got from the Internet. "Do you sell VHF radios?"

"Yes, we have a couple in stock."

"Great. We're on a houseboat that is hard to handle. I'll be there in a couple hours. Could you have someone help us when we get there?"

"Of course, just hail us on channel 16 or channel 10 when you get close and we will have a dockhand meet you," came the pleasant reply.

"Sorry, we don't have a VHF. That's why I was checking to see if you have one. I'll call you on the phone if that's OK?"

"Sure thing Skipper! We will stand by."

When they were approaching the marina, a young man ran out to help them dock. Nelson jumped off and hurried to the marina store to purchase a handheld VHF. It was pricey, but that didn't matter. They needed one for the bridges and emergencies. He also purchased a *Waterway Guide* for Florida's west coast. It had a mile-by-mile description of bridges and facilities, marinas, and anchorages. And a bonus was information on local history and points of interest. When he saw it on the shelf, Nelson thought, "What a helpful find to have to guide our trip – current information!"

Nelson brought some ice, water, pop, and sunglasses back to the boat, along with the radio and guidebook. They were ready to cast off and get underway again. While Nelson was at the store, Thompson topped off their fuel.

Once they were on their way again, Nelson asked Thompson, "Can you take it for minute. I want to study the route ahead. Here's the iPad with the route plotted out. It looks pretty straight forward." Thompson was getting familiar with how to enlarge the image on the screen and liked seeing where the boat was on the moving chart.

"Well...I've got to admit this thing is pretty useful. It's better than trying to look at a paper chart and figure out where the next marker is."

They hadn't counted on having to wait at bridges until a specific time. Some bridges opened on demand; others were on the half hour. The *Waterway Guide* was helpful in figuring out the schedules. Thankfully, they didn't have to open every bridge they came to.

Getting close to the next bridge, Nelson joined Thompson at the helm station. "Bridgetender, this is *Épave* houseboat on VHF channel nine requesting an opening. Over."

The reply came quickly. "This is Manasota Bridge. Our next opening is on the hour, in 14 minutes. I have you in sight on the south. Keep comin'."

"Thanks. It looks like we will make it in time. Over."

"Do not enter the bridge until the spans are fully open."

"Thompson, that was easy. I'm glad we have the VHF. Can I plug in the charger somewhere?"

"There's a cigarette lighter plug by the cabin door. That should work."

Nelson backed down the ladder and plugged in the charger. Thankfully, the VHF battery indicator light came on. The outlet would also be useful for recharging his iPad so they could continue to have the Navionics electronic chart. Passing through the next few bridges was easy. One was tall enough to pass under without having to open it.

"Nelson, I used to get stopped on bridges because of the boats passing under and always resented the interruption. Now on the other side, I see how it works. Guess some of the folks up there waiting on the bridge might imagine they'd like to be on a boat traveling on the water instead of in a car going over the water."

"Sure. I'm kind of liking this cruising. We're only an hour or so from where we can overnight in Lemon Bay. We've made better time today and won't have to anchor in the dark. Here's where I'm thinkin' we could stop for tonight." To get Thompson's approval, Nelson pointed to a spot on the chart.

"Looks good to me. Maybe we can even fish for a bit."

More boats passed their slow boat heading north and they met boats heading south. Sailboats, power yachts, sportfishing boats, even kayaks crossed their path. Watching the birds and occasional dolphin was a treat. Seeing the homes on the waterfront, crammed together, with manicured landscaping, and massive docks wasn't so heartening.

Thompson waxed, "You know, all these people crowded together in little spaces, in houses that are so much larger than anyone needs, is not the life I could ever imagine. It might be each one's special piece of paradise, but I just can't imagine living that way. I think of all the natural places they bulldozed and filled for their mansions and how only the rich get access to what God gave to all of us. Well, it kind of bothers me. Reckon, each to his own."

Nelson nodded in agreement, "You know, we, well you especially, have had a special communion with nature, living

214

a simple austere life. I have a passion for the public parks, the conservation lands and waters that protect the natural places and provide for everybody, rich, poor, city people and country folks, to get outside and enjoy what needs to be protected in trust for the future."

"Well, ain't that just a little sentimental? But, yes, the natural areas are a treasure. I don't like rules, but who does? The big problem is that there are just too many rats on the ship!"

Their philosophical conversation ended abruptly when the houseboat bumped and they saw mud stirred up behind the outboard motor. "Quick, we're out of the channel!"

Their serious conversation had distracted them from watching the plotter. They were on the wrong side of the marker, in a shallow shoal area. Both of them knew better. Fortunately, they hadn't run hard aground; they were just humbled by their momentary distraction. They were able to back off and adjust their course to get back into the channel.

They soon found a suitable place to anchor. Anchoring was easy, in a charted 6-foot depth and out of the channel. Boat wakes rocked their houseboat every time one of the big cruisers passed by in the channel. But, they were secure and hoped they wouldn't be run over by someone else who was not paying attention to their course and wandering out of the channel.

Nelson and Thompson stopped with enough light left in the day to do a little fishing. Thompson caught a speckled trout and filleted it for grilling. They enjoyed the fish along with a can of beans and some fresh cabbage salad. Retiring early, after their night cap and a little more trivial musings, they hit the sack.

The weather was decent over the next few days. The farther north they traveled, the more intense was the development. High rise condominiums created a wall at the oceanfront. Homes and seawalls lined both shores. There were fewer green spaces and so many people. The two boaters wondered, "How could there be so many rich people?"

Rising with the dawn, Thompson asked, "How 'bout some eggs and toast this morning before we head out?"

"Sounds good."

They were at the south shore of Tampa Bay, watching the sun rise and change the sky from a pale pastel pallet to a robust red and orange glow surrounding the bright yellow disc of the emerging sun.

Thompson observed, "We better check the weather. Red sky at night, sailor's delight. Red sky in morning, sailors take warning!"

Nelson took the VHF from the charger and tuned in the NOAA marine weather forecast. The drone of an artificial voice repeated the weather statement:

"Marine weather forecast for the KHB 32 listening area. Breezy northerly winds will continue through the day today and overnight with corresponding elevated seas expected through morning. All local water zones are under a Small Craft Advisory through this evening. In addition, a high rip current risk is in effect from Pinellas to Lee County into this evening. On and off shower chances will continue into morning as a weak front passes. Weather conditions will rapidly improve tomorrow and Bay conditions are expected to be calm for the next several days."

"What do you think 'bout hanging out here for today to see what the weather really is. They're saying it's going to be a little frisky today and Tampa Bay could be rough with a small craft advisory. Of course, that's the forecast and now it looks OK. But it could be uncomfortable when we get out there."

"I'm with you. We can stay here and wait to cross the Bay until we are sure we've got the weather. Looks like once we start we have to go all the way."

EIGHTEEN

It was good to take a day off, spending time on the houseboat, reading the *Waterway Guide* and fishing, even if they were only catching catfish. Thompson poured over the *Guide*, learning as much as he could about his destination.

Crossing Tampa Bay the following day was not difficult. They carefully watched a large container ship as it headed towards the Port of Tampa, but it remained well off their location. They encountered another bridge to get into the waterway behind St. Petersburg Beach and they saw more dense development with not a green space in sight.

They continued north until they were near Dunedin, where there were anchorages shown on the guidebook maps and on Navionics. Once they found a suitable spot, they dropped the hook. Surrounded by spoil islands, their chosen anchorage would be calm.

After dinner Thompson retrieved the bourbon from the camper cabin and brought two cups to the table. "Well, Nelson we're more than halfway there and it looks like the next passages will be a little less built up. Want to celebrate our odyssey?"

At night the bright lights of the city diminished the visibility of the stars. It was not like the inky darkness of the Everglades where the Milky Way revealed its splendor on cloudless nights. Here, the humidity reflected the urban illumination like a pastel glowing nightlight.

Nelson pulled up a chair while Thompson poured. "Yes sir, we've done pretty well so far without any real problems. Though, I have to admit that narrow opening down by Placida made me nervous."

Thompson nodded, "Me too!"

As they sipped their nightcaps, Thompson said, "You know, you've asked a lot of questions about me, but I don't know anything about you, except that you are a park cop."

"As you say, well….I grew up in a city, a middle-class kid, in the Atlanta suburbs, with dreams of outdoor and sea adventures, like Jack London, Zane Grey, and Robb White's *The Lion's Paw*. I started out studying biology in college at the University of Georgia and got interested in their natural resource program. I graduated with a degree in resource management. That led to a forestry job, but I really wasn't keen on tree extraction and timber sales. After a couple years I decided to take a temporary Florida State Parks job for a year before getting hired on in Tennessee with their state parks. Unfortunately, those jobs didn't pay the bills, but I loved the work. The basic problem seems to be that politicians appear to think that, if you love the job, they can pay you less and demand more of you. There are some really dedicated people working for natural resource agencies, state and federal, for a lot less than they deserve."

Thompson said, "Ought not to be that way. Exploitation and greed go hand in hand."

219

"After I got married to the wonderful girl I met in college, we found we couldn't both have careers. If I was working in my field in some remote place, she couldn't get a job in her profession. Shirley was an environmental chemist. Not much call for that out in the sticks, so she either did substitute teaching, or waitressing, or volunteering. One day she was driving to a temporary job when a truck went into a skid on a slick road and hit her car. She died at the scene. I was devastated and that heartbreak in the cold mountains froze my emotions. I had to find a warmer place to thaw out my heart. That's when I applied to the National Park Service. It was better pay and benefits and the park I started at was in the Caribbean. After my wife died, I guess you could say I married the National Park Service. Suppose it's my 12-year anniversary now."

"I went to the Federal Law Enforcement Training Center to be certified as a law enforcement officer. My Park Service career went from the US Virgin Islands to a little historic park in Georgia to the Dry Tortugas. Then the problems with refugees at Dry Tortugas overwhelmed me, so I transferred to Everglades, hoping I could get back to normal Ranger duties there."

Thompson was sarcastic, "Well, looks like that didn't turn out so good, unless getting shot at is normal."

Sighing, "Yep. Not what I hoped for. Love the Park and the normal challenges, but it has been one wacky situation after another. Seems like I jumped out of the pan into the fire."

Thompson consoled him, "You know, what you are doing is worthwhile, even if it's tough. It still seems like you are important to protecting the Park, even if it involves rescuing stupid people or fighting poachers," adding after a short pause, "and hassling old men."

"I know, but being a biologist is at my core. The law enforcement duties are necessary but secondary. Some have joked giving badges to wildlife biologists is like using a butter knife to eat soup."

Silence filled a void in the conversation. Finally, Thompson changed the subject, not really having anything to say to respond to Nelson's story. "I'm glad you came along so I could teach you how to run a houseboat. Tomorrow, I'll let you drive all the way. Want another shot for the road?"

In the morning, leaving out of Dunedin, they stopped at a marina just off the channel to gas up. There was nothing but open water ahead from Anclote Key up to Suwannee River. Every place they could get fuel would be a long way off the direct route and the channels they would need to take to get the gas all looked tight and twisty and especially shallow.

After passing under the Honeymoon Island Causeway bridge, the most dominant landmarks were the Anclote Island lighthouse to the west and the very tall power plant smokestack to the east at Tarpon Springs. Straight ahead was 150 miles of Gulf to Apalachee Bay. Cedar Key lay about halfway. Keep going west and it would be 700 miles to the Texas shore.

Even close to the Florida coastline, no more than 20 miles offshore, it felt like the wide wild ocean. The houseboat was not an ocean-going vessel, so they were happy with a flat calm, glassy sea, at least for today's segment.

An hour out, Nelson said, "Mr. Thompson, I have a present for you, kind of a thank you gift for saving my bacon back at Shark River."

"Hell, there is no need for that." Grinning from ear to ear, he remarked, "My reward was shooting that fat fucker in the ass!"

Nelson knew his use of salty language was an out of character off-color remark to cover his modesty. "Seriously, this is something I suspect you will need in your new cruising grounds." He handed him a box containing a Garmin GPS chartplotter. "I saw this in the store at the marina. It's like what I have on the iPad. You can use this to find your way around. We can go over how it works tonight over a few shots."

Thompson was grateful, but perturbed at the generosity. He had never depended on anyone's charity. "I should say thanks, but all I want to say is, let me pay you for this thing. I didn't need this kind of thing down in the Ten Thousand Islands, but I reckon this will be useful up here as I explore more in my new home turf."

"Nope. It's a gift! And a selfish one, because I don't want to find you run aground and have to come to pull you off. Now you won't have any excuse."

"Well, guess I just say thanks and don't be doing this again!"

While Thompson steered north, Nelson hooked up the new chartplotter. He ran a wire down the helm tower to the battery, attaching it with zip ties to the tower structure. Then, he carefully attached the plotter's bracket near the steering wheel in a position where it was easy to see and touch while steering.

That night was spent a couple miles off New Port Richey, anchored in what the new Garmin showed as a mere 4 feet. Thompson was learning how to operate his new electronic chart. "Damn, the water is really shallow up this way. Two miles off and it's only four feet deep? I will need to be careful!"

Nelson said, "It's not only the shallow water but there are rocks, not a lot but if you hit one you might put a hole in one of your pontoons."

Thompson was intent on learning how to use the chart plotter, realizing the limitations of his lack of experience in a new kind of sea bottom. With this instrument and a thorough reading of the Big Bend cruising guide, he'd be a lot better off.

With the new day and calm weather, they hoped to make it all the way to Cedar Key. Starting early and keeping an eye on the weather and an ear on the NOAA weather channel, they set a course straight for Cedar Key. At 52 nautical miles, it would be the longest day of their trip. If they couldn't make it they would need to adjust course to motor miles to the east to be closer to the coast for a shallow anchorage.

Bolstered with confidence by their success so far, they were ambitious and the weather window looked decent. For hours the motor droned on. They only stopped to add oil and refill the fuel tank from one of the extra jerry cans of gas, quickly getting back underway.

Checking the charts, they were making good progress and, if they could maintain speed, they would beat the darkness to set the hook near Seahorse Key. Then the next day they could navigate the reportedly tricky channel around the island to get to Cedar Key. Morning light would be better to see the channel markers.

In the late afternoon, a dozen miles west of the entrance to the long-defunct Cross Florida Barge Canal and about three hours from their destination, they were startled by Nelson's phone ringing and flashing. It was the ring setting for Ranger Smith at the Park. Nelson jumped to answer.

"Hey Buddy, what's up?"

"Oh man, I'm glad I finally got you. We hadn't heard any report from you for several days and I could never get you to answer."

"Sorry." Nelson looked at his phone and saw a lot of voicemail messages. "I guess I had the phone on silent ring. I really didn't want you to worry. Everything is fine here. We're almost to Cedar Key."

"Glad to hear that. There's no real problems here, but there have been a number of calls from a marina in Marathon and some lady in Atlanta who wants to get in touch with Mr. Thompson. I assume he's with you. Can you give me his cell number so I can pass it along and get them off our back?"

"Ha! Are you kidding? Thompson would no more have a cell phone than a TV. He shuns most all technology. I bought him a chartplotter and he has finally come to accept that it is useful. You can pass along my number. But let them know we are in and out of cell service on the boat. We should be reachable after 9 tonight or tomorrow. That is if Cedar Key has reception."

"Thanks. I will give them your number so they can speak to Thompson. So, how is it going?"

"Great. This has been a wonderful respite from the Park. Traveling up the coast, we've seen a lot of interesting territory I never imagined. I'll look forward to showing you some photos when I get back. How's the crew? Any problems at Flamingo?"

"Everybody is fine. Cooper stopped in to show he's still on the mend and missing us. No problems yet. If any come up, I'll save them for you."

"Buddy, it's been an unexpected pleasure to cruise on the boat with Thompson. He's quite an interesting guy. I admire his self-reliance and simplicity. I want to sign off now, before I lose cell service and you call out the Coast Guard."

"Okay, Nelson. Take care and I don't think the Coast Guard would come. You've used up all your credit with them."

"Probably so, but maybe they have a loyalty program and I have earned enough points for a free rescue. Bye. I'll be in touch."

Thompson asked who was on the phone. Nelson relayed that some people were trying to get in touch with him and they would call on his personal cell phone. "My co-workers were checking up on me since they hadn't heard from me and were getting worried. I'm ashamed to confess that I hadn't thought about work for most of this trip."

Three hours later, they were at the entrance marker to the south channel into Cedar Key. The sun still hadn't set. There would be enough light to anchor before dark.

About a half mile off Seahorse Key, they turned to be well out of the channel. They'd seen a few commercial crab boats as they were making their way up the coast and they didn't want to be in the path of those boats if the skippers used the channel at night or before daybreak. Circling around, they monitored where they were by the position on the chartplotter and iPad. Eight feet of water should be more than enough, even if the tide got really low. Dropping the anchor, Nelson payed out plenty of rode to have a long scope. More than 7 times the depth, plus a few feet for extra measure. Since they were so exposed and there was an island they could drift into if the anchor dragged, they wanted to be sure they were hooked well.

Thompson gently backed down, until the houseboat jerked, pulling directly on the anchor. It was well set, dug into the mud.

Before dinner, they toasted their accomplishment and traded barbs on who deserved the credit. Now they could relax. They were close enough to their intended destination that they could claim success. They spent a couple hours enjoying the breeze and rum. Tomorrow they could get to the dock, reprovision and maybe even eat at a restaurant.

The night breeze fell off to a flat calm. With no moon, both were delighted to see the brilliant celestial display filling the dark sky with twinkling stars. Worn out, they were asleep soon after they called it a night.

About 2 in the morning, the boat was rocking and waves were banging on the side of the boat. It was an unusual motion and the sound was disturbing. Thompson bolted from his bed first, nearly tripping over Nelson still emerging from his sleeping bag cocoon. On deck Thompson shined his powerful spotlight over the boat and out onto the surrounding waters. He couldn't see anything except the distant shore of the Key and its lighthouse pulsing a regular blink.

The wind was blowing hard with a definite chill. At night the wind feels so much stronger and ominous than it does at the same speed in daylight. Nelson went to the bow of the boat to look for the anchor line. He couldn't see it when he shined his small LED flashlight to where he figured it should be.

Bending over the bow, he traced the line from the cleat to discover it was very tight and instead of being ahead of the boat it was leading back to the stern. "Hey Thompson, the anchor line is going backwards, under the boat."

Water seemed to be rushing by the pontoons like they were underway, but clearly they weren't moving forward or in any direction for that matter. Waves were still slapping the starboard pontoon and resonating on the hollow aluminum tube like a drum.

Thompson passed through the storage shed. His bright light shone down on the Suzuki outboard. Through cloudy greenish water he could make out a faint line stretching out from the lower unit. It was the anchor line.

He paused to collect his thoughts and confer with Nelson. "I see a line. Think it's the anchor rode, hooked on the outboard, maybe wrapped on the prop. It's not going in the direction the wind is coming from, but definitely, the water is flowing from the same direction the line is pointed."

"Think it could be the tide?"

"Yes! That's it. The tide is pushing us one way and the wind is pushing us another. It must have fouled the motor prop when the wind came up and the tide turned."

Nelson said, "I think this is a wind blowing out from shore because the land is cooling off and the wind is rushing from the temperature differential. It's really strong. What should we do?"

"We could wait it out and see if things settle, but I'm worried the line may chafe through from the strain against the prop. If we cut it loose, then we might end up beached on that island, or even out into the Gulf."

"Guess we better straighten it out."

Thompson found a boat hook pole in his storage shed. "Here, see if you can grab the anchor line and pull it up to where we can get a hand on it. I'll hold the light for you."

Nelson reached down to try to hook the line. After several attempts he had it. It was tight with the force of the tide pushing sideways on the houseboat. The camper and shed structures on the pontoon platform created a lot of windage. Finally, Nelson made some progress getting the line up close enough for both to get a hand on it.

"Pull it up to get enough slack to get the strain off the motor." Both pulled, the old man and Nelson, who was half his age. The teamwork slowly released tension on the motor and they retrieved enough line to tie it off to a stern cleat, leaving a fair bit of slack drifting back, past the motor."

"Let's catch our breath" Nelson was winded.

Thompson cajoled, "What's the matter Sonny. Hard work too much for you?" But, he needed a break too, now that the immediate crisis was averted. After catching their breath, they could attack untangling the motor. With the boat hook, Nelson pushed down on the line releasing its chokehold on the lower unit. Pulling it up to check out the rope's condition in the light, they could see that it was not chafed or cut.

Now they needed to get the line back to the bow so the pull would be tight against the tide.

"How should we do this?" Neither had ever had a strange experience like this.

Surveying their predicament, they saw that the stern was facing the tide and the wind was forcing the boat sideways. They determined that the tide was stronger than the wind.

They came up with a plan. They got more line ready to let out, tying 20 feet of line to another bow cleat. Then, slowly, they let out line from the stern cleat, keeping the excess line that had been wrapped on the motor from getting snared again. When the wind pushed the boat sideways, they released all the line from the stern so the boat drifted back from the force of the tidal flow. As they were executing their maneuvers, they hoped there was nothing under the boat for the line to snag on.

The boat drifted sideways. The stern swung around slowly without tension on the anchor line. Nelson ran to the bow to ease out more line that was attached to the back-up bow cleat. Now the boat swayed as the tension increased. Then it jolted, taking the full force of the tide.

Both men watched the water flow by the pontoons. In the darkness, there was no reference for orientation. However, the steady direction of the wind, and the lessened slap of the waves on the hull indicated their fix had worked. Disaster had been averted.

It took a half hour for them to calm themselves enough to return to bed. They had spent an hour fighting the wind and tide and the fluke entanglement of the line on the motor. Neither would sleep easy until daylight. In the dawn the wind was calm again, the sky was a beautiful mix of colors, and the waters were still. It was as if the challenge in the night had been a bad dream.

After coffee the next morning they could head to town, crossing the finish line.

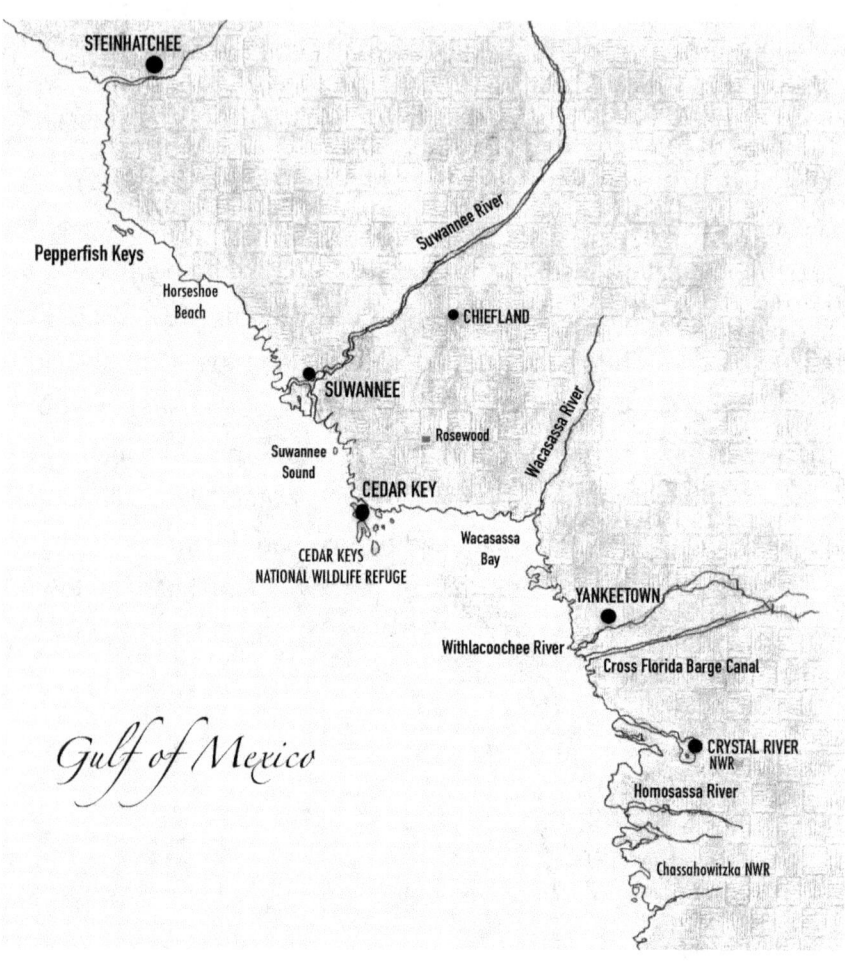

STEINHATCHEE

Pepperfish Keys

Horseshoe
Beach

Suwannee River

CHIEFLAND

SUWANNEE

Rosewood

Wacasassa River

Suwannee
Sound

CEDAR KEY

CEDAR KEYS
NATIONAL WILDLIFE REFUGE

Wacasassa
Bay

YANKEETOWN

Withlacoochee River

Cross Florida Barge Canal

Gulf of Mexico

CRYSTAL RIVER
NWR

Homosassa River

Chassahowitzka NWR

NINETEEN

The chartplotter displayed the route from their anchorage off Seahorse Key to the Cedar Key waterfront. Just like the guide books advised, there was no dock or services, only a small boat basin cut into a point of land. It looked like the basin may have been a marshy wetland at one time in the distant past. It had been dredged to make it deep enough for small boats and the spoil was piled on the marsh edge. Now there is a road with a low bridge and restaurants and gift shops lining the waterfront. There were remnants of piers and docks sticking into the shallow waters between the town and Atsena Otie Key; none were set up for landing or docking. And there was a modern concrete pier sticking into the channel that was being used as a fishing pier.

The entrance to the "port" was under the low fixed bridge. Once under the bridge and in the center of the basin there was a dilapidated floating dock for temporary tie-up of small fishing boats. There was also a boat ramp for launching small boats.

A few boats that couldn't make it under the bridge were anchored off the town. Kayakers and small sailboats were making their way back and forth across the channel to Atsena Otie Key where there was a nice white sand beach. There was a trail on the island that meandered through the forest to ruins of an early 1900s pencil factory. A small ferryboat took day-users from the town boat ramp to Atsena Otie, part of the Cedar Keys National Wildlife Refuge.

Only a few buildings in Cedar Key looked modern. There were a number of old pilings and ruins of old waterfront structures, evidence that the place had been battling the Gulf for a long time. All and all, the place exhibited a rustic, old-Florida flavor.

After seeing there was no place suitable to tie up the houseboat, Thompson asked Nelson to look at the chartplotter to find a place to anchor. "Something close and out of the channel so we don't get turned around in the tide."

Nelson found a spot near an abandoned looking pier on Atsena Otie Key. The decrepit dock was posted with No Landing and Refuge Closed Area signs. Anchoring near the dock would provide enough water and the spot didn't appear to be in the drainage of vast shallows like their position was last night. There was even a symbol on the chart indicating the place was an anchorage, so they wouldn't be hassled by a Refuge worker. It would be a half-mile paddle to the boat basin, farther than they liked but not really that bad.

After anchoring, the problem was how to get the two of them to town in a one-man pirogue. Thompson said, "I'll wave down a passing fishing boat to see if they would take you and I'll paddle."

Thompson tried to hail the passing boats. A couple of them just ignored him and one just waved back at him. Nelson said, "Just get ready and go in your pirogue. I'll keep trying and catch up." Thompson started off. The next sportfishing boat Nelson waved at passed and then turned back. "Hey, do you need help?"

Nelson said, "I need to get to Cedar Key. My friend is paddling his one-man boat." Nelson pointed to the pirogue, now more than halfway to the shore. "Can you give me a lift?"

"Sure. Don't know how you will get back, but we'll get you over there."

Nelson passed Thompson on the way and yelled, "Meet you at the dock!"

The boat operator said, "Now that's not something you see every day 'round here. An old black man paddling a canoe."

It wasn't hard to catch the thinly-guised racism in the boater's remark. Nelson wouldn't take the bait to be engaged in a conversation about race or Thompson. Ignoring the topic, he replied, "You from Cedar Key?"

"No, I live up the road a bit at Fastrun Springs on the Suwannee River. I like coming here 'cause it's pretty good fishing and close. It's better than putting in at the town of Suwannee and going a long way out to get to decent places to fish. My buddy's got a camper trailer he parks on a lot nearby. We come a few times a month."

When they were at the boat ramp in the boat basin, Nelson jumped off the boat with a bow line and said, "Thanks for the lift. Sorry, I need to run over to help my Dad get out of his pirogue. He's not as spry as he used to be." It was a conundrum he wanted to leave the guy with, guessing. From the confused look on his face, it worked.

Nelson met Thompson at the dock. They secured the boat and headed over to a kiosk that had a map of the town. Taking a tourist leaflet with a map, they started exploring the small town. There were art galleries, tourist shops, a convenience store, gas station, and a lot of bed and breakfasts. Mid-morning the streets had a fair number of people wandering around. After his earlier experience, Nelson was now sensitized to race more than usual. The town was overwhelmingly white and middle-aged, with a lot of fishermen pulling small boats on trailers.

On their agenda was getting a little familiar with the town so Thompson would know what was available and how to get around. They would need to reprovision so finding the little grocery store was important. It would be good to get a five-gallon jerrycan filled with gas and another filled with potable water. Thompson left the jugs in his pirogue, pending finding a place to get them filled. Ice would be good too, but given the time it would take to get back to the houseboat, it would melt so that was off their list.

It only took an hour to walk the streets and locate the places they would need to revisit after lunch. Back at the boat basin they checked out a Refuge kiosk. It had some information on the thirteen islands managed by the U.S. Fish and Wildlife Service, noting that one of the islands, Seahorse Key, has a historic 1850s lighthouse and research outpost for the University of Florida. Part of the refuge was a wilderness area, off limits to motorized boats, and most of the islands had restricted public access. It was interesting to Nelson to compare the refuge to NPS administration. He saw that it was part of several refuges on the north Florida coast that were headquartered in St. Marks, a hundred miles north on Apalachee Bay.

After checking out the map, Thompson was growing impatient with Nelson's reading all the information on the sign boards. He asked, "You 'bout ready for lunch or you going to read all day?" Clearly it was time to go. Nelson grabbed leaflets on the refuge and agreed, "Yep, let's go. Something smells good!" It was the greasy exhaust wafting in the wind from the fryers at several restaurants.

As Thompson walked ahead, Nelson noticed a slight limp to the old man's gait. It was not really prominent, but showed an unequal footing. Nelson asked if Thompson was okay with all the walking. The answer was a scowling gaze back. He realized that subject wasn't open to discussion.

At the restaurant, all eyes turned to the two men as they entered. They were out-of-the-ordinary clientele that usually consisted of fishermen, tourists, and a few locals. Seated by a window they could see the houseboat safe at anchor off Atsena Otie Key. Boats transited in front of the restaurant and the fishing pier dock was busy with activity by sightseers and bridge fishermen.

Lunch was good. Having a meal prepared and served was rare for Thompson. After a week of Thompson's cooking canned and dry goods, it was a treat for Nelson. Fried mullet and fried flounder, with French fries, and fried okra. It was all too southern and all too much. Both wanted something fresh, like a salad or vegetables, but were seduced by the smell of the hot grease. They knew they were going to pay the price of this heavy lunch when they had to tote their purchases back to the boat.

Before running their errands, they decided to sit on a bench for a spell to let their bellies settle. It was still up in the air about how they both would get back to the houseboat with all of the supplies they bought.

Nelson's phone rang. The screen showed a number in area code 404 that he didn't recognize. He thought it might be the NPS Regional Office in Atlanta, but then it was a Sunday. He answered it, even while thinking it was probably spam.

"Hello, this is Bob Nelson. Who's calling?"

"Hello Ranger Nelson. I'm Ashley Clark-Greene. You may not remember me, but me and my husband Cameron were rescued from a disaster on an island last year when we were on our honeymoon."

"Oh yes, indeed! I remember you! How are you doing? And how are the men who were injured. We don't get many crocodile attacks."

"Oh, they are fine, but we're still angry with them. Chad has had a couple surgeries to repair his hand and Bill has a scar from the crocodile that he shows to everyone he meets. My husband and I are OK, too, thanks to the old gentleman on the houseboat. If he hadn't been there, things would not have worked out. And, of course, with the help of the Park rangers, it turned out OK.

"I was told by Ranger Smith you could put me in touch with the houseboat owner, Mr. Thompson."

"Yes, I can. He's right here. Would you like to speak to him? Let me get him on the phone."

He put his phone on mute and asked Thompson, "It's the young girl you saved at Pavilion Key last year, the couple that the pranksters messed with. Want to talk to her?"

Thompson nodded OK. When Nelson took it off mute and gave him the phone, he said "Hello, Hello, Hello? I'm sorry I can't hear you," handing the phone back to Nelson.

Nelson told Ashley, "Wait a minute and let me turn up the volume and put you on speaker."

Handing the phone back to Thompson, Ashley asked, "Mr. Thompson, can you hear me now?"

He replied, "Yes. What can I do for you?"

"You saved us from a very bad outcome last year when we were camping on our honeymoon. I told you then we would be forever grateful. I saw you were attacked by illegal fishermen a couple months ago. When your houseboat was shown on TV, I knew it was you. I prayed you were alright."

"Yes ma'am, I'm fine. I hope you are OK. That was a bad thing your friends pulled on y'all."

"Yes, it's all worked out. But I wanted to let you know we have patched things up with the stupid friends who caused the trouble. Well, almost. They still have more groveling to do before we trust them again. But I'm calling to let you know we put together money to cover the cost of your new outboard motor. We paid your bill at the boatyard in Marathon. The manager said you were going to return the motor if you couldn't pay back the person who paid the bill."

Almost crying, she pleaded, "Please don't return the motor. We want to pay for it. And we made the guys who harassed us contribute most of the money. You shouldn't have to spend your money to fix something that wasn't your fault. Please. Please, accept the donation."

Thompson said, "Well…. That's mighty nice of you. You know, I pay my own bills, and don't like to be wanting charity."

"Please, Mr. Thompson, take our gift of appreciation. And take the contribution from our friends as their atonement for their stupid practical joke. You are our hero and giving you a new motor is the least we can do in gratitude." Firming up her voice, "I will not accept no for an answer!"

Thompson was moved and quiet for a moment before saying. "Well…if you won't take no for an answer, then I suppose I will just have to say yes. Thank you. Maybe I can say thanks in person one day."

"Oh, you have made me sooo happy! We have been worried that you would return the motor."

"Thank you, young lady, and thank your husband and friends. God bless you. Goodbye." He handed the phone back to Nelson. She was still on the line.

Turning off the speaker, "Ashley, this is Ranger Nelson. What you just did was wonderful. His new motor is working out well. He's moved up to around Cedar Key in North Florida and your motor made it easier for him to get here. Thank you, again. Bye now."

Thompson said, "Now don't that just beat all and restore faith in this younger generation. Makes me a little sad that the world we're leaving them is in such a mess."

Nelson nodded his head in agreement. "There are a lot of good people out there. I just hope they outnumber the bad ones. That was nice and kudos to you for accepting their generosity."

Not much for sentimentality, Thompson barked, "OK, enough of this. We have things to do. Let's get on with it."

They purchased some groceries and struggled with the two jerry cans. Carrying 80 pounds of liquids for several blocks back to the boat basin was more of a work out than Nelson wanted. Thompson had the bags of groceries. In the store, he was treated well by the cashier but customers kept looking him up and down. Back at the dock, Nelson suggested Thompson take the groceries back to the boat in the pirogue. He would try to hitch a ride with another boater and bring the jerry cans. "Good idea. I'll wait for you on the boat. Hope you find one soon."

Nelson watched the old man paddle back to the boat, assuming that he made it. He didn't see any other boaters in the basin, so he went to the launch ramp to see if someone was putting in that he might befriend. Everyone seemed to be taking their boats out after a day out fishing.

He was starting to get worried that he couldn't make it out to *Épave*. He thought he might have to wait until morning when the fishermen were launching. He figured he could find a room somewhere in town, but how would he let Thompson know where he was since the old salt didn't have a phone.

Then, as luck would have it, a Refuge employee was launching to go out to Atsena Otie Key to check that the island was secure for the night. Nelson introduced himself and asked for a lift. After thinking about regulations about transporting civilians, the refuge worker, Ira, decided it would be okay to take a fellow federal employee out.

"Thanks! I really appreciate the ride. I don't know if I could endure the no-see-ums much longer!"

"They are brutal. We must be the capital of bugs!"

Nelson disagreed. "Have you ever been to Flamingo? Or the Shark River in the Everglades? There's no place buggier than where I work."

"Wow! I can't even imagine a place that's worse than here," respecting the somewhat older Ranger's experience.

Nelson said, "It's not really a competition. It's like cold – it's not a number on the thermometer. When it gets to a certain point, you are cold and it doesn't matter what the thermometer reads. Either you have tolerable insects or intolerable insects!"

On the way out to the boat, the refuge worker told him a little bit about the refuges along the north Florida coast and bragged about how there was 200 miles of coastal marsh in the Big Bend in conservation management by several agencies, state and federal. It had been a tremendous accomplishment that could never be repeated, partly because there wasn't that much land to buy, but mostly because political winds had shifted to be under an anti-environment majority in government. Even money already set aside for land purchases was being withheld or used for spurious unrelated purposes. The two men had a lot in common, although they worked under different agencies but still within the same Department of Interior. To Nelson the refuge work seemed a little more hands-on with nature and less in policing the public.

Back at the boat, Nelson offloaded the gas and water cans. The Refuge officer left, traveled a few yards, beached his skiff and began surveying Atsena Otie for stragglers who might not leave the island at sunset.

"Hey Thompson, let's fire up the grill. I bought a steak at the grocery."

"Yeah I found it. I'm still full from lunch! Let's do it tomorrow. I can find a place in the small electric cooler to keep it."

"No argument from me! I will wrestle with all that grease all night long. It sure was good, but I can't eat like that often."

"I'll just make some noodles and onions." Thompson's diet was as austere as his whole lifestyle.

They stayed up late, settling their stomachs with coffee. While Thompson read, Nelson searched the Internet for information about the nearby communities, marine facilities, and local demographics. He came upon a history of Rosewood.

Nearly a hundred years ago, a nearby town was obliterated in a violent racial attack. He read that in 1923 a black settlement attached to a sawmill was a thriving community until a white woman lied about an affair gone wrong claiming she had been assaulted and raped by a black man. The Ku Klux Klan was entrenched in the area and vigilantes from the nearby area came to seek justice, killing many inhabitants and burning Rosewood to the ground. Many black residents were killed and more than a couple hundred black people fled for their lives, never to return. Rosewood now was a ghost town.

Just like the persistent feelings of victimization that permeated Everglades City over the drug busts 40 years ago, the echoes of guilt, rationalization, and racial prejudice still rippled in the descendants of the perpetrators of the Rosewood conflagration. Racial prejudice always simmered under the surface, but political rhetoric of recent political campaigns seemed to open the lid and give permission for open discrimination. Nelson noted that what was once politically-correct speech had been replaced with vulgar language.

Nelson was bothered about what Thompson might face as a lone hermit outsider. Naively, he thought he should warn Thompson of the potential problem.

"Thompson, can I talk to you about something serious?"

"What's on your mind, Ranger?"

"I've been looking into the culture and history of this area. It really is a great natural landscape that I'm sure you will fit into very well, but I'm concerned about the human aspect. From what I've found on the Internet, this community has a deep stain of racism. The counties in this area have a very low black population and are very segregated. There's a lot of poverty and a lack of opportunity for folks. I just want for you to be careful, as an outsider."

"Nelson, you might not have noticed but I've been black all of my life. Racism – I've seen it. I've lived it. I know what you are talking about, but I have survived in good times and bad by watching my back and minding my own business. So, you don't have to tell me about what I know firsthand."

Nelson felt humbled that he thought his few minutes of research could be informative to someone who had a long life's experience. Being white, he could have sympathy and empathy but never truly understand without having had the same experiences. He realized that the legacy of enslavement is lasting and some folks are still fighting the Civil War.

Trying to back out of the uncomfortable conversation, "I just wanted to give you a head's up on the community. And suggest that some other places along this coast might be more accommodating, both in political persuasion and, especially, facilities for you to get supplies."

Thompson said, "I didn't know any specifics, but I had a feeling that I might not be welcome by everyone in this port. It was hard to avoid seeing all the Confederate flags and all the vulgar bumper stickers. Then there's the American flags on pick-ups, not being displayed as the flag for love, but as a symbol of hate. But, I did see a few of those rainbow flags and a few peace symbols on the art galleries and bed and breakfast places, even one BLM sign, so there are some different people living here. It must be hard for them."

"I do plan on looking around this coast to see if there is a better fit, especially for a better place to get fuel and water at a dock. I won't have you around to tote my water forever." He smiled and was chagrined that Nelson was worried about him.

"Don't get me wrong, I'm sure there are a lot of good people here in Cedar Key, residents and visitors. There's just a few…"

Thompson interrupted him, "Nelson, enough of this. I'm a grown man and will work it out. Always have, always will." And that was the end of the awkward conversation.

Nelson was happy that the uncomfortable topic was over. Now he brought up his leaving to get back to Flamingo. "You know, I've got to get back to work in a few days and I have no idea how I'll get back to south Florida. I didn't see any taxi cabs in town, or rental cars, or even a bus station.

"I'm going to call the office to see if I can extend my leave a few days to figure out how to get back. I know this was your intended destination, but wonder if you might take me down to Yankeetown to see if it is an easier place for me to catch a ride to connect with transportation. From what I see in the books, there are marinas with docks there and a Coast Guard station. It's got to be easier to navigate the channel if the Coast Guard works out of there."

"Well...that's not a problem. I was thinking the same thing. I would need to check it out sooner or later as I learn this coast. It will be a little easier with the GPS you gave me and that *Waterway Guide* book."

"Good. I'm going to hit the sack. It's been a long day for me. You can stay up and read, but I'm going to bed."

TWENTY

Cedar Key was interesting and Nelson and Thompson were glad they had found what they needed there. Thompson now had an idea of what the facilities were and how difficult it would be to get to town. The islands looked intriguing, but the town was too overrun with tourists and too many locals stared at him with a "stink eye."

Motoring out the way they came in, Nelson set a course for the entrance marker to the Withlacoochee River channel. It was about 20 miles southeast to Yankeetown. The town is only a few miles off US Highway 98 and a few miles up the Withlacoochee River from the Gulf.

Thompson studied his new GPS and noticed an area that looked promising for him to spend some time. The spot was off to the southeast, in between Cedar Key and Yankeetown, where the Waccasassa River flowed into the Waccasassa Bay. It looked like a wild coast, remote, with shallow waters and protected by the surrounding state park. He made a mental note that he would need to add it to his list of places to explore after Nelson departed.

The channel into the Withlacoochee River was well marked. Nelson was at the helm, being careful to stay in the middle. A couple of boats passed on their way out to fish, followed by a U.S. Coast Guard patrol boat with four Coasties on board. They waved as they sped by. The houseboat rocked as the boat's wake overtook them.

Looking back, he saw the Coast Guard inflatable make a sharp U-turn and race back toward them. He yelled to Thompson, "Hey, looks like we are going to be stopped by the Coast Guard. Prepare to be boarded!" Nelson stopped the motor and took it out of gear. Thompson came out of the camper and looked to the stern to see the Coast Guard boat getting closer. One of the Coasties was on their bow waving.

As they pulled up, the Coast Guardsman was smiling, "I bet you don't remember me!" reaching to catch the side of the houseboat. Another man was at the stern ready with a line.

"I was with the crew that responded to the incidents in the Everglades! I recognized your houseboat. I figured it had to be you – there couldn't be another boat like yours. I transferred up to Yankeetown a couple months ago."

Thompson was relieved that this was a friendly call, not an inspection. Nelson backed down the ladder to the deck to meet the Coastie.

"Hey, you were down in the Everglades too, with the Park. I didn't recognize you out of uniform," extending his hand to shake Nelson's.

Nelson replied, "Good to see you again Lt. Shaffer. I am on leave, helping Mr. Thompson move his boat up this way. Actually, he's teaching me how to live on a houseboat. It's been a great trip up the coast and this looks like an interesting area."

"It's sure different from Florida Bay and the Keys. I like it. There are a lot fewer people."

Thompson was a man of few words, but commented, "I've got a lot to learn about the waters around here. I need to find a peaceful place to hang out and some place to get supplies when I need them. We're heading down to Yankeetown to check it out."

Lt. Shaffer said, "It's a small fishing community, a pretty friendly place with more fishermen than tourists. A hundred years ago wealthy Yankees came here to fish. Maybe that's how the place got its name, I don't know. They even built a fishing lodge on the river, but it burned down and was rebuilt 20 years ago. You need to check it out."

"We will. Maybe we can catch up when you get back from your patrol."

With that, the Coasties were off and the houseboat resumed course. "Isn't it a small world? Who would have ever expected to run into somebody who was from Marathon way up here?"

Nelson agreed. "Yep, guess you've got a recognizable boat that makes quite a memorable impression."

"So much for my anonymity."

Later in the day, at a marina dock, Lt. Shaffer came by. "Can I come aboard?"

Thompson reprised his standard gruff response, "Not without a warrant!" Then he grinned. Nelson recognized that Thompson's attitude had lightened up a lot as a result of all the social interaction of having him aboard and meeting people on the long cruise up the west coast.

They all sat enjoying a six pack that Shaffer brought, recalling the events of the Everglades. Shaffer shared what he knew about this part of the coast. He was new on the scene, but after two months of daily patrols and may-day calls, he was getting his bearings.

"You know, this Big Bend area is really wild, without the traffic of the Keys. It's a different kind of boating. Nearshore fishing brings out a lot of day-users. The commercial crabbers operate at all hours and go further out than I would expect. If they are stone crabbing, they have to go out to rock bottom and that's deeper."

Nelson said, "Bet you are glad not to have the emergency calls about refugee boats."

"Yes sir. You can bet on that. It was very stressful and sad. So many Cubans and Haitians risk their lives and untold numbers never make it. All that risk only to be interdicted and, most often, returned."

Nelson said, "That's what drove me out of Dry Tortugas. But when I got to Everglades there were a lot more problems, just a different kind of problem. The gun battle with the poachers really set me to thinking about my career."

"Now, that's just the beer talking. You Park guys got it good. There's got to be something good happening between the emergencies. For us, every mission is a response to a problem."

Thompson said, "You two going to complain who has it worse? Shame on you. Just do your jobs! You got another beer or do I have to drink mine?"

Shaffer and Nelson were duly chastised on the shop talk and got back to talking about the Big Bend. Thompson listened intently.

"You know there's a lot of wildlife areas along this coast and a lot of different agencies involved in managing it. There aren't any national parks, but there are a few federal wildlife refuges. You ought to consider getting on with them. Except for the bugs, snakes, Bubba-brained yahoos, gators, unbearable heat and brutal cold, oh, and hurricanes, this place is a paradise!"

Nelson wise-cracked, "Sounds perfect! Everything a Florida Man could ever ask for!"

"I've got to go walk back to the station. The guys will wonder where I got off to. Y'all should stop by before you head out again. I'll show you around. You need anything while you are here? Ride to the grocery store?"

Nelson said, "As a matter of fact, I could use a ride back to someplace where I can catch a bus or rent a car to get back to Homestead. I don't have but a few more days of leave and I haven't figured out how to get back home."

"I can give you a lift. Just figure out where you need to go. Dunnellon or Crystal River are the biggest nearby towns, but there's always Ocala or Gainesville. Be happy to take you!"

"Thanks, I'll look on-line and give you a call later, if I can work out a plan." Nelson's first thought was "Gainesville, the home of the infamous Florida Gators? No self-respecting Georgia Bull Dog would ever want to go to that swamp!"

Nelson found several options. A bus seemed the most practical. From Ocala to Homestead was cheap, but 10 hours, twice as long as a car ride.

He called Shaffer and set a time to go to Ocala the next day, spend the night in a hotel and catch the bus the following morning. One of his ranger friends would pick him up in Homestead and take him back to Flamingo. After buying the tickets and making hotel reservations on-line, he was all set. This would be a quick exit with no time for drawn out goodbyes. Nelson informed Thompson about the plan.

Thompson was quiet and then expressed his appreciation. "Nelson. I didn't think I needed anybody to help me get up here, but I was wrong. You really helped. Don't think I would have made it so easily without you and those modern gizmos. Thank you." He reached to shake his hand.

"Let's go out to dinner for a farewell supper." They chose the Izaak Walton Lodge. They were impressed with all the pictures of the old days in Florida hanging on the lodge walls. The photos included lots of fish, fly fishermen, and trophy tarpons. "This place must have really been something a hundred years ago. Even today the town is a pretty remote outpost on a wilderness coast."

The waitress was very engaging. She worked at the Lodge to fill the gaps in her time and income. The gig was part-time. Her main job was at the hospital as an admitting nurse. She'd moved down as a traveling nurse and got planted in the Florida sands which offered more than her native Cleveland. She'd decided to stay. Nelson thought her a "comely lass" and they seemed to have a connection. After the waitress left to get their drinks, Thompson poked Nelson saying, "That gal had her eye on you. Why didn't you ask for her number?"

"I'm married to the National Park Service!" Nelson poked back. "She is nice. Haven't been in the dating scene since my wife passed."

The next day, farewell was bittersweet – and fast. Nelson loaded his gear into Shaffer's truck and they were on their way. Thompson watched as they drove away and muttered a lie to himself, "Finally I can get back to some privacy. It's good to be on my own again."

Nelson was preoccupied with worry about Thompson's immediate future to be much of a conversationalist with Shaffer.

He was thinking, "How would Thompson cast off the dock without help. Was he familiar enough with the GPS plotter? Where would he go? Would he run aground?" It was as if he was leaving his kid at college to be on his own for the first time. He was bemused that he was worried about someone who was so resourceful and experienced at living alone for a such long time.

Back at Flamingo, Nelson had a good bit of work stacked up on his desk. Reports for the Park, reports for the Regional Office, phone calls from the federal attorney in Key West, and setting work schedules were all waiting for his attention. All of the paperwork that built up when he took time off was incentive not to go away for so long. It had only been about two weeks and he had at least two weeks of backlog work to do. He knew he wouldn't be enjoying any Ten Thousand Islands patrols for a while.

One particularly onerous task was responding to a Congressional inquiry regarding the alligator attack on the Afghan hound. The couple had filed a complaint with their U.S. senator.

Ranger Smith and Fuentes wanted to hear all about Nelson's adventure with the houseboat hermit. During every coffee break, he'd recall some part of the trip and share a few photos on his iPhone. It was good to reminisce about the recent journey up the coast. His cohorts were enthralled to hear the stories and incredulous that the hermit could have been so hospitable. Nelson held close Thompson's secret life and did not reveal anything personal to his coworkers.

Fuentes said, "That's amazing! I'm glad you had a good time helping him. What do you think he will do now?"

"If I know him, he will find his way, explore the area and find a place somewhere that suits him. He will be expert at cruising that coast just like he knows ours. I just hope he doesn't run afoul of the various agencies that manage the area or the creepy rednecks. He will be fine."

Nelson wasn't completely confident. As far as he knew Thompson would be alone with Lt. Shaffer being the only person he knew. He wished he had bought Thompson a cell phone so he could check up on him.

"So enough about my adventures. What's been going on here while I've been gone?"

Fuentes lamented, "The usual stuff with the excitement of a drug bust during a traffic stop and a domestic dispute in the campground that had to be referred to Homestead. Other than that, it has been pretty quiet."

"Good. Now I've got a lot of catching up to do. That's the price we pay for taking time off!"

Nelson had a lot to do but he took time to look on the Internet for information about the northern Gulf area. He was curious about where Thompson might be but he had no way to check on him. He could call Lt. Shaffer, but that seemed like meddling. He would just look at the chart and watch the weather forecast. If he saw that severe weather was predicted, he might call Shaffer to ask for him to keep an eye out for the houseboat.

Getting back to the paperwork, Nelson was bound to his desk for days. Every time he thought he was making progress some new urgent request for data would appear. He felt he would never catch up.

Finally, he was free enough to schedule himself a patrol to the western boundary. What a relief it was to be back on a patrol boat, screaming across Whitewater Bay out to Shark River. As usual, there were fishermen out and Nelson greeted a few kayakers on the canoe trail. Time alone among the mangroves reinvigorated his enthusiasm.

Nelson approached a trawler anchored at Little Shark River to review the regulations for boats transiting the Park. What should have been a routine check turned out to provoke a heated, belligerent response from the crew. "What do you mean, I have to pass a quiz on boating in the Everglades? I am on the water. I have not stepped foot in your park. You can't expect me to pay your damn entrance fee!"

"What an unpleasant, irritable couple," he thought. Everything Nelson said was met with an argument. He did not want to issue any citation and was relieved when they were leaving in a huff. That was just fine; he wanted nothing more to do with such unreasonable people. They pulled anchor and gave him a rude hand gesture salute as they were leaving.

He moved on to make a few more checks of the campsites at Pavilion Key and Lostman's. On his way back, he was entering Whitewater Bay looking forward to enjoying a leisurely ride to Flamingo when the VHF radio hailed on channel 16. "Any boat in the vicinity of Cape Sable, this is the *M/V My Way*. Over."

Nelson responded, "To the vessel hailing on 16, this is the National Park Service. Please switch and answer channel 68."

"*My Way* to 68," was the response, followed in a minute by, "This is the motor vessel *My Way* on 68."

"This is NPS on 68. *My Way*, please respond. Over."

"We are on a trawler and our engine has overheated. We need a tow or a mechanic. How long will it take you to get here to tow us? We want to go to Marathon."

"*My Way*, this is NPS Ranger Nelson. Can you restate the nature of your emergency?" Nelson was certain this was the couple who had just left the anchorage at Little Shark River. He hadn't seen the name of the boat on the stern when he first met them. But, the skipper's attitude over the radio confirmed it was the same trawler.

The skipper responded with information about how many persons were on board, that there was no medical emergency, and that they were not taking on water, just having engine trouble. They were anchored in choppy seas, but not in immediate danger.

"*My Way*, this is Ranger Nelson. I have alerted the U.S. Coast Guard in Marathon to make them aware of your situation. Stand by for a communication from them on Channel 16 or 22. I can also alert a towing company out of Flamingo if you would like, but the National Park Service cannot take your vessel under tow."

The response was a stream of expletives, complaining about how they pay taxes and expect, no, demand government assistance. Still on VHF 68, Ranger Nelson responded politely, "M/V *My Way*, can you provide the latitude and longitude for your position? Please provide details on your vessel. I am in Whitewater Bay."

My Way responded with their position and stated, "I am on a 45-foot Marine Trader Yacht, white hull, 1995."

Nelson asked. "What is your power and displacement?"

After receiving the boat's details, Nelson radioed back, "My boat is not capable of towing your vessel. I am about an hour and a half away from your position. Have you heard from the U.S. Coast Guard?"

"No, damn it! I've been on the radio with you – and that's been useless. That's to be expected from the National Parks."

Nelson suggested, "You might monitor channel 16. I have heard the Coast Guard trying to hail you. I am switching back to Channel 16." Nelson was happy to turn this over to the U.S. Coast Guard. He legitimately could pass this on. His boat was too small and there was no emergency. Even if he could help, a tow to Marathon across Florida Bay was out of the question.

Nelson enjoyed listening in on the exchange with the U.S. Coast Guard. The *My Way* skipper was no more polite to the Coast Guard than he had been with him. He admired the USCG radio operator for keeping his temper. Nelson heard the Guardsman tell *My Way*'s skipper that the USCG would be happy to pass along the boat's location and information to a commercial tow. Then, the radio operator broadcast an announcement:

"Pon pon, Pon pon. This is United States Coast Guard, Key West District. U.S. Coast Guard Marathon has received a report of a disabled 45-foot motor yacht located 2 miles south of East Cape Sable requesting assistance. All vessels are asked to keep a sharp look out and render assistance if possible. Report all sightings to U.S. Coast Guard on channel 16. Out."

The Coast Guard radio officer communicated back to the *My Way*. "We have broadcast a general announcement on channel 16 reporting your position and request for assistance. Would you like us to refer you to Sea Tow or TowBoat US for a commercial tow?"

My Way responded. "Hell no! That will cost a fortune! We will wait here for assistance."

"This is U.S. Coast Guard Marathon, *My Way*. We will stand by on channel 16 and 22. Please keep us advised of any change in your situation. Skipper, can we be of further assistance?"

As Nelson docked at the Park Service basin, he heard a call from *My Way* on channel 16. It was a woman and she was frantic.

"This is the *My Way* boat. My husband has hurt himself trying to tow our boat with the dinghy. I can't see him over the side, but I heard him yell for help. Please help!"

USCG responded first, "This is U.S. Coast Guard Marathon, on channel 16. Please restate the nature of your emergency."

The woman was panicked, "My husband is hurt and missing overboard. Please hurry!"

"This is U.S. Coast Guard Marathon, ma'am, please stay calm. Was your husband wearing a PFD? What is your location?"

"We are in the same place that we were when we called you a couple hours ago requesting help. You didn't come, so he tried to tow our yacht with the dinghy. He's gone! Help!"

Nelson jumped on 16. "This is Everglades National Park Flamingo Ranger Station. We will respond to the scene. Estimated ETA 45 minutes. Please confirm."

The woman barked, "Can't you get here any quicker than that?"

"This is U.S. Coast Guard Marathon. Message received. Confirm ETA 45 minutes. We will begin preparation for a helicopter search. We are about out of light. Stand by on channel 16 for an update. USCG Marathon out."

Nelson and Fuentes boarded the park patrol boat moored on the saltwater side of the water control structure on the Buttonwood Canal. They raced out through the Flamingo channel, with the blue light on. Fuentes said, "We are running out of light. The sun has set and there won't be much light left when we get there."

Arriving at the scene, they saw a body hanging on the side of an inflatable dinghy. The engine was running and out of gear. Approaching slowly, they both observed movement. A head turned and yelled, "Get me out of here!"

Nelson and Fuentes struggled to pull the heavy man up from the water and onto the dinghy. He clumsily rolled over glaring at his rescuers, "I've been in the water two hours waiting! I yelled for help, but I guess my wife didn't hear me, so I gave up. I couldn't get back in the dinghy over these damn rubber tubes."

Nelson thought, "To be fair, it is nearly impossible to climb into an inflatable from the side, but pretty easy from the stern, using the motor as a ladder. He could have killed the engine and saved himself."

Ranger Fuentes called the Coast Guard to provide an update on the rescue. "We have retrieved the victim. He is in good condition with no obvious trauma. Says he is fine. Will update after we check further."

U.S. Coast Guard Marathon responded, "We will stand by. Please advise if extraction is necessary. We're delaying launch for a few minutes while you assess and report back."

The rangers took the skipper to the stern of the boat and helped him get up to the deck. His wife was happy that he was found alive and was being helped into the boat, but perplexed about where the ranger found him.

"Ma'am, he was at the bow of your boat, hanging onto the dinghy. We pulled him out of the water. Couldn't you see him from the bow?"

"No. When I looked out the front window I didn't see him or the dinghy. I only heard him scream for help. The generator that runs the air conditioner is so loud I only heard him call for help once and he didn't answer when I called out for him from here. So I called on the radio for help. You could have been quicker! Harold, are you OK?"

"Karen, I'm wet and tired. Thank you for calling for help."

Fuentes pulled the first aid kit from the patrol boat to take his blood pressure and temperature, while Nelson asked more about his condition. Harold strongly asserted that he was fine and required no assistance. His vitals were within a normal range, so Fuentes again confirmed with him that he did not require any medical attention.

"Young lady, I told you I was fine! Weren't you listening the first three times I told you?"

Ranger Nelson asserted, "Sir, before we leave we need to confirm you are OK and do not request medical attention. We need to inform the Coast Guard. They are standing by with a helicopter to airlift you to a hospital if necessary."

"Shit, I don't need a hospital. I need a tow to Marathon! You can tell them that!"

Nelson affirmed, "Yes sir. We will be happy to pass that along. We are going to depart. Can we help retrieve your dinghy?"

"I'll leave it in the water, just be sure it's tied up. I guess I should thank you, but I need a tow."

Nelson nodded, "Yes sir, I will pass that along to the Coast Guard as well. Good night and stay safe!"

As they departed, Ranger Fuentes couldn't keep herself from sarcastically chirping, "You're welcome!"

The rangers raced back to Flamingo in the dark, following closely the "bread crumbs" they had dropped on the chartplotter on the way to the scene. "That was interesting. What a joyful couple!"

"Yep, another one for the books. I'm glad it turned out OK. But, wow, how ungrateful for the assistance. By the way, you did great. Thanks for coming along!"

"Thanks for taking me. I don't think they know what they are doing and the boat looks like an old junker. I don't think the Coast Guard has seen the last of them, but I hope we have!"

What had started out as a great day to get back to normal ended up as a long day with a neo-Florida Man and his wife.

TWENTY-ONE

Thompson was getting more comfortable in his new domain. He'd learned how to use the GPS plotter to get around in the shallow waters and liked having information about his boat speed and the distances he traveled. With the GPS showing tracks of where he had been, he could retrace his route with a degree of confidence.

In his ramblings around for the past few months he had visited the main ports along the coast. The old guide book was helpful but out of date. He learned to not depend on it except for general information. The book also contained some narrative about water-related activities along the coast: scalloping, fishing, crabbing, collecting oysters, and clam farming. The *Waterway Guide* was more up to date but the information was sparse about this little-visited part of Florida.

Thompson learned to recognize the pattern of the crab boats and daily recreational fishing boats. At night, he could see lights on boats traveling back and forth across the Gulf between north Florida and the peninsula.

Thompson was settling in well, staying at an anchorage for a week, exploring and fishing. And the fishing was good. He rarely needed to open a can of tuna or Spam. The houseboat was well stocked with dry goods like rice, noodles, and oatmeal. Everything was working on the boat. Solar chargers and his spare battery kept his small refrigerator powered. If he didn't collect rainwater in a bucket, he tapped his jerrycan supply.

The most northerly port he explored was Steinhatchee. There was a marina there that was easy to dock at. The grocery was a little far to walk, but not unreasonable. The town was nearly as quiet as Everglades City and the people were mostly friendly. It even had an excellent restaurant. The river flowed a little fast, so he learned to watch the tide to time his arrival and departure and call for docking help on the VHF radio Nelson left for him. Thompson liked the technology and reluctantly accepted its utility. Now he was dependent on the convenience of the plotter and the ability to easily find the marine weather forecast.

When he stopped at the ports to resupply, he was able to supplement his library with used books. He traded what he had read for new ones. In addition to his Bible, he was keen to read anything and everything.

So far, he had a couple of favorite anchorages, places where he was rarely bothered by the fishermen and crabbers. One was the Pepperfish Keys, a couple of islands with some sandy beach and a little higher elevation supporting an oak hammock. While exploring the Big Bend, he discovered that islands like Pepperfish Keys were rare in the area. They were different from the low shrubby pine islands surrounded by muddy salt marsh that he saw more frequently. On Pepperfish, he could land his pirogue on the beach and scavenge the shore for things he might use like abandoned crab traps and floats so he could set his own blue crab traps. He found driftwood for his grill, fishing lures and bobbers and, sometimes, a bucket or boat cushion. The wrack line provided entertaining beach combing. Not far off the island, there was a deep-water hole that became his private anchorage. Surrounded by very shallow water, exposing flats at low tide, most of the time the wave action was light. Only high winds from the changing sea breeze pushed his houseboat around. Fishing was good in his hole during each turn of the tide.

He was as happy at some of these new places as he had been in the Everglades and Ten Thousand Islands. Yet, here there was no old farmstead to harvest like Cane Patch. When he was sure he was alone, he occasionally used his pistol to shoot a bird, feeling guilty each time, but enjoying grilled duck as a change from his regular seafood diet. He rationalized that his law breaking wasn't hurting the waterfowl population and it was his marksmanship practice.

Patrols never seemed to stop to check on him like he experienced in South Florida. Boats passing by often waved when they were nearby. It was quiet and friendly enough. The only time he thought he might be uncomfortable was during scallop season in the summer. At that time, the areas around Steinhatchee and Crystal River were crowded with boats, snorkeling for the shellfish. He had overheard when he was in town that there would be hundreds of small boats filled with people.

Sometimes he anchored at the mouth of the Suwannee River, in a cut between the main channel and West Pass, where he was in a mostly fresh to brackish marsh between two islands. Boat wakes rocked his houseboat during the day, but at night it was dead calm, sheltered in all directions from the weather. It was a good place.

On one of his stays at this anchorage, a Florida Fish and Wildlife officer who was headed down the main channel slowed and turned toward him. This would be the first time any law enforcement had shown any interest in his houseboat since he left the Everglades. He was anticipating being hassled, but thought he would be all right because he had all his equipment and lifetime senior fishing license that Nelson had arranged.

The skiff pulled alongside. "Hello! How are you doing today?" It was a young officer, decked out in his uniform and safety vest. He handed a line to Thompson who met him on deck.

"What can I do for you Sonny?"

"I just stopped to see if you were OK. I hadn't noticed you here before. Staying for a while?"

"Yes sir. I have been here a couple days and plan to be here a couple more."

"Fine, it's a nice spot. I've seen cruising boats stop here to avoid heavy weather when they are crossing from Carrabelle on their way to Clearwater. You catching any fish?"

Thompson relaxed with the friendly tone of the young man. "Not much here, a couple bites. But I haven't tried much. The fishing is better out there," as he motioned towards the Gulf.

"Yes sir. A lot of folks come here to fish. Well, just checking on you. I've got to run out to check fishing licenses. You have a good day."

It was a courteous interaction and no problem. Thompson couldn't quite figure why the officer was so polite since he didn't ask for a fishing license or do any safety inspection. He was used to being inspected when marine law enforcement stopped by for a chat. He chided himself for being overly suspicious.

Over the months of exploring, he pondered his options for getting settled in the area. He considered what place might be good to set up a post office box and he was running low on cash.

He'd tapped into the stash he had hidden in an old paint can in his shed. Counting his funds, he had about $1,100 left. That was plenty to sustain him for a few months or more, yet, at some point, he would need to straighten out his banking. He decided it was now time, but he had no idea about how to find a bank. If Nelson was here, he could use his phone to find one. He reckoned he would need to go to a town where maybe the library could help him. He only needed to visit every couple of months, so it didn't matter what town the bank was in, but it needed to be in a place where he could tie-up long enough to get his mail and cash a check.

Thompson decided to visit Suwannee, where his main mission would be to find a bank. Moving up the Suwannee River, he found a marina dock. The list in the *Waterway Guide* gave directions on how to get there. When he arrived, he called on his VHF radio for help docking. He could see docking was going to be tricky because the marina was at the end of a pretty narrow canal. He could get in but, with a clumsy boat, it would be awkward to turn around. He hoped maybe, with help, he could manage.

He did manage to dock successfully, but it was difficult. After asking the dockhand if he could stay a little while, Thompson headed to the town library. The marina was OK with him being there as long as he didn't tie up at the fuel dock.

The volunteer at the library welcomed him. "I don't recall seeing you in here before. What can I help you with?" The small building was stuffed with books on shelves and narrow aisles.

Thompson took off his cap, and said, "I'm trying to find a bank."

"Oh, the town has an ATM at the Zippy Mart. Would that help?"

"No ma'am. I need to find a real bank where I can set up an account."

The closest is up in Cross City, but it's a far piece from here. Most everyone I know uses the Cabbage Palm Bank up there. It's on U.S. 98."

Thompson was disappointed. "I'm on a boat and don't have a car, so I want something I can walk to. It doesn't have to be here, in this town. Any place from Cedar Key up to Steinhatchee would work. I don't know how to find one."

"You can look on the Internet," she suggested, directing him to one of two computers on a desk by a window.

"Sorry ma'am, but I don't know much about the Internet or computers. I'm not too up on electronics."

"No problem, let me help you. I can show you how to do a search." She began a lesson on how to use the Internet to search for information. She was kind and patient while showing him how to type in a topic in the search block and then scroll through the results.

"Let's see – there's no bank in Cedar Key, only a few ATMs but you already said that won't work. Let's try Yankeetown. Just put the pointer arrow here in this block and type in "BANK YANKEETOWN."

The results flashed up with several banks in Crystal River. The librarian said, "It looks like Crystal River has a few choices that are close to Kings Bay," as she tapped on the dots on the map.

"Crystal River might work. You know anything about that town?"

"Why yes, I do! I was born near there. As you can tell that was a long time ago! It was a quiet place when I was a child. There were only a few motels and restaurants. It was a place where people came to fish. Then it exploded with tourism when people discovered there were manatees in Kings Bay, especially during the winter. Development followed the tourism and more people settled around Kings Bay. The commercial fishermen left for other places or just quit and took whatever jobs they could find. I left with my late husband when we just couldn't stand all the construction, traffic, and ticky-tack businesses on the highway. It's so citified now."

"That doesn't sound quite what I'm looking for. Can we try Steinhatchee?"

"Sure, type it in here."

There was a bank in Steinhatchee and the map showed it was close enough to the dock Thompson had visited. It was located a little further than the grocery store. The map also showed a post office.

"This will be good." The librarian gave him a slip of paper and pencil to write down the phone number and address. He copied the information from the computer screen.

"Thank you. Much obliged!"

"I'm happy you found what you were looking for. Do you want to get a library card? I can sign you up!"

"No ma'am, thank you. I like reading but docking here is a little hard for me on my houseboat. I wish I could. Thanks."

After he filled up with gas and water, it was a fiasco leaving the marina, an episode Thompson wanted to never repeat again. Without the dockhand's help, it would have been a disaster. He was pretty sure that he wouldn't be welcomed back. If he ever stopped again, he would need to anchor in the river and paddle his pirogue to town. Once away from the dock and into the river proper, he decided to explore a little more before heading up to Steinhatchee to "put down roots."

Being in no particular hurry, over the next days, Thompson made his way to Waccasassa Bay. In his favorite anchorage, at night, he could see the glow of lights from Cedar Key in the north and Crystal River to the south. He wondered why people needed so much light; it spoiled the night stars.

This anchorage rated high on his list. It was very isolated. Channel markers led the way up to the Waccasassa River, but the GPS chart didn't show any boat ramps upstream. That accounted for there being little fishing boat traffic, except for the flats boats coming from Cedar Key or Yankeetown. The water was shallow, yet deep enough for his boat, except at very low tide. It was a place to fish and read in solitude. Birds were everywhere. The brown pelicans were diving to scoop fish while ospreys and eagles glided, performing their aerial ballet. Shorebirds scavenging exposed oyster bars fluttered back and forth in amazing synchronization. Gangs of gulls harassed any bird with a fish. Wading birds patrolled the edge of the marsh to stab fish. It was serene, especially in the placid fading warm glow of sunset.

Departing at sunrise after a couple of days of quiet, Thompson was greeted at the last channel marker by a U.S. Coast Guard patrol boat. He slowed to a stop to allow their inflatable to come alongside. Lt. Shaffer was on board.

"Howdy, Mr. Thompson! How's it going?"

"Just fine, and you?"

"Fine. Just another day in paradise. I've been looking for you for a while. The other day a state fish and wildlife officer said he spotted you up by Suwannee. Got a message for you from Ranger Nelson."

Thompson asked, "What now?" in an exasperated tone so as not to let on that he was curious.

"Nelson called to let me know he's coming up here for a job interview with the national wildlife refuge. He's considering transferring jobs to work at Lower Suwannee Refuge. Everglades has got him burned out."

Thompson joked, "Probably misses annoying me!"

"Yep, you and he are quite a pair for excitement. More than likely he needs a change of scenery."

As he cast off from the houseboat, Shaffer said, "I've got to go, we have a call. Where are you headed now?"

"Up to Steinhatchee. Got business to attend to. Probably be there a bit."

"Good. I'll let Nelson know! He will want to catch up." Then the boat raced off toward the horizon.

Getting to Steinhatchee was easy enough with the chartplotter and his previous experience coming up the river. He timed it to arrive at a slack tide and, using the VHF, called the marina for assistance docking. He asked if he could dock for a few days, paying the nominal fee for the space. Once settled at the dock, with his 110-extension cord plugged in and his water jerrycans filled, he walked into town.

Getting a post office box did not take much time. The postmaster was helpful in filling out change of address forms and even called the Everglades City post office to have any accumulated mail forwarded.

The bank was different. He couldn't just open an account. Although he now had a post office address, he had no street address and that was not pleasing to the representative.

He tried to explain, "I live on a boat. I moved up here months ago from Everglades City. My bank at Marco never had a problem with me having no address other than a PO box."

"Sorry sir, but we need a physical address for an account. I will see if the manager will make an exception. In the meantime, we can fill out the rest of the form."

He showed his identification, a nearly out-of-date passport, while she completed the form. "Next of kin?" she asked. She wouldn't accept his reply of "none".

Thompson paused. He had a daughter in a previous life, but he left her behind when she was an infant and he was declared dead. There was no telling where she was. "I guess put down Robert Nelson, Flamingo, Florida."

It was frustrating and he was losing patience with this unhelpful agent of the bank. He was sitting in front of her desk thinking, "Maybe this isn't going to work out. I might have to go to Crystal River, after all." He really didn't want to get involved with a bigger city so he persisted.

The representative asked, "What kind of account do you want. Checking or savings? The minimum deposit is $500." She was not expecting him to have that amount when he unrolled bills and gave her twenty-five 20s. She counted carefully.

"I get funds automatically deposited to my account each month and I need to cash U.S. government checks from time to time."

"Sir, you will have to set that up with whoever sends you money. I can't help you with that."

Just then, Mrs. Johnson entered the lobby. She was the lady who had given him a ride from the grocery store to the dock on one of his previous trips. She saw him at the desk and immediately came up to greet him like a long-lost friend. "Well, hello, my old friend. I see you've come back here. So good to see you. I hope my niece is taking good care of you!"

The desk clerk was taken aback that her aunt knew this old black guy and was being nice to him. She'd not known her to be so, well, liberal.

"Yes. Good to see you too. I'm trying to set up an account."

The niece's attitude changed in the presence of her aunt and she became more pleasant and helpful. "Sir, I'm sure we can help you with all of your needs," and began showing him options for checks, debit cards, and even helped him fill out a credit card application.

Mrs. Johnson went over to the counter turning back to say "I look forward to seeing you again. I'm happy to carry you to the grocery or wherever." Neither Mrs. Johnson or Thompson knew each other's names, but no matter, they were friends and all the people at the bank saw that.

To complete his banking, he needed to contact the bank in Marco to arrange transfer of his funds and close his account there. The representative helped him call and the Marco bank manager said she would mail the paperwork to his newly opened post office box. She told him that he would need to return the paperwork with a notarized signature. He decided these were details he could wait to arrange until the next time he was at Steinhatchee.

As they were leaving the building at the same time, Mrs. Johnson said, "Can I drive you back to your boat? Need to stop anywhere on the way?"

Thompson accepted the lift and they formally introduced themselves. Thompson told her that he'd moved up the coast because Everglades City had become too rough. She told him that she was born in Jena, across the river from town, and moved away for a career in newspapers. After her husband died, she returned to a family homestead. She didn't tell him that she was an iconic matriarch of the community with deep family ties. Now they knew a little something about each other.

At the marina, Mrs. Johnson gave Thompson her number and said he could call if he needed anything when he was in town.

"Thank you, but I don't have a telephone. I appreciate the kindness."

"Well, just use the marina's phone to call. I don't have anything to do but read and watch the river! Bye now."

TWENTY-TWO

Thompson was content to stay at Steinhatchee for a few days. He had some things to do on the houseboat. He wanted to buy some Christmas lights or solar yard lights for his screened deck so he would be more visible at night, that is, when he wanted to be visible. He could find these things at the local hardware store. And, maybe the letter from the bank would be at the post office and he could complete his transfer and close his Marco bank account.

He was awakened at sunrise with someone banging on his boat. Dressing quickly, he yelled, "What is it?"

When he was at the doorway, he saw Nelson on the dock, silhouetted in the sunrise. "Ahoy there, Captain! I came up to see you. Lt. Shaffer said you might be here."

Thompson was heartened to see Nelson, but he didn't want to show it. "Are you here to harass me again or did you just come for free coffee?"

"Can I come aboard?

Thompson wanted to say 'not without a warrant', but decided to just say, "Yes, OK. I'll put some coffee on."

"Hope I didn't interrupt your beauty sleep!"

"No, I was just about to get up anyway. What brings you up here?"

"Thompson, I'm thinking of taking a job with one of the refuges up here. They have an opening and I might be able to transfer from the Park Service. I'm really worn out at Flamingo."

"Well…I can tell you that this place isn't any better for bugs. Shark River had biting flies and mosquitoes, but up here it's no-see-ums like you can't believe! Air is thick with 'em!"

"Yeah, I know. Waiting for you outside the screen, they almost carried me away!"

Thompson caught him up on what he'd been up to since they departed company. His eyes crinkled with his enthusiasm for the fishing and the wild coast. "It's not as isolated as the Ten Thousand Islands, you know. There are more towns along the coast, but less hassles. There's more fishing and boating activity around here, but nobody bothers me. And, there are a lot of good old boys who I don't trust behind my back, but there have been some really kind folks too."

Nelson didn't want to rant about the troubles that were causing his career crisis. It was his own problem and maybe the change of venue would be a fresh start to reinvigorate his passion. The Big Bend was as good a place as any to try. Instead of complaining, he merely said, "I've got a job interview this morning. Well, not actually a job interview. It's more of a discussion with the manager of the Lower Suwannee Refuge and his boss. She's coming down from St. Marks, up near Tallahassee, and the manager is coming up from Fowlers Bluff on the Suwannee to talk to me about the possibility of a position with the U.S. Fish and Wildlife Service. They're meeting each other halfway, here in Steinhatchee. I'm not sure it's going to work out but I need a change."

Thompson said, "If you do come up here, I think you might like it. It's more laid back. Even if there's a lot of 'bubbas', there's not as many dumb tourists. I miss my old place, but this area is growing on me as I get more familiar. I've only run aground twice, but there's been no shoot-outs with poachers!"

"How about I catch up with you for dinner tonight? I'll get a room here and drive back tomorrow to Flamingo. In the meantime, I gotta go meet with these folks."

"Sure. Why not stay on my boat and save the money?"

"The floor is too hard and I didn't bring my sleeping bag. Thanks for the coffee."

The two men were pleased to see each other. Nelson was happy that Thompson looked like he was getting acclimated and liked the place. Thompson was pleased to see the closest thing he had to family and learning that he may be relocating nearby.

Later, as the sun was getting low on the horizon, Thompson heard Nelson knock. "Hurry up! The bugs are horrible!" Once inside the screened deck, Nelson brushed off his bare arms and neck that were covered with the biting gnats. "These things are terrible. I don't think Shark Valley can claim bug capital of Florida anymore! You ready? There's a restaurant a couple blocks down the road. I'll drive, 'cause if we walk we might not make it. The bugs will have us for supper!"

The restaurant had an open dining room with a nice salad bar buffet dividing the booths from the tables. They were seated at a window to watch the big orange disc melt into the Gulf.

Speaking to the waitress, Nelson said, "I'll have a bourbon and water on ice. How about you, Thompson?"

"Same for me."

The waitress brought crackers and smoked mullet dip, telling them they could take their time with the menu.

Nelson looked it over, "Not gonna do another 'grease feast' this time! They claim they have the best prime rib. Think I might give that a try."

"I think I will get broiled grouper. I've been eating redfish, flounder, and trout for weeks. But, I haven't caught a grouper."

When Nelson said, "Let's make sure it's not a goliath!" Thompson smiled. "Think the poachers down at Everglades City may have got 'em all?"

Sipping the cocktails, Thompson asked, "So how'd your meeting go?"

Nelson said, "Fine."

"Just fine? What's the skinny? You gonna get a job up here or not?"

Nelson said, "I'm a little up in the air about this. I like the folks and from what they told me, and the little I've seen, this area looks wonderful, except for your no-see-ums. The refuges are grouped together in a complex. St Marks is the headquarters and they have Lower Suwannee and Cedar Keys, as well as one or two refuges farther west, under their supervision. Each refuge has a small staff and a small field office. I'd be at Lower Suwannee and could live in a government trailer or find a place, say in Suwannee or Yankeetown."

"Well… that ain't bad. There's a pretty little waitress nurse down at that fishing lodge that had her eye on you."

Nelson let the quip pass. "Living in one of the rural communities wouldn't be so bad. The government housing at Flamingo is a pretty decent place, but it's so far away from everything."

"The job sounds interesting. It would be a Senior Refuge Ranger position, not with law enforcement authority, at least not at first. That would be a welcome change. The job is managing public use and the refuge lands and, by what they said, mostly "other duties as assigned." That means it could be anything from prescribed burns to replacing boundary signs to building bat houses."

"Bat houses?" Thompson queried.

"Yep, the refuge claims to have one of the biggest bat houses around and a very healthy bat population. I knew the manager at St. Marks. She was the manager of the Florida Keys National Wildlife Refuge a few years ago. We were at the same meetings about Florida Bay. There's a Deputy Manager at Lower Suwanee. I'd be reporting to him. It's a small staff, with a few maintenance workers and a wildlife biologist and tech, and a refuge officer, who's about to retire.

"They were encouraging me, thinking it would be a good fit. I might have to go somewhere for Refuge Officer LE Training, even though I've had an NPS badge for years and both agencies are in the same Department of Interior. I'm going to think hard on this."

Thompson agreed, "You got a lot to think about. I had to move up here after it became obvious I couldn't stay at Everglades City. Seems you have a choice, to stay where you are worn out or start a new chapter. Whatever you decide will be the right choice."

Nelson appreciated the guidance and support. It was going to be a thoughtful drive back to Flamingo.

"I've still got a lot of traveling to do on this coast. I've found a few great places to drop my hook, but there's so many more. I study the GPS thing you gave me and look at all the creeks and rivers that flow into the Gulf. I haven't been here through all of the seasons and I'm not looking forward to the winter. I think it's going to be colder than I like."

"You better get some long johns and a coat!"

"Yeah, thinkin' about going to Goodwill next time I'm down to Crystal River."

"Ready to go? We can have a night cap back on your boat or across the street at my motel."

"You got anything to drink in your room?"

"Yes sir, some good coffee-flavored rum and a couple plastic cups."

In Nelson's room, they spent a couple hours chatting over the rum until they ran out of conversation and were repeating themselves. "Guess it's time for me to get back to the houseboat. I'm waiting here for a letter from my bank in Marco so I can move my account up here. After that, I'll be moving on."

Before he left to walk over to the marina, he gave Nelson his address. "Not that I check my mail too often, but here's the address for my post office box."

Nelson was gone the next day. Thompson got his letter from the Marco bank and returned his notarized form. He figured out how to get his checks direct-deposited into the Steinhatchee bank. All his tasks were done, so he was free to go.

He was about ready to leave when he was surprised to see Mrs. Johnson walk down the ramp to the shaky wood floating dock. Thompson went over to her to give her a hand.

"Mr. Thompson, I was curious about your houseboat. I knew you would be moving on, so I wanted to catch you before you left. Oh my, is that it?"

"Yes ma'am. It's my humble home." For the first time, Thompson was concerned about its appearance. He was suddenly conscious how this nice lady would see his functional craft that had been assembled from salvaged parts, with no concession to aesthetics. It was clean on the inside, but rather cobbled together.

She took his arm to steady herself on the wobbly dock and they walked to the houseboat together. Standing on the dock, she said, "Your boat looks very," pausing, "interesting. I bet you find it comfortable. How long have you been living on it?"

"Nearly a dozen years. It's saucered and blowed to suit me."

"How creative! It looks like you put together something very functional. I brought you some cupcakes as a bon voyage gift."

Thompson was speechless. This woman, whom he barely knew, was being so generous and kind. Being seen with her was a signal to the community that he was OK and probably moderated some of the community's apprehension. He wasn't sure if his improved stature by knowing her was at the expense of her reputation.

"I don't know what to say."

She said, "You could say 'thank you,' but you don't have to say anything. I just hope we can meet again when you make your way back to Steinhatchee. Will you walk me back up the ramp? This dock isn't a good place for a dizzy old lady."

"Yes ma'am, happy to." Taking her arm, they walked together back up to solid ground.

"I'll look you up when I come back for my mail. Thank you for all your kindness."

Thompson motored out the river to the straight channel that goes out to deep water. He decided to work his way back to Waccasassa Bay, stopping first at Pepperfish Keys. So far, these were his favorite places.

At anchor at Pepperfish Key, he smelled smoke. The fragrance was a wood fire. He looked around to see if there was a forest fire on the island or from the mainland. Maybe it was from a prescribed burn. The wind was from the south and he could see a wisp of smoke coming from the Keys. Thompson retrieved his binoculars and scanned the shore. Two kayaks were pulled way up on the beach, partially obscured by brush. A small pup tent was pitched in an opening. The smoke was from a campfire.

Relieved that the fire was probably under control, Thompson relaxed. He watched for activity, but didn't see any people. It was likely that they were in the tent taking refuge from the bugs that invade in the late afternoon to evening.

Later at night, he could see a couple of people at the beach, casting lines out to deeper water. Sound carries over the water on still nights; he could hear talking but couldn't make out what was being said. This was reminiscent of the kayakers he'd seen back at Pavilion Key. He didn't think this was an official campsite with a portable outhouse like the Everglades had, but it was the place he would pick if he was paddling along this coast.

Thompson stayed up late reading. He read a book from his Bible and then resumed a book on contemporary politics. The world was going crazy. He was thankful that his off-grid existence insulated him from the insanity. A long time ago he figured out there was nothing one person could do to fix sick politics. People were such lemmings.

Although he was not really worried, he checked on the campers before retiring for the night. His experiences with the kayak campers back in the Everglades were mostly good, even if a few intruded on his privacy. These paddlers must be on an uncharted adventure.

Waking with the sun, he first checked the island. The campers were up and they had a fire going. With the wind out of the east, there was no smoke wafting his way. He made coffee and oatmeal. While deciding on where the next stop would be, he saw on the GPS a couple of deeper holes around Shired Island.

After a few days here, he'd move on to Shired Island, a little farther south but still north of Suwannee. Thompson followed the chartplotter route carefully in towards Shired Island. A satellite image feature on the GPS showed a white sandy beach and a boat ramp was noted on a nearby creek. He could anchor safely in 4 feet, about a half mile offshore.

Later that week, as he anchored in the spot he chose off Shired Island, he was thinking, "Deep is relative." He learned from experience that along this coast where the shallow waters are marked as 1 or 2 feet, or even exposed grass flats at low tide, a spot that is marked on the charts as 8-feet deep is considered deep. The tide ranges 3 or 4 feet. If he could make it into an anchorage with the rising tide, there was less of a chance of running aground and getting stuck. In each location he chose, Thompson was careful to watch the tide and the numbers on the charts. He knew the houseboat was too heavy to push off of a shoal.

Once his anchor was down and set, he relaxed. He used binoculars to watch the activity on the nearby beach. Several RVs were parked at campsites backing up to the water's edge. People were at picnic tables and using the park grills. A few kids were wading in the water. This was a nice anchorage, but the nearby activity made it less appealing for a longer stay.

Kayakers came by the houseboat. They looked like the boats he had seen at Pepperfish. They waved as they passed by on their way to the beach. Once on the beach, they pulled the kayaks up above the high tide line and began making a camp, setting up their pop-up tent. He thought, "Yep, just paddlers on an adventure. I wonder how far they've come and what their destination is." Because of their shallow draft, kayaks could skim over the thin waters and were perfect for getting close to the shoreline. But if the wind was blowing it could be hard paddling in bumpy waters.

Late at night he could hear the RV generators and music coming from the campsites. The sound was not loud but distracting enough to be annoying. Thompson resolved to move on. Now that he knew this place, he could check it off and go discover another. He was creating a mental picture of the coast and making a list of places to stay. This one would not be a first-tier choice.

Thompson studied his GPS. A couple miles away, on the other side of a place called Pine Island, there seemed to be a decent prospect for an anchorage. It was a series of deeper holes surrounded by marsh. There would be no protection from wind, but the location should be flat calm in all sea conditions. The challenge would be finding the narrow entrance to the cove.

He would have to time his entrance with the rising tide. About 10 AM it should be slack, so by 11 he should be able to slowly poke his way into a private, quiet spot. On the way in, he bumped the bottom, feeling the pontoons slid over a shallow spot. Thompson hoped that by going slow he would not run hard aground, allowing him to back off if he got stuck. He made it to just about where the chartplotter indicated it would get deeper and then he hit the bottom. Trying to reverse only stirred mud behind the houseboat. He was stuck and he was so close to his final destination.

Throwing out the anchor to be sure he wouldn't drift when the tide rose and dislodged his boat, he launched his pirogue.

With a cane pole, he measured the depth around the houseboat, probing into the spot that was supposed to be deeper. He said aloud, "Darn, if I had only been 20 feet to the right, I would have had enough depth, even six feet – 3 ½ feet more than I need."

Since he would have to wait for the tide to rise, he decided to explore the cove in his pirogue. The depths were good, deeper than he could touch with the cane pole. He flushed a couple of rails from the reeds. They were upset with Thompson for trespassing on their private space, quickly disappearing with ease into the marsh grass that looked impenetrable. A six foot, or larger, gator watched and then slowly retreated to sink into the dark water. If there was one thing Thompson liked least about this coast, it was the water. It was either too green or too dark to ever judge the depth by sight.

When the houseboat finally floated free he moved it slightly to re-anchor in the cove, Thompson decided this would be the place he would stay. He found it very hospitable and far enough away from people to consider himself all alone in his own world.

For the past few months, Thompson had made his way poking around the coast. Living it every day, he was getting accustomed to this new environment. This was his pattern – find a place, check it out. If it was good, stay, if not, move on. In time he would know the Big Bend as well as a native and he could settle on which were his favorite spots, reducing his explorations. For now, he needed to keep wandering until he knew this coast as well as he knew the Everglades.

When he stopped periodically in Steinhatchee to collect his checks and junk mail, he would make a point to see Mrs. Johnson. He enjoyed his conversations with her. She told him that she was lacking anyone to talk with about literature and current events. Most of her acquaintances in the community were obsessed with grandkids, gossip, and the gospel. Talking with someone her own age who was so well read was stimulating.

Thompson was glad to have a friend in the community who valued him as a person and not a just a suspicious outsider. They would have coffee at the restaurant overlooking the entrance channel to the Steinhatchee River. Mrs. Johnson was intrigued about his gypsy lifestyle and even more curious about his past. He would deflect any question that would lead to exposing anything about his life before the houseboat.

During his latest trip to pick up his mail, it was scallop season and Steinhatchee was buzzing with people. The place was packed and his houseboat was taking up dock space. After a day, the marina manager politely invited him to leave saying he could rent the space to two or three smaller boats. It wasn't a hard sell; Thompson was ready to go. While he liked visiting Steinhatchee, he was always anxious to get back to his anchorages south of the Suwannee River. Life alone in the wild was his asylum. He'd stay there until the swarm of boaters subsided.

While checking the VHF for the marine weather, he stumbled on an alert from the U.S. Coast Guard.

"Pon, pon. Pon, pon. This is United States Coast Guard, Station Yankeetown. We have a report of a scalloper injured in a shark attack in the vicinity of Horseshoe Beach. Be advised rescue teams are underway. All vessels should keep a sharp lookout and assist if possible. Report all sightings to U.S. Coast Guard, Yankeetown on Channel 16 or 22 Alpha. Out"

The site of the attack was not far away. He had often wondered if all the people snorkeling in the shallow seagrass ever saw sharks. Getting help to a shark bite victim so far away from a medical facility would be difficult and slow. Thompson hoped the victim would be OK.

The news of this shark attack spread like wildfire through the communities on the coast. The attack cast a pall on the scalloping activity and media attention was on the story like flies on stink. Without access to news outlets, Thompson didn't know why he noticed a sudden decline in boats in the scalloping areas that had been packed as he made his way to his anchorage to the south of the Suwannee River where it was out of the way and quiet.

TWENTY-THREE

Jenny begged Rhett to take her scalloping on one of his days off. They had enjoyed the activity in the past but it had been years since they had been out on the boat together. Rhett seemed to only go fishing with his buds on his day off or on Sundays when she was at church.

Rhett made his living running a live bait shrimp trawl. He'd make drags and collect the shrimp to supply the marinas along the coast. He had a regular schedule running from Steinhatchee to Crystal River. He'd start late in the afternoon and drag at night, timing his collections to arrive at the marinas at dawn to stock their bait tanks. Each marina had a day for its weekly delivery. He also had a day of the week reserved for emergencies, if the weather was bad or if a marina had an emergency shortfall. He stayed pretty busy and the money was good. He could pull in enough cash to fund his sports boat, four-wheeler, and hunting club membership.

His wife Jenny had her own life. She kept a garden and took care of his dogs. She worked part-time at the convenience store up on U.S. 98 to earn her own money since her household allowance from him was too little to cover expenses. She was addicted to daytime TV, watching a number of her "programs" on satellite dish.

Their families had lived in the area for generations. They had been in school together and gotten married young.

Jenny dreamed one day they could get a new double-wide to replace their old worn-out trailer. There was always a reason to put off an upgrade. Expenses always seemed to come up to keep them short of funds. The washing machine would break, the air conditioner would need to be replaced, or the refrigerator or chest freezer would go out. And, there were truck payments to make. It was impossible for them to get ahead, but they got by.

"Rhett, please take me out scalloping! It's been a long time. I think we need some time together like we used to have."

Rhett didn't answer until she said it again, louder, "Rhett, did you hear me? I want to go out scalloping!"

Rhett turned to answer, "You don't have to yell at me. I heard you. I was thinking. What?"

"Rhett, I want to go scalloping like we used to. Remember?"

"Oh yeah, we had some good times. But we can buy scallops so cheap. It will cost a lot to get gas for the skiff. You know how the Democrat President has screwed up the prices."

"I don't care. We need some time together. You are always running off at night to shrimp and when you're not doing that, you're fishing with Zeke and Sam, or at your hunting lease. You can find time to go with them, but not take a day for your own wife!"

"Well, OK, but next week. On Wednesday, if the weather is OK." He hoped it would not be.

But, come Wednesday, the weather was perfect. They launched his boat at Cedar Key, loaded it up with their snorkeling gear and an ice chest for lunch and the scallops they might find. It was a late start, but they could get an afternoon in and, with luck, they could limit out.

"Rhett, let's go up to the Suwannee Sound and try there."

"Why? It's a longer run than down to Waccasassa Bay. We know the scalloping is good there. Besides, that shark attack happened up north of Cedar Key."

Rhett had already accepted that there was no use arguing with Jenny about scalloping and was resigned to doing what he had to do to keep her quiet. So, he acquiesced with, "Yes dear. We'll go up to the Sound and try there, but no complaining if we don't get anything."

Jenny was pleased, "Thank you darlin'. You're so sweet." She gave him a squeeze and kissed his neck.

Getting into the water, it was not nearly as clear as what they remembered. Maybe the dark water flowing from the Suwannee was reducing the visibility. They found a few scallops, but the density was low. An hour into snorkeling, they got on the boat with only one gallon of unshucked shells.

Popping a couple beers, they sat in silence and rested before going in the water again. When Rhett was done with his beer, he crushed the can and threw it into their five-gallon bucket. Jenny placed hers in a cup holder by the wheel.

"Rhett honey, I have a surprise for you. But you need to turn around for a moment." He faced the stern as she stripped off her bathing suit and wrapped herself in a beach towel.

"Okay, you can turn around now. Opening the towel like a butterfly's wings, she wiggled her hips and shimmied her breasts.

"I thought we could do what we used to do when we went scalloping. You know, do it in the water."

Rhett was more enticed than he had been in a long time. Their intimate relationship had declined with his work routine and their impulses being out of synch. Rhett smiled, "Oh yeah, for old time's sake!"

Jenny said, "Go ahead and get in the water and I'll be right there. I want to prepare myself."

Rhett shucked his duds and jumped off the back in the expectation she would be joining him soon. When she didn't jump right in, he grew impatient, "What's taking so long?" He heard the motor start and saw that Jenny was back in her bathing suit.

"Rhett honey, a few months ago the store called me in to work late while you were on one of your emergency trips. I saw your truck parked at that Mexican woman's house. She really needs better curtains."

"She's not Mexican. She's from Puerto Rico." Maybe that wasn't relevant, but Rhett didn't know what else to say. "I, I… was just parked there waiting on a friend."

"You have been waiting on a friend a lot, 'cause I checked there every time you had an emergency shrimping night. You seemed to be there a lot."

"OK, OK. So we can work this out. Just turn off the motor and let me back on the boat."

"Don't think so. You can swim back to Cedar Key, that is, if the sharks don't get you." She unwrapped a frozen chum bag and threw it at him, narrowly missing his head.

Then the boat was in gear and she disappeared back south towards Cedar Key.

Rhett pondered his predicament. He was naked and alone, thinking first about how the mainland shore was a couple of miles away and there were no boats out in the area this late in the day.

Then the panic about sharks set in. He needed to get away from the chum, so he started swimming east, fast at first and then slow and steady in an effort to make it to shore. But, if he reached it, there was nothing but salt marsh at the shoreline.

After swimming for what seemed to be an hour, he felt something sharp hit his knee. He reached to find what had happened and his hand scraped oysters. It was shallow; he could stand up. He was on a shoal, scattered with clusters of oysters. As he carefully walked on the bottom, he emerged in a place that was only ankle deep. Blood was oozing from where oysters cut his knee. The tide was running out so it would be exposed soon. Sharks wouldn't be able to get him on the bar.

Jenny was on her way, not to Cedar Key, but down to Waccasassa Bay, where she knew it was popular with scallopers. When she arrived, she would run up to a boat and ask for help.

In the late afternoon, there were only a few boats in the bay, several fishing boats and a couple boats with dive flags out. She headed to a larger skiff that looked new. It would be well equipped and have a radio.

In a Tony Award-winning performance, she breathlessly told the two men on the boat that her husband disappeared while scalloping just a mile or so south of their position. "I don't know what to do!" Crying, she pleaded, "Please help me. I don't know how to operate this boat."

"Lady, where did this happen?"

She pointed to the horizon south of their position, well south of where she had actually abandoned Rhett by at least twenty miles. Suwannee Sound is north of Cedar Key.

The boaters pulled their anchor and said, "Follow us. We will go that way to look, while we call the Coast Guard for help."

While one man piloted the fishing boat further south, to where she had pointed, the other kept an eye on Jenny's boat to be sure she was following along behind them. He called the Coast Guard.

"Coast Guard, this is the fishing boat *Fin Chaser* on channel 16. We have an emergency. Come back."

On the speaker, the response was, "U.S. Coast Guard, Yankeetown on channel 16 to the vessel calling. Please respond and switch to channel 22 alpha."

The *Fin Chaser* answered, "Channel 22, U.S. Coast Guard. This is *Fin Chaser*. We, ah, just had a woman come up to our boat to report her husband is missing while scalloping. We are at Waccasassa Bay south of Cedar Key. She is following us to the general location where she last saw her husband."

The USCG asked for a latitude and longitude position and information on the two boats, the *Fin Chaser* and the missing boater's boat. Coasties mobilized immediately to run up to Waccasassa Bay from Yankeetown. Time was of the essence due to it being late afternoon. They would be losing light soon. The Coast Guard broadcast a notice to mariners about the missing boater and asked for assistance from any nearby vessels.

Two other vessels that heard the broadcast joined the search and the FWCC sent an officer. The local Levy County Sheriff boat that was in Cedar Key headed south. A half dozen boats were wandering the area when the Coast Guard arrived.

After briefly taking a report from Jenny, they tried to narrow the search area. They continued searching until well after dark. Some of the volunteers gave up and headed back to the Cedar Key launch ramp. Jenny stayed into the night using her spotlight to feign searching. She ran out of gas.

The *Fin Chaser* towed Jenny's boat back to the ramp. A local sheriff's deputy was there to meet her. He helped get her boat out of the water, onto the trailer, and parked in the lot. Then he drove her back to her mobile home. "Do you have someone to call. Do you need help?"

"No," sniffling and genuinely tired from her exhausting act, she continued, "I'll be OK. I got a friend who will help. I can let Rhett's family in Cross City know what happened."

The Coast Guard, sheriff's boat, and FWCC continued searching through the night. At dawn more boats arrived to run a grid search. Nothing turned up. Jenny waited at the boat ramp with a deputy. Visibly overwrought, she sat alone in her car, surfing the Internet on her phone. The weather was predicted to turn bad, which was good news for her. She was hoping the search would be suspended.

Due to the marine weather report, Thompson decided to move his houseboat to a little more protected area. It was calm before the storm. On the way out he saw someone standing on an oyster bar. He was too far off to tell if it was a kayaker or a fisherman. As he got a little closer, he couldn't see a boat or a kayak. Curious to see a lone figure, standing in the middle of nowhere, he grabbed his binoculars. It couldn't be, but the guy looked naked and was waving his arms over his head.

Thompson decided to alter course to get a closer look. His eyes did not deceive him. It was a naked man, all alone on the shoal. Because it was too shallow for the houseboat to get to the guy and with only a one-man pirogue, the guy would have to wade out to him. He figured that, in the worst case, he would have to get in the water to trek through the mud over to the guy. It was not the best option because, while his prosthetic was workable on land, in mud it would be nearly impossible to walk. He was hoping the guy could make it to him.

Thompson got as close as he dared, and yelled, "Do you need help?" It was an obvious understatement.

"Yes!" the naked man shouted back. "I can swim over to your boat!"

Thompson helped him get on board and asked the guy, "What the hell are you doing out here?" while he grabbed a towel for the naked guy to cover himself. The man was scratched up, with cuts on his knee, hands and feet. Thompson used a bucket of fresh water to wash him off and gave him some hydrogen peroxide to pour on the wounds.

"My wife tried to kill me! If you hadn't come along I would not have made it." The man was weak and cold from being exposed for nearly 24 hours. Thompson got him a blanket and sat him in a chair at the table.

"Let me make you some coffee. Here's some water. Drink it slowly."

Shivering, the guy said, "I need a cigarette. Thanks for rescuing me. Now I'm gonna kill that bitch when I get back."

By the time Thompson returned with coffee, his guest was asleep, leaning back in the chair.

Now there was time for Thompson to call for help. His first thought was to call the marina at Suwannee, rather than the Coast Guard. They would be closer and could get to his location more quickly. Thompson was concerned about getting caught in the weather.

Thompson radioed the marina, "I'm down in Suwannee Sound and just picked up a guy who was stranded out here. Any chance somebody could come get him?"

An FWCC officer happened to be in the marina store when Thompson's call came in. The officer got on the radio, "This is Officer Watkins with Florida Fish and Wildlife. Can you switch to channel 10?"

Thompson replied, "Channel 10." He then proceeded to give his location and report the victim seemed to be in stable condition. "I will stay at this location 'til you arrive. I'm on a houseboat near the Lone Cabbage Reef."

FWCC officer Watkins replied with an ETA of about a half hour. The marina called the local Dixie County Sheriff and the local EMT at the Suwannee Volunteer Fire Department. They would be at the dock when the FWCC officer brought him in.

As the FWCC officer was about to depart, a U.S. Fish and Wildlife Service vehicle pulled into the marina parking lot. Officer Watkins asked the Refuge employee if he wanted to go along on a rescue of a disabled swimmer. "I could use some help. It doesn't sound too serious, but you never know. I'll explain on the way."

As they boarded the FWCC boat and moved away from the dock, they discussed the emergency call. The FWCC officer didn't have much more information, but relayed to the refuge employee that the call came in just a couple minutes before.

"In the haste to get going, I didn't introduce myself. I'm FWCC Law Enforcement Officer Watkins. I haven't seen you here before. Are you with the Refuge?"

"Yes, just started a few days ago. I'm Bob Nelson. I transferred here from Everglades National Park where I was a senior ranger. I decided to take a job as a Visitor Specialist Refuge Ranger here at Lower Suwannee. I don't have law enforcement credentials here yet but I have had training with the Park Service."

"Good to meet ya. What happened to Ranger Donner?"

"She was promoted to their Regional Office. The park specialist position opened up, so I applied." Being new to the Fish and Wildlife Service he was often substituting the familiar term 'park' for 'refuge.'

"I liked her, but this wasn't a great place for a single woman. There's not much to do around here for a city girl."

The two wildlife officers, one from the state and one from the federal agency, zoomed down the East Pass toward Suwannee Sound. Skimming over the mirrored black waters, it seemed like they were flying upside down on the clouds. It did not take long for them to spot Thompson's houseboat.

"I can't wait to see the expression on that old man's face when I show up with you. We go back a few years, in the Everglades. Interesting guy. I know he's not expecting me!"

TWENTY-FOUR

Thompson was surprised when he saw his old friend in a new uniform, momentarily forgetting that he had a naked castaway sleeping at his porch table. "Hey, what are you doing here? You give up your 'flat hat' for a ball cap?"

"Yes sir. Good to see you too." Nelson smiled, "I'm here with Officer Watkins to pick up your rescue. How is he?"

Once the FWCC boat was tied to the houseboat the two officers boarded and started attending to the survivor. They checked his pulse and saw to his wounds.

"What is your name? Do you know where you are?"

Disoriented, as if he were drunk, he replied, "Rhett Webb." He was exhausted and had just been startled awake. As he woke up, he remembered his predicament and said, "Yes, I'm on an old black guy's houseboat. He rescued me from being stranded by my wife. Damn bitch!"

Officer Watkins got on his cell phone to the Dixie County Sheriff's office. This situation seemed more like it was a crime than a straightforward rescue of a stranded swimmer. They all waited for a return call from the Sheriff's office. Thompson poured the coffee. Rhett cupped his hands around the mug to absorb the warmth. He was cold to the core. Even though the air temperature wasn't bad, his core was sapped from exposure and exhaustion.

When Watkins' phone rang, the others could only hear one side of the conversation. "So, we can wait here. I don't expect that an hour will be a problem. Yes, seems fine, maybe a little hypothermic after the night in the water. Yes, at Lone Cabbage Reef. Understand it's Levy County not yours. Probably a good idea. Bye."

Watkins relayed the result of his conversation with Dixie County. "The Sheriff is passing this along to Levy County. The Coast Guard and the Sheriff will be here to pick you up Mr. Webb and take you to the Crystal River hospital to be checked out. It's not Dixie's jurisdiction, unless you are critical. We're waiting here for about an hour."

Webb was fine, too tired to care about anything except being pissed at Jenny. He rested his head on the table and slept.

Thompson wanted to know how it was Nelson was up here at Suwannee. "Tell me about what's up with the new job?"

"After visiting you a few months ago, I decided I needed to change the channel. The constant routine of emergencies at the Park, especially the urban problems and people, were souring my outlook on life and drained my job satisfaction. When I met with the Fish and Wildlife folks and discussed my interests, this place seemed like a better fit."

"So, you think this is better?"

"Well, I didn't expect a rescue like this in my first week. In fact, it's my first solo patrol and I happened to be in the right place at the time the FWCC needed a little help. But it's not as bad as some of the petty stuff I was constantly dealing with in the

Everglades. You know one of our visitors complained to a U.S. Senator that we weren't fencing the squirrels and alligators?"

Thompson chuckled, "You mean you don't!"

Officer Watkins butted in, "You know, most of the problems up here are more small fishing violations. Used to be this was a big area for drug smuggling, but somehow, the DEA has quashed the activity. Well, most of it anyway." Thompson choked back a laugh.

Nelson said, "I have to do some training with the U.S. Fish and Wildlife Service to get my law enforcement certification for the refuge. You'd think that 15 years of experience as a National Park officer, in the same government department, would be enough to transfer, but I have to go to a two-week course at their national training center to get certified. 'Til then, I'm working as a Park Ranger for public use. But it's not bad and I'll learn the park."

Watkins asked, "Don't you mean refuge?"

"Yes, refuge. It's taking me a while to adjust to the new terminology."

Watkins pulled out his laptop and wrote a brief incident report while he was waiting on the Coast Guard. Nelson and Thompson caught up on what they'd each been up to over the past couple months since they'd been together at Steinhatchee. Thompson told Nelson about the kind Mrs. Johnson who had befriended him and immediately regretted mentioning her.

"So now you got a girlfriend? You old dawg!"

Thompson threw it back at him, "Sure, just like your waitress down in Yankeetown. Don't tell me that's not why you decided to settle there?"

Nelson replied, "I'm not there yet. I'm staying in refuge housing for now. She is pretty and smart. Who knows maybe I'll end up at Yankeetown. Maybe you'll wind up with your gal in Steinhatchee."

Shortly, the Coast Guard arrived to take Mr. Webb on board. It was a quick transfer. Lt. Shaffer was in charge with a crew of three plus the Levy County Deputy. They gave Webb a new disposable jumpsuit, returning Thompson's towel and blanket. Before leaving, Lt Shaffer had time to tease Thompson and Nelson about their latest adventure together. "Well, it looks like Batman and Robin are together again to save the day! Trouble seems to follow you two!"

Officer Watkins and Nelson also departed in the FWCC boat to return to Suwannee. As they were casting off, Nelson asked Thompson, "Where you going to be for the next few weeks."

"I'm hanging around here, until after the front passes and then I don't know. Eventually back to Steinhatchee to get my mail. But, not until the end of the month when scallop season is over. You better get going if you're gonna beat the squall!"

Nelson would have quite a story to relate to the Deputy Refuge Manager, guessing there would be some paperwork protocol to complete. Not knowing the Fish and Wildlife system, he realized he had quite a bit to learn about his new agency, as well as the lay of the land.

TWENTY-FIVE

Nelson spotted Thompson's houseboat docked at the marina in Steinhatchee. He walked the rickety dock to the boat. Knocking on the side, "Permission to come aboard?" There was no answer. He tried again, "Permission to come aboard?" Again, there was no reply.

If Thompson was OK, he was probably out running errands at the post office or bank. Nelson would wait at the restaurant. As he entered the restaurant, he saw Thompson and Mrs. Johnson at a table by the window. "Why, hello Mr. Thompson! Glad I found you here. Won't you introduce me to this nice lady?"

Thompson was caught off-guard, which was not a common occurrence. He stuttered, "This... this... is my Mrs.... lady... friend, friend Mrs. Johnson."

Nelson reached for her hand as she said, "Nice to meet you. You must be Mr. Nelson. Mr. Thompson has told me a lot about you and your times together." Nelson smiled.

"I see you are in a Refuge uniform. Are you working at Lower Suwannee or Cedar Key?"

"I'm at Lower Suwannee. Just started a month ago. I'm still learning the ropes. Pleased to meet you!"

"Please pull up a chair. Won't you join us for lunch? Or I can leave if you have some business with Mr. Thompson."

"No business, just a friendly visit with an old friend. I'd love to join you!" and turning to Thompson he inquired, "If that's OK with you." Thompson's quick retort was, "Have a seat!"

They chatted over lunch. Mrs. Johnson was fascinated with the relationship of the two friends. They had such adventures together in the Everglades. She was an accomplished interviewer, ferreting out their stories.

The men stood as Mrs. Johnson rose, saying, "Gentlemen, may I take my leave? It's been delightful, but I have some appointments I must attend to. I have enjoyed meeting you Mr. Nelson and lunching with you. I hope we might do this again sometime."

Thompson and Nelson reseated themselves. "That lady is very nice!" Nelson told his companion. Thompson expected kidding but Nelson's compliment was genuine and not teasing.

"Yes, she is very nice. She helps me a lot when I'm up here. I enjoy the conversation. I reckon she enjoys it too, since she doesn't have anybody here that is more.... well, for lack of a better term, intellectually stimulating."

"I've never thought of you as an intellectual! I've considered you more of a reclusive curmudgeon!"

Thompson wasn't insulted. He preferred being perceived as a grouchy hermit. "Let's go back to my boat. I've got a new bottle of rum we can test."

"Sorry, I'm on duty. Don't think the boss wants a drinker on the staff, but I'll go back to sit with you while you enjoy a drink."

On the boat, Thompson percolated a fresh pot of coffee. Rum could wait for another visit, when Nelson wasn't working.

"I've got an idea. Why don't you pack an overnight bag and that bottle of rum and come stay with me at my new place down at Yankeetown?"

"Yankeetown? I knew it, you are chasing that nurse who's a waitress, aren't you?"'

"I'm at Yankeetown because I don't want to live too close to the folks who use the refuge. It's better if I can keep a professional distance from the neighbors."

"Say what you want, but I know you are chasing that skirt!"

"OK, think what you want. I will pick you up tomorrow and carry you down to my place. On the way, we can stop at a store if you need anything. I know it's the first night you will be spending ashore in ten years!"

The next day, they passed a lot of forested land as they drove up from Steinhatchee to U.S. Highway 98. They then turned south. As they got closer to Old Town, the natural forest turned to farm fields and small rural residences. U.S. 98 was a wide, four-lane highway without much traffic. A bridge crossed the Suwannee River at Fanning Springs, some 25 miles upriver from the town of Suwannee. The Lower Suwanee Refuge office where Nelson was stationed was on the south side of the river, only a hundred yards across the river from the town by boat, but 80 miles by road.

On the drive, Nelson was able to update Thompson on the craziness around Rhett Webb and his wife. "You recall that naked guy you saved at the oyster bar?"

"Sure! I can't unsee that!"

"Turns out, his wife stranded him out there, hoping he'd drown or a shark would get him. She had heard about a shark attack on scallopers up toward Steinhatchee. That gave her an idea on how to get rid of her cheating husband. She seduced him into getting into the water and then drove off in his boat, leaving him there, but not before chumming the water!

"Then she took the boat down south of Cedar Key to report he was lost there, hoping nobody would search up north of Cedar Key, 20 miles away. If you hadn't found him, she might have gotten away with it.

"Now she's in jail awaiting trial on first degree attempted murder and a host of other charges for causing the unnecessary Coast Guard search. Don't think she's gonna get off easy."

The highway passed through the small community of Chiefland. The town showed some evidence of neglect, like time had passed them by. A few chain stores and restaurants were active, but there were a number of vacant buildings with well-weathered "For Sale" signs. This was the "Other Florida," not the tourist image of coconut palms and white sand beaches and new construction everywhere. Unlike Marco, these places were hardscrabble, working class towns living in a different climate and a different economy. Thompson was interested to see what the area inland of the wild area on the water that he had been exploring looked like.

They arrived at Nelson's rented cabin on the Withlacoochee River. It was a small place on a large wooded lot. Live oaks were dripping with Spanish moss and cabbage palms lined the sandy driveway. The screened back porch overlooked the dark water stream. It had the vibe of Old Florida, reminiscent of a time when small camps and cabins were getaways for sportsmen and their families. His rental cottage was built in the 30s or 40s, when Yankeetown was a real backwater, not that it had developed to any kind of urban community now. It was still a fishing community and rural resort, just located closer to encroaching development.

"Well…looks like you've got quite a nice place here!" Thompson was impressed that the residence was set in the woods and felt natural.

"When I found this spot, I liked it immediately. It's a little far from my Refuge office, but the drive's not bad. I thought I'd start here until I get more familiar with the area." Nelson tried to pick up Thompson's bag, but was immediately rebuffed.

"Sonny, I ain't so old I can't carry my own bag!"

They sat on the porch for a spell, watching the Withlacoochee flow by. A couple of otters playfully slithered by and disappeared into the swamp across the river. Songbirds fluttered by. Nelson identified some by sound.

"You ready for a shot before we go to dinner?"

"I think that would be good, wondering when you were gonna ask to get into my rum."

Nelson got a couple tumblers from a cabinet, while Thompson pulled a bottle of Venezuelan rum from his bag. "Found this down at the liquor store in Suwannee and thought I'd give it a try."

"It's smooth. Cheers."

After sipping their libations, they moved to the restaurant. "I knew you would take me to this place – the place with the pretty waitress!"

"It's the best restaurant I found so far, but I admit I like her. Don't be speculating there's anything going on between me and her. It's just friendly. She might not even be working tonight. She's a nurse first, you know."

As luck would have it, she was working. Nelson wasn't disappointed to see her and Thompson was grinning, knowing he could gig Nelson later about the woman.

After a nice dinner and cordial conversation with Flora, the friendly waitress, they returned to Nelson's place. A full moon illuminated the river and, when their eyes acclimated to the light, the woods seemed to glow with a magical blue cast.

Nelson broke the silence, "You know, so far, I'm pleased I made the move here. I'm feeling a lot more at ease with the job and I'm liking getting to know the refuge. It's been a lot more mellow than the uncertainty of each shift at the Park."

Thompson responded. "I told you whatever you decided to do would be the right choice. You've got to follow your own path. You only have one life before you get your reward in heaven."

Nelson, "I know you are religious. But it's not so much my thing. I respect your beliefs."

"I don't think you really know my beliefs."

"You are right. I do hear you saying your blessing at each meal and know you faithfully read your Bible."

"Well...let me tell you, Nelson, I pray at each meal because that's the way I was brought up. My mother was very devoted, in the AME Church. When she was dying she made me promise to give thanks every day. I do it for her and in respect for her belief that regardless of what someone has in life, good or bad, rich or poor, everyone needs to recognize their life, whatever they have, is a gift. She believed life was a direct gift from God. God, she was a good person. I think of her every time I give thanks."

"But you study the Bible. Seems you have a quotation for every situation."

"Nelson, for whatever you come up on in life there's an answer in that book. You can find anything in the Bible. I'm not really religious. I just find there are answers for anything you want, whether it's justification or rationalization, for anything your heart desires. I got nothin' against the true believers, especially the ones that follow their faith. So many people use the word of God for good, like my mother. And, many use it as an excuse for evil, couched in words that make the evil sound good. Where I put my faith is in nature and humanity. All our trials, good or bad, are tests of our own character, and the hell or heaven we find is in the life we lead here on Earth, not in some imaginary clouds or furnace."

"That's not what I suspected."

"You don't know this about me, but I told you I went through some very dark times after I was on my way back from my injuries. I was looking for answers in a bottle and angry at everyone, feeling life was all against me. Somehow, I found my way back. You recall I told you about my "do nothing career" that my handlers arranged for me?"

"Yes, you had a government job that was boring, with nothing to do. Don't know how you could get through that."

"Well…. After I got over the mad, I decided to go back to school. I'd started out as a literature major before I was drafted. Then my injuries in the special operation ended that and the government planned my life. It's probably what I needed, but it wasn't what I wanted.

"Long story short, I got my degree. Then I got a Masters in psychology, lookin' for answers to questions that were on my troubled mind. I quit before I finished my doctoral dissertation. All the teaching was about nature or nurture and tracing problems back to somebody else or some kind of traumatic experience."

Nelson was astounded and chagrinned that he had underestimated Thompson's education. He respected that he was smart, and resourceful, but had no idea he was a scholar. "Wow, then what?"

"I decided for myself that people are either ignorant, indoctrinated, ingrates, or insane, and the world has a shortage of altruism, self-reliance, and virtue. When I couldn't find these attributes in society, I started looking for these things in myself and nature. That's when I was reborn, but not in the Christian sense, on my houseboat. I am blessed and still searching. I guess I'm Christian by values, but atheist by faith."

Nelson said, "That reminds me of an Audubon Society guy I met a long time ago. His quote was 'People, generally, are pretty stupid.'"

"Yep, pretty much sums it up. No offense, but present company included."

"Seems like the troubles of society are infiltrating the wilderness, like all the drama and craziness back in the Everglades. Just can't seem to escape the problems. Even here, we had another episode with that guy who you saved."

"Yeah. He was rescued, but not "saved" in any sense. There's a chance, not likely, that he might find a path out of his trap, like I did."

"Thompson, we both came up here looking for something. You think maybe we'll find it?"

Thompson answered, "There's a chance. We're meeting good folks that don't succumb to the backwards attitudes of their neighbors. Kind, thinking people, mixed in with the folks who are who they are by birth and culture. They are not bad people. Many have good hearts buried deep under generations of delusion or hypocrisy.

"The folks we meet that are flying those rebel flags and hating people they don't know weren't born that way. Many of 'em are just living the life they were born into, finding comfort in what bolsters their own identity. Any circumstance they don't like, whether of their own making, direct choice or by inherited birthright, needs an excuse. Many find personal validation in devaluing other folks who aren't like them, either richer, poorer, or just different.

Nelson queried, "Is it a reason or an excuse?"

Thompson shrugged. "Best thing I can do is live my own life and deal with my own problems and try not to hurt anybody. For me it's the life on my boat, out in the wild, to find my peace in the back-country."

Nelson mused, "Thompson, we moved here to get away from our problems in the Everglades. I think we're better off. It's certainly different. It's a new venue, but not utopia. Seems to be the same old dilemmas in another wilderness."

"Kind of proves that you can run but you can't escape. There's no refuge in the wilderness."

"Cheers!" as they clinked their glasses of rum.

If you enjoyed this book, try the sequel!

CAN'T OUTRUN THE PAST
Enjoy the sequel to HOUSEBOAT HERMIT as trouble follows Thompson and Refuge Officer Bob Nelson, formerly a NPS Park Ranger, in North Florida's Big Bend wilderness. Unknown agents target Thompson to secure the secrets of his past only to be thwarted by the local sheriff and new friends.

Other Books by Marvin Cook

ACROSS FLORIDA STRAITS
follows a bastard son of a young Cuban dancer growing up in an all-inclusive Soviet resort on the south shore of Cuba. Matvey's larceny leads to entanglement with a traveling London art professor and his desperate need to escape Cuba. The story spans post-revolution life in Cuba through the Special Period and into modern time. His perilous journey takes him to Key West and a chance for a new life.

ADRIFT IN THE GULF STREAM
Matvey escapes his captors, but is alone in the Gulf Stream, drifting in the current. A sequel to *Across Florida Straits,* this book continues the story of Matvey, thief of antiquities and wanted for assault by Cuban authorities. Will he survive to find his way to a new life in The Bahamas and leave his past behind?